CLOSE TO
THE EDGE

CLOSE TO THE EDGE

Toby Faber

**MUSWELL
PRESS**

First published by Muswell Press in 2019

Typeset in Bembo by M Rules
© Faber Productions 2019

Toby Faber asserts the moral right
to be identified as the author of this work.

Printed and bound by
CPI Group (UK) Ltd, Croydon CR0 4YY.

*This book is a work of fiction and,
except in the case of historical fact, any resemblence
to actual persons, living or dead, is purely coincidental.*

A CIP catalogue record for this book
is available from the British Library
ISBN 9781999613532

Muswell Press
London
N6 5HQ
www.muswell-press.co.uk
team@muswell-press.co.uk

To Matilda, Lucy and Amanda

Monday, 27 July – 2.45 a.m.

Near the top of the second escalator, Laurie released Paul's hand. They had climbed from the darkness of the Underground, back into the light of Euston's deserted ticket hall. The CCTV cameras meant she had to hide her face. To soften the feeling of separation, she turned around and gave him a kiss, a reminder to them both of why they were there, before using the hands she had freed to pull the back of her t-shirt over her head. They were smiling at each other as they created their makeshift hoods. Then Laurie led the way up towards the barriers.

She only saw one of the men at first. For a moment Laurie thought he must be a night worker, but in that case he would surely have been wearing a fluorescent jacket, not a vest. Everything about him spoke of aggression: his stance, legs slightly apart, poised on the balls of the feet, his arms thickly muscled and tattooed, and the way he was staring at the mid-riff Laurie had exposed through her misuse of her t-shirt. She felt naked beneath his gaze.

'Well,' she heard, 'this is an unexpected bonus.' The words came from another man, somewhere to the side. They were

1

almost drawled, such was the relish that lay beneath them. For an instant, Laurie swung her head around, tunnel-visioned by the neck-hole of her t-shirt, desperately trying to locate the voice's source. Then common sense took over. She turned to flee.

Paul, on the stairs immediately below Laurie, was unable to see the reason for her alarm. 'Run!' she shouted, powered by fear. Then, while his face was still digesting the news, and with his body still blocking the more obvious escape route, she leapt to sit on the escalator's rubberised handrail.

Laurie had seen this done once before, by a man only a little older than her – late twenties perhaps – who had drunk one too many. The speed of descent had taken him by surprise, and he had ended up tearing his suit halfway down. She, at least, knew what to expect.

From the moment Laurie started to slide, it was clear that there was little friction between the rubber and the cotton of her leggings, but she took a moment to pick up speed, and while she was travelling slowly past the still-immobile Paul, she managed to bring her top back down behind her head, regaining the full use of her arms. That was just as well. With one hand holding the torch, she could trail the other behind her on the handrail, for balance as well as a brake. She was glad of the glove that protected it from the worst of the friction as she slid into the darkness, heart pumping with terror.

Soon enough, Laurie felt the curve that indicated the handrail was coming to an end. She flew forward a few metres more before her feet hit the ground with a jar that required all the strength in her knees to absorb. If she had not been so frightened she might have tried to stop and regain control; perhaps then she would have stumbled. But instead she ran, maintaining the speed she had built up during her descent, not even bothering to look round, although a drumbeat of rapid thuds told her the pursuit was under way.

Pitch black, the entrance to the staircase down gave a hint of safety. Before Laurie even reached it she had ripped off her gloves and transferred her torch to her left hand, ready to grab the right handrail she knew would be there. She took the stairs two at a time, keeping her knees soft, spiralling down, absorbing the occasional changes in rhythm every time she reached a landing. Down and round she went until there were no more steps.

Could she allow herself to use the torch now? She had to if she was going to maintain her speed. She flicked it on. There was the T-junction she expected: southbound or northbound, left or right. She headed left, round a curve in the passage and down another flight of steps.

It was her running belt that Laurie worried about now. Its reflective strips made it a liability. As she ran she was unzipping it with her left hand, feeling inside for its contents: the three keys she had taken off the ring earlier, her mobile phone, her Oyster card, and the key with the numbered tag, the cause of all the trouble. She stuffed them down the front of her leggings. Why had she not worn pockets?

She was at another T-junction: left to the Northern line, or right to the Victoria. The belt was empty now. Not wishing to make a sound, cautious in her terror, Laurie laid it on the floor. The pause amplified her hearing. Footsteps echoed somewhere behind her. There was no time to waste.

Left again, and Laurie came onto the platform, at the end where the trains emerge. She switched off her torch and sprinted noiselessly along towards the southern end, anxious only to get further ahead of her pursuers. The sound of her breathing filled her ears, competing with the thud from a heart kick-started by adrenaline.

She must be approaching the end of the platform. Laurie slowed to a walk, arms in front, feeling for the end wall. There it was! If she could just hide in the tunnel then perhaps they'd give up looking for her. A look behind: she couldn't hear footsteps, but she could see the faint glow of a torch from the passage through which she'd come. They must have found her running belt: let them go right, let them go right.

Suddenly, Laurie felt a sickening sensation: her mobile phone, slipping down inside her leggings. But there was something else: before Laurie even had time to react, she heard the tinkle of a key hitting the floor. Had her pursuers heard it? To Laurie, no sound had ever seemed so loud. Frantically, she crouched down and swept around with her left hand. She couldn't risk the torch now. Meanwhile, her eyes glanced towards the far end of the platform. Was that glow getting stronger?

Finally, Laurie's hand caught the hard edge of curved metal, almost at the end of the platform: that tagged key again! As she grabbed it, the glow coalesced into a definite beam. They were coming this way. What to do with the key? She was still holding the torch in her right hand and had to retrieve her mobile from somewhere around her knee. She didn't have enough hands. No time to think. She'd just have to dump the key. Was there anywhere to hide it? Laurie pushed out with her left hand, searching.

Yes! There was some sort of grille. That would have to do. Still crouching, Laurie pushed the key through it and then reached down through her waistband to grab the errant phone. There was a definite circle of light at the far end of the platform now. Was it strong enough to pick her out? Laurie didn't waste time finding out. She manoeuvred herself to the side of the platform, and slid down onto the near rail. As she did so, the torch in her right hand fell.

The clang reverberated down the platform. There was no possibility Laurie's pursuers hadn't heard it. No longer caring about the noise she made, she moved as quickly as she could into the tunnel, edging along by the platform with the rail as her guide. In seconds, the wall to her left was lit by a torch beam. The only reassurance was that her shadow did not appear within it. Laurie risked a look round. Without even realising, she had come into a tunnel that bent round to the right. The curve of the wall obscured the platform. To any-body there she was invisible. The torch moved away. She was in darkness once again.

Then a shout. Laurie's stomach lurched. She must have been spotted. No, of course not. The shout was not at her.

'Brian. Come here. Northern line, southbound.' Was that the man whose voice she'd heard before? She thought so.

They must have split up to follow her. He was calling for backup, but why wasn't he chasing her? Surely he knew she was in there? Now was no time to wait to find out. Laurie moved on down the tunnel, but carefully, containing her panic as she strained for sounds of pursuit. Perhaps it was worth staying silent after all.

For the first time since she'd started running, Laurie had time to wonder what had happened to Paul. He couldn't have been far behind her as she slid down the escalator, but he hadn't followed her down the staircase. She'd have heard him. Had they caught him? Laurie had a sudden vision of him beaten up and bleeding somewhere in the tunnels beneath Euston. Casting the image aside with a shake of the head, she forced herself to be rational: she'd surely have heard some-thing. Presumably he'd cut either left or right at the bottom of the escalator and had the luck not to be followed.

Laurie walked on. She'd been going for a few minutes now and there was still no sound behind her. From ahead, on the other hand, there were scuttlings and an occasional squeak. Rats! Laurie had never thought of herself as squeamish, but she still didn't relish the idea of treading on something. Could she risk the torch again? It was as dark behind her as ahead. She must be well out of sight of the tunnel entrance. And what time was it? She checked on her phone: just coming up to three; no particular need to hurry, but what wouldn't she give to be back home in bed?

There were no shouts from behind when Laurie turned on the torch, no quickening footsteps, but ahead half a dozen pairs of small red eyes fled the beam as if it were a flamethrower. The light meant she could move faster. As for what she was moving towards, she still wasn't sure. The next station south of Euston was King's Cross – not far away – but so large that it was bound to be well protected with CCTV and locked doors. It was no place for trying to leave the Tube network.

And what about her pursuers? In retrospect, Laurie was not surprised that they had not chased her into the tunnels. At some point an 'unexpected bonus' stopped being worth the hassle. Nevertheless, she had few illusions about what they might have done if they'd caught her. Now that she seemed to have got away and the adrenaline was leaving her system, she could allow herself to imagine the worst. Her jaw stiffened at the thought. What if they had not given up? What if she found them waiting for her at King's Cross? The answer, she realised, was to run.

In less than a minute, however, the light from Laurie's torch picked out a junction with another set of train tracks coming in from the right. The sight brought her up short. What was going on? For the first time she faced the terrifying possibility that she might be lost, that she might be stuck down here until the morning switch-on. All she could do was make a note of the intersection and press on. If she had to turn back, she could try going down that other track instead.

Reassurance came within seconds, when the beam showed an exit to the tunnel. Laurie was coming into a station. She turned off her torch and moved forward carefully until she felt the ground fall away from her feet: the 'suicide pit' that ran along every platform. A clatter echoed from somewhere to the right. It could have been anything, but it forced her to contemplate another unpalatable possibility. What if her speed had been in vain? What if she was heading for an ambush? In that moment she reached her decision: she would carry on through King's Cross and get off the line at the next station, Angel. Surely no pursuer would expect that?

Laurie negotiated the step down into the suicide pit and felt her way along the track, using the rails as guides. At the end, she clambered out and back into the tunnel, the atmosphere closing around her once again. After a minute or so more of careful walking she turned the torch back on, to reveal – what? – more track, more tunnel. But once again it meant she could move faster, to safety, away from any pursuit. She was developing confidence, but even as she picked up her pace a low glow ahead brought her to a sudden halt. Were there workers on the line? Or was this the ambush she was dreading? In an instant, Laurie had switched off her torch, ready to flee back towards King's Cross if the glow got any stronger. But it stayed there unwavering and, she soon realised, entirely silent. What was it?

Laurie watched and waited, ruled by uncertainty. Until now, despite her sudden conversion from excited discoverer to prey, despite almost overwhelming panic, she had always, at her core, known what she was doing. This light, however, represented the unknown far more powerfully than the gloom it displaced. She yearned for the comforting familiarity of the dark. It would be so easy to turn around. Perhaps she could go back through King's Cross and Euston as far as Camden?

Madness – that's what it was. Whatever the source of the light ahead, it couldn't be worse than stumbling around on the Tube network until the line went live at half past four. Laurie had to press on; she had to get out. She was tired of running. Why try to hide any longer? Resigned to discovery, she stepped out towards the light. She could explain how she had ended up here, couldn't she?

Tuesday, 21 July – 8.30 a.m.

Six days earlier

Of the ten fingers splayed out before her, the little one on the right hand seemed at least reasonably clean. Laurie used it to hook a loose strand of hair out of her eye and tuck it behind her ear. That was the fifth time her chain had come off in the last two miles; she'd spent an hour on a journey that should take twenty minutes.

Enough: there must be something wrong with the bike that roadside repairs could not put right. It had sounded a bit creaky yesterday. Perhaps that solitary adventure along the Parkland Walk on Sunday had been too much for it. Well, at least she'd got to within spitting distance of Euston. She could take the Tube to Green Park and walk to Berkeley Square from there.

Laurie pushed her bike up the steps from Eversholt Street, locked it to the racks outside the main concourse, unhooked the pannier, checked she still had her Oyster card, and set off for the entrance to the Underground. She was going to be late for work and she'd be travelling on the Tube when the morning crush was at its worst.

There was an attendant by the turnstile into the toilets. Laurie considered explaining that she only wanted to wash her hands, that she'd been cycling and had no change, but thought better of it. Until she got into the office, a wet wipe would have to do.

The Victoria line platform was as bad as Laurie had feared. A mass of commuters lined the edge, waiting to squeeze onto the next train. Behind them there was more fluidity; people moved along looking vainly for a space. Laurie joined the flow, heading gradually for the far end, trying to ignore the way her cycling shirt was sticking to her back. It would be a relief when she could finally change into the dress in her pannier.

At the end of the platform, by the tunnel's mouth, things were marginally quieter; there was at least a prospect of getting on the next train. Laurie positioned herself near the edge and stared down at the tracks beneath her feet. The heat and the crowd were not just physically oppressive; she felt the weight on her soul too. The frustration she had been feeling after her abortive cycle ride was magnifying into an awful, all-encompassing lassitude. The sense of despair that came in its wake was familiar but no less unwelcome. What if she were just to let herself go, fall onto those tracks, leave it all behind?

Once, in the terrible months after Mum died, Laurie might have followed through on her impulse. But not now: that behaviour belonged a decade in the past. She pulled her gaze away from the tracks and looked around, deliberately reconnecting with the world around her.

Almost as if he knew what was required when she caught his eye, the man beside her smiled. He was too old for it to be a come-on and Laurie felt her cheeks crease in response, pushing away the wisps of depression before they could take hold. He was wearing a surprisingly smart but quirky suit, with patch pockets and pleated trousers – a bit out of place among the more uniform offerings of Laurie's fellow commuters, and a sharp contrast to her own Lycra.

The man was trying to talk to her; he was leaning over and pointing at his nose. Something shiny was hanging from his hand. Laurie watched it swing as she bent her head towards him, straining to hear against the sound of the station tannoy, continuing her smile in response to his. Then the mood of the crowd around them changed. The roar from the tunnel to their left increased; the next train was approaching. People were moving into position, jockeying for spots where doors would soon be opening.

The swell of humanity seemed to catch the man by surprise. Laurie saw him shift his stance to accommodate the sudden pressure and was still looking at him when he realised that one foot was no longer on the platform. She just had time to register the change in his expression from amusement to horror, time to see his hand reach out in an attempt to regain his balance, and time to scream – an involuntary reaction to her own helplessness – before, with shocking suddenness, he was gone. The southbound train came out of the tunnel, slammed into his falling body, and carried it relentlessly into the station, before screeching to a premature halt halfway down the platform.

Laurie stood there, her scream stopped as rapidly as it had begun. She stared at the train carriage that had appeared in front of her where the man had been only moments before. Inside, she saw faces turn from shock to bewilderment: this was not how their train was meant to stop. She saw commuters recover the dignity they had lost from being thrown into each other by the unexpected deceleration. She heard an announcement that due to an incident at Euston, Victoria line services were suspended until further notice. She watched passengers gather themselves together and leave the carriage, joined by those from further down the train, still stuck in the tunnel. She felt the platform start to empty around her.

A chill spread from Laurie's scalp, leaving a numbness in its wake that only amplified a sudden and overwhelming sense of claustrophobia. She had to leave. She had to be ahead of the crowd, be out in the open air. She raced down the platform, spared only a glance for the rubberneckers gathered round the front of the train, and began to shove her way through the queue for the up escalator, ignoring the mutterings around her.

Whatever Laurie might have wished, the journey up was painfully slow. With both escalators packed solid, she could only stand on successive slowly rising staircases, waiting her turn. Forced into immobility, she began to calm down. Now she recalled her earlier panic with embarrassment. She looked around, wondering how close she was to people she had been pushing aside only moments earlier.

Finally, Laurie reached the top. Another wave of her Oyster card brought her into the ticket hall. In forty seconds she was back in the plaza outside, looking across to the bike she had abandoned only a few minutes earlier. Nothing had changed. The sky was the same deep blue it had been for days. A helicopter overhead was pulling a banner advertising insurance; she had seen that earlier too. People were still rushing to work with the same air of hurried purpose. None of them caught her eye, let alone smiled like the man below had.

The tiredness Laurie had felt underground came back upon her, but this time it brought no suicidal thoughts in its wake. Somehow, seeing the man fall had put paid to them. She walked over to her bike. It looked forlorn, with its chain hanging useless – like a horse that had cast a shoe. There was only one thing to do. Laurie pulled her mobile phone out from the pannier, swiped the unlock pattern, and pressed the green button twice. 'Home' flashed up on the screen. She could hear the ringing at the other end, and then the answer: 'Laurie love. What's up?' She managed to get as far as, 'Oh, Dad.' Then she burst into tears.

Dad was useless on the phone really. Laurie had known that before she called him. But even the sound of his voice made her feel better, and she had to smile when he suggested coming to her rescue, all the way from Somerset. Her breathing returned to normal. Eventually she was able to speak with a measure of self-control.

'I've just seen someone fall under a train at Euston.'

As Laurie told the story, standing there in the open air, only a few hundred feet from where the accident had happened, the tightness within her began to release. By the end, she was still exhausted, but with an accompanying sense of relief. She did not, of course, pass on the thoughts she had been entertaining just before the man fell – no need to burden Dad with that. She had moved from home; she was doing OK, honest.

Dad didn't reply for a while. Feeling the silence down the line, Laurie suddenly realised what she had done. Of course he would be thinking of Mum. Laurie had never seen her body after the accident, but he had. Was that the image that would now be forcing its way into his brain? Was that what she had brought upon him by calling home so unthinkingly?

'Dad. I'm sorry,' she began.

'It's all right, darling. I'll be fine. But I'm still worried about you. Why don't you come back here? I'll meet you off the train. Get a bit of fresh air. You know.'

'Dad. I'm not fifteen any more. I can't just run away. I need this job.'

'What, you mean you're still planning to go into work?'

13

'Isn't that what you always say? If you fall off the horse, get straight back on.'

'This isn't quite the same thing. Still, you might be right, I suppose. But you're probably in shock. Lots of sweet tea is the thing for that. Don't rush anywhere until you've got your blood sugar up. And of course you're still coming down this weekend, aren't you? I imagine Fitzbillies can spare you then.'

'It's Fitzalan, Dad, Fitzalan Capital.' Laurie was more amused than exasperated, but she had heard the note of entreaty in his voice. 'And yes, of course I'm coming down. I'll call you this evening.'

'Good.' Dad sounded more like his usual self now. As if to prove it, he threw in two final pieces of advice. 'By the way, you might be a material witness to the accident; I know you don't have particularly happy memories of the police, but you really should give them your name. As for your bike, it sounds to me as though your back wheel's misaligned. That will be why the chain keeps slipping.'

'Dad! That was years ago, and didn't they swear there wouldn't be anything on my record, as long as I went on that course?'

'Well, I guess this will be your chance to find out, and to show that you are now a fine, upstanding citizen.'

Laurie thought about things for a few moments after breaking the connection. Then she squatted down beside the bike. Dad was right. The axle at the back wasn't fully engaged in its brackets. A spanner would put it right, but that could wait. She straightened, ready to go to work – and was instantly light-headed. Dad had been right about that too, of course. Sugary tea held no appeal, but some other treat would do the trick.

Laurie was eating chocolate Brazil nuts as she walked through the station to the British Transport Police office.

There, a buzz lock let her through to an anteroom dominated by a glass security screen: nothing like her memory of Cambridge police station, and all the better for it. The yellow-jacketed WPC behind the screen looked doubtfully at Laurie's cycling shorts and t-shirt, but heard her out to the extent of taking down her contact details and promising that if an investigation was required then an officer would be in touch.

That done, Laurie considered how to get to work. She couldn't face going underground again: the inevitable announcement that 'due to an earlier incident there are severe delays on the Victoria line', the crowds even worse than before, the smell and the memory it would provoke. She would take the bus.

Tuesday, 21 July – 10 a.m.

'Laurie. You rock that Lycra look. In the immortal words of Big Cook, you are "hot, hot, hot". Did you wear it just for me?'

So much for being able to sneak in and change before anyone noticed her. Laurie should have guessed Nick would be here. He seemed to spend as much time leaning outside the front door nursing a cigarette as he did at his desk. Laurie could never have got away with that sort of behaviour, but then fee-earners always were cut more slack than support staff. Anyway, should she be offended by his remarks? She couldn't be bothered; it was better, surely, to give as good as she got.

'So, Nick, to all your other bad habits, do we now have to add a liking for children's television? You are one sick individual.'

Nick smiled back, enjoying the banter. 'I've got children, haven't I? So how come you know *Big Cook, Little Cook*, then? Please don't tell me you're young enough to have watched it first time around?'

'No.' Laurie smiled. 'Old enough would be more accurate.

I do the recipes with my god-daughter. If you like I can sing you the song.'

'Why spoil a wonderful moment? By the way, did you know you had a smudge on your nose?'

It was just as well Laurie was walking past Nick as he spoke. His comment immediately brought to mind an image of the man on the Tube platform, leaning across to talk to her and pointing at his nose just before he fell. As it was, she was able to go downstairs to shower and change and reflect that at least she knew now what he had been going to say. She arrived at her desk as composed as on any other day.

With Henry and most of the team on holiday there was little routine work to do, and certainly no prospect of over-time. Only one of Laurie's nominal bosses was in the office. Michael was young enough to have grown up typing his own emails and had never shown the slightest inclination to use a Dictaphone. Did anyone under fifty? Nevertheless, he grunted assent when Laurie offered to do his filing, and even seemed mildly impressed by the energy she put into it. The work was hardly interesting, but it beat surreptitiously scrolling through Instagram until lunchtime.

Tuesday, 21 July – 5.30 p.m.

Laurie and the other two assistants stood up from their desks and headed for the door, weaving their way past analysts who would be there for hours to come. She had successfully negotiated a day at work. So far so good. It had been the right idea to go into the office.

Spending the day at work was one thing; taking the Underground was another. Just thinking about it immediately reminded her of feeling helpless while the smiling man fell. Instead, Laurie returned to Euston on the bus and headed straight for the bike racks, determined to use the spanner set she had bought over lunch. Kneeling down beside her bike, she took off the lock and pondered the problem in front of her. Could Dad guide her through what to do on the phone? Perhaps she could YouTube it?

Laurie was just about to pull out her mobile when she became aware of a presence behind her. She looked over her shoulder. A dark figure was silhouetted against the still-blue sky. Her heart quickened with the shock, but before she had time to react any more than that, the man spoke in a Home Counties accent: 'Can I give you a hand with that?'

Laurie stood up to see that this was another cyclist. Unlike her, however, this man clearly had not bothered with changing after work. Instead, bicycle clips at his ankles spoilt the line of a blue suit worn over a white open-necked shirt. The leanness of his neck suggested he must be fit, but his helmet made it hard to guess his age. Brown eyes looked into hers with friendly concern, holding her attention. Laurie registered elegant eyebrows and cheeks shadowed with a slight stubble before looking across to the bike he was holding: so shiny it might have been brand new, but just a Raleigh, nothing flash.

The cyclist smiled as he waited for Laurie's reply; perhaps she'd been checking him out for longer than politeness required.

'Thank you. That would be lovely.'

Propping his own bike against a pillar, the man retrieved a spanner from a little bag hanging behind its saddle and turned Laurie's bike over so that it rested on its handlebars and saddle. In a matter of seconds, he had realigned the back wheel, checked that it spun freely without catching the brake pads and set the chain back on the cogs of the two gear mechanisms, first on the wheel, then by the pedals. A quick turn of the latter with his hand ensured that the chain was totally engaged, which allowed it to slip into its correct gear settings. Finally he flipped the bike back over and presented it to Laurie with just the slightest hint of a flourish, as of a waiter in a high-end restaurant serving the chef's signature dish.

'Oh, but you must have got oil on your hands. I've been scrubbing mine all day, and they're still icky.'

The man held his hands in front of him and turned them over: muscular and elegant; a pianist would have hands like that. And yes, the two fingers that had grasped the chain were both slightly oily.

'Here, let me.' Laurie found herself saying. She retrieved a wet wipe from her pannier and, holding his hand, removed the worst of the oil. Tending to this stranger's fingers, Laurie couldn't help remembering that last unsatisfactory date, months ago, the attempt at a kiss that had got nowhere before she broke it off. This felt so much more intimate, despite the innocence of her actions.

He was speaking. 'You'd better just try the bike. Make sure the gears change OK. I can always adjust them a bit more if not.'

Laurie hoped she didn't look as flustered as she felt. She got on the bike and cycled to the steps and back, checking out the gears as she did so. Everything ran fine. In fact, there was a smoothness to the ride that she was sure had not been there before. When she returned, the man was holding her pannier. He hooked it on her bike in the usual place above the back wheel. Oh God! She'd left all her stuff with him. What had she been thinking? Laurie was itching to get off her bike and check nothing was missing. Only embarrassment at the possibility of appearing rude made her stop.

'Looks like you're all set then ...' The man hesitated. 'I don't suppose you'd fancy a drink.'

Laurie relaxed slightly. Surely he wouldn't have made a suggestion like that if he really was about to run off with her purse? Nevertheless, her reply was automatic: 'I'm sorry. I really am grateful, but I've got to get going. I'm already late as it is.'

'Hot date?'

'Well, something like that,' Laurie replied, starting to regret her refusal. 'It's just, you know ...' She tailed off, not sure how to continue the conversation. What if she asked for his phone number?

'OK. Well, safe cycling.' The man held up his hand, almost

as if he was issuing a benediction. Then pulled his bike from the pillar and wheeled it away.

Laurie stared after him, disappointed, although whether with him or herself, she wasn't quite sure. She briefly considered cycling after him, but she really did have to get home. Quite apart from anything else, she had decided to cook, and that would mean buying some ingredients. A quick check in her pannier revealed that nothing was missing – the man had been as trustworthy as he looked – before she started wheeling her bike towards the road.

Laurie shouldered her way through the front door of the flat. Jess was on the phone in her bedroom, first giggling and then letting out a full-voiced, throaty laugh. Presumably she was talking to one of the Marks.

Going through to the kitchen, Laurie unloaded the shopping and started stripping an onion. Then she got out her mobile and put it on speaker while she chopped.

The phone rang twice at the other end before Dad picked up. She pictured him sitting there, waiting for her call, the crossword resting in his lap.

'Hello darling. How are you feeling? What did the police say?'

'Much better, thanks. They just took my address. I got the impression they weren't interested, really. Anyway, I was glad I went into work. It took my mind off everything.'

As usual, Dad didn't ask for specifics and Laurie knew better than to offer them.

'Well done you. Have you thought any more about this weekend?'

Laurie swept the onion into the frying pan, sloshed in some oil, and turned on the heat. 'Yeah. I promised to babysit Tessa on Friday. So I thought I'd probably get the lunchtime train down on Saturday, if you could pick me up at the station, the one that gets in at twenty to three.'

'Sounds good. So you're not going to bring your bike down? How is it, anyway?'

'Fine, thanks. You were right about the back wheel. A nice man ended up fixing it for me. I've just ridden it back. And yes, I will ride in again tomorrow, but the weekend is something else.'

'OK darling. Be careful, won't you. And try not to fret about this morning. I'm afraid that sort of thing must happen all the time.'

'Right. Love you Dad. Bye.' Laurie put the phone down and concentrated on dicing the carrot she had been peeling.

'What's that about a nice man?' Jess had come through from her bedroom and caught the tail end of the conversation.

'Just a man at Euston station. He mended my bike for me.'

Jess raised her eyebrows and Laurie was surprised to find herself colouring in response. 'If you must know, he asked me out for a drink as well, but of course I said no.'

'Of course,' Jess said, with a wry twist to her mouth that suggested she might have behaved differently. 'Laurie, I'm not going to try telling you to get out more, because last time I did you thought I didn't like you hanging around the flat, and that's not what I mean at all. But you've got to take a few risks, you know. London's a great place to be young. Just give it a chance.'

Laurie didn't try protesting. She knew Jess was right. She'd known it even while she watched the man wheeling his bike away.

Jess smiled. 'It's all right. Lecture over. Who am I to talk, anyway? Here I am, over forty, no one special in my life, having to exploit young cousins to help pay the mortgage.' She looked at the pan. 'What brought this on?'

23

Laurie wondered what to say: that she'd been rescued from a moment of despair at Euston by the friendliness of a man who had immediately fallen under a train? That she had decided that a bit of cooking was the best way to take her mind off things?

'I dunno really. Just felt like it. Plenty for you if you want some.'

'Lovely. Here, have a glass of wine. Save me from being a solitary alcoholic.'

Wednesday, 22 July – 7.30 a.m.

Getting out of bed was as difficult as ever, but Laurie was still grateful for the alarm. It rescued her from dreaming about Mum for what seemed like the first time in years: Mum reaching out, yearning, her hands imploring for something – what? Help? Mercy? Forgiveness? And how had her car got onto the Underground?

The sunlight streaming in around the blind lifted Laurie's spirits. She stretched, rubbed the sleep from her eyes and wandered through to the kitchen in her pyjamas.

Forty minutes later Laurie was freewheeling down Fortess Road. The lights at the end were red, and she slowed down in case a pedestrian started to cross, but she certainly wasn't going to bother with stopping. At this point yesterday morning her chain had already come off twice. Now she felt like she was cruising, weaving round cars, exulting that they were now the ones feeling frustration.

Euston Station merited a second glance as Laurie passed by. Then came the junction with the main road. The traffic here was as heavy as ever. Only a madman would jump these lights. Laurie stopped and rested her left foot on the pavement. Within seconds, however, another bicycle drew up beside her and she heard a familiar voice: 'So, how was your date?'

Yes, it was man from the station! Laurie's heart gave a little jump. Was it just shock? What were the chances of that? Why was she grinning so inanely? She covered up her embarrassment. 'Do you specialise in creeping up on people?'

The light was green now. The man moved across to his left to allow the cars behind to move. It also meant that he was blocking Laurie. She didn't mind. Besides, she owed him an answer. 'Not that it's any of your business, but it wasn't really a date. I just had to phone home.'

As she spoke, Laurie was aware of how feeble the words sounded, but to his credit the man didn't probe any further. 'You're right. I was being nosy. And to answer your question, no, I don't specialise in creeping up on people, I just recognised your cycling gear.'

The light was back to red again. Laurie straightened, sitting upright in the saddle, emphasising that she was in no hurry to move off. She felt the man's eyes on her. Then he spoke again. 'So, if you won't drink, how about a coffee?'

He was called Paul – Paul Collingwood.

They locked up their bikes where they'd met the evening before and went into the station. She had a cappuccino to his espresso. They shared a chocolate brownie. She said she couldn't stay long. He said he couldn't either.

Laurie looked at the man sitting opposite her – at Paul. Now that his helmet was off she could see his hair: close-cropped, dark – almost black – eminently strokeable. A few flecks of grey somehow emphasised the contrast with the rest of his colouring – hair and eyebrows, of course, but above all, his eyelashes. Why hadn't she noticed them before? They gave his eyes a gentleness that might almost have been feminine, if it wasn't for the bone structure of the face beneath. What could a man do with eyes like that? Even the barista had been flustered, blushing slightly as she handed over the change for their coffees. It reminded Laurie of her own mini-crushes – never obviously reciprocated – during the two years she'd drifted between waitressing jobs in Wells.

They talked about cycling in London, about lorries that turn left without indicating, about tourists who look the wrong way when they cross, about how you never notice the wind until it's against you.

'So have you always been a cyclist?' He seemed genuinely curious.

'Well, I was brought up in Cambridge, and everyone cycles there – a combination of poor academics not being able to afford cars, and it being so flat, I suppose.'

'So is that what your Dad is, an academic?'

'Yes, well, he's semi-retired now. He moved us back to Somerset after Mum died.' Laurie hadn't meant to say so much, but now she'd started she didn't feel like stopping. There was something about Paul that made him easy to talk to: the way he was clearly giving her his full attention, the sense of understanding conveyed in the looks they were sharing. Perhaps it was easier because he was a stranger, except that he didn't feel like a stranger.

'She'd been ill, but she was getting better, looking forward to getting back to work. She was at Cambridge too, in the MRC – Medical Research Council. She was driving back from outpatients when her foot slipped on the accelerator. Apparently it would have been very quick.'

Laurie stopped, remembering Dad coming to get her out of school, trying to explain, using exactly the same words with her, attempting to assuage her rage and grief. She didn't tell Paul about the open verdict, about the suggestion that her depression medication might have been to blame. It was an accident, wasn't it? Mum would never have done that, however ill she was.

'I'm sorry. I can't even begin to imagine something like that. Is it still very raw?'

'Well, it was almost ten years ago, but I still miss her, if that's what you mean. And I was pretty bad immediately afterwards. That's why Dad moved us to Somerset, to get me away from Cambridge, and all the memories. God we fought about it, but he was right. I'm so much better now than I was then. He was great. He is great.'

Paul smiled. 'That's good. Dads aren't always given the credit they deserve.' He paused, as though considering whether to say more, before taking Laurie by surprise with a change of subject. 'So what's your happiest memory of your mother?'

Startled, Laurie still had to smile in return. It was the perfect question. 'Just listening to her laugh – before she was ill, you know. She loved those old silent movies. We used to curl up on the sofa together to watch them.'

That got them onto Buster Keaton versus Charlie Chaplin, then to how many times you had to watch *Groundhog Day* to appreciate its full genius. They talked about their favourite parts of north London. He said that a walk on Hampstead Heath was as good as anything you could get outside London. She boasted of her explorations along the towpath.

Paul was looking at her. Why did she have the sense that she was being appraised? Why didn't she mind? 'So what is it you do that means you're cycling past Euston Station at eight-fifteen in the morning?' he asked.

The question brought Laurie back to reality. It was now well after nine. She'd be lucky if she got to Mayfair before

28

9.30. 'Shit, I'm going to be late for the second day in a row. Look, it's been lovely, but I've really got to go. How about trying to have that drink this evening? Meet by the bike racks – usual place, six-thirty?'

Paul nodded his agreement with a smile, standing up as Laurie left, before leaning forward to give her a goodbye peck on the cheek. At least that must have been what he intended, Laurie was sure, but for one electric moment the corners of their lips met. Laurie gathered her things together and rushed out. What had just happened?

It was just as well Laurie didn't have much work to do that morning. She kept thinking back to the hour she'd spent with Paul, and remembering the feel of his lips on hers. What did that grey in his hair mean? He must be in his thirties at least. Their meeting this evening was, presumably, a date. Might it be the beginning of something? What would it be like to date an older man? Well, she could cross that bridge if they came to it. Right now, it just felt good to have met someone she could talk to.

And why had she suggested they meet in such a ridiculous place? If this was a date, she couldn't wear her cycling gear again. And – this would please Jess – she wanted it to be a date. She'd clearly have to leave her bike at work and get up to Euston by public transport.

That still didn't solve the problem of what to wear. The dress Laurie had changed into on arrival had done two days in the office. It felt like work clothes and that wasn't right. A lunchtime trip to Oxford Street was in order.

A dress in the window of French Connection caught Laurie's eye. It was black, V-necked, stopping just above the knee, with an air of sophistication that felt right somehow. She took it to the changing room and examined herself in

29

the mirror outside. Did it look like she was trying too hard? If only she'd brought someone along for a second opinion. Someone? Who was she kidding? Apart from Jess – and God knows what she'd say – there was only Lizzie, who would never spend her lunch hour shopping.

'That looks lovely. I wish I had the figure for it.'

Laurie knew the sales assistant was just doing her job, but was grateful all the same. She happily accepted further advice, picking out an embroidered clutch bag to go with the dress.

Walking back to the office, Laurie eyed her shoes: black flats. They'd looked OK with the dress, but no more than that, and she'd been thinking of buying a pair of sandals for weeks – something strappy, with a hint of heel. Kurt Geiger was right there. Laurie spotted exactly the style she was thinking of, interrupted two sales assistants deep in conversation and got the less grumpy of the two to track down a pair of size sixes. Within a couple of minutes, she was handing over her credit card at the till.

Back at her desk, Laurie reflected guiltily on the ease with which she'd got through two weeks' overtime money in an hour. It had all been a good distraction from thinking about the man on the Underground, but Dad would not spend that much on clothes in two years. Well, at least she could phone home, if only to warn him that she wouldn't be calling again this evening. The news certainly made him curious, but he knew better than to probe further. The next conversation – with Jess – was slightly trickier.

'Well, I suppose I should be pleased that you've taken my advice so quickly, but honestly, darling. You're meeting at Euston Station, of all bloody places. And all you know about him is that he's called Paul Collingwood, that he lives somewhere in north London, and that he's a dab hand with cycle maintenance. Have you had a common-sense bypass?'

30

'Look. I am being sensible. That's why I'm telling you his name. It's not as if I'd know any more about him if we'd just met on Tinder. Just don't forget it, OK?'

'Good point, well made. But at least tell me you've googled him.'

'Well, yes. But it didn't help much. It turns out there's a cricketer called Paul Collingwood. I guess he must be quite well known, because he's the only one I could find. Anyway, that's not him.'

'Fine, fine. Paul Collingwood, but not the famous one. Have a lovely evening. Text me when you're with him to let me know you're OK. Make sure you get his phone number this time. And don't do anything I wouldn't do.' This last exhortation came with a raucous laugh that implied it wasn't much of a limitation. Not for the first time, Laurie wondered what her cousin's employers at the Barbican made of their senior press officer.

Laurie put down the phone to realise Michael was watching her. How much had he overheard? What was Fitzalan Capital's policy on personal phone calls? Laurie had a vague memory from her induction last year of some fairly draconian rules. Michael might, like her, report to Henry, but there was no doubt that, as an analyst, he stood above her in the hierarchy. Anxious not to catch his eye, she looked back down at her desk.

When Michael spoke, however, he referred only obliquely to what he'd heard. 'If you're not particularly busy, perhaps you can give me a hand with this. How familiar are you with Excel?'

Laurie let her gratitude for his discretion seep through into eagerness. 'It was a module in my diploma. I use it to do Henry's expenses. Happy to help if I can.'

Michael's sigh conveyed the disappointment that he lacked

the tact to hide. Almost to himself, he said, 'I suppose there's no harm in trying.' Then he looked up at Laurie. 'Right, I need to run a sensitivity analysis on my model. Check how it performs under different assumptions. With me so far?'

Laurie nodded. Encouraged, Michael continued, 'I've got four variables: one-year bond yields, five-year yields, ten years and twenty years. Where each of them will be in a year's time has an effect on the success of this trading strategy. I need to test it for point-one per cent increments, from zero to two-point-five per cent.'

By now, Michael seemed to be talking to himself as much as Laurie, persuading himself that it really was necessary. He seemed slightly surprised when Laurie responded, 'So that's twenty-six possibilities for each variable. You've got four of them. You'll need to run your model an awful lot of times.'

'Twenty-six to the power of four,' Michael responded, with the defeated air of someone who knows that he has no prospect of leaving the office before midnight any time soon. 'Now you know why I need some help. If you could test all the scenarios from zero to one per cent and I'll do the rest. You'll need to tabulate your results somehow.'

Laurie knew she had no choice, really. 'OK. I'll have a go. What's your deadline? It's just that I'm going out tonight.'

'I know.' Was that a hint of a smile? Laurie had never seen one on Michael before. Then he got more businesslike. 'I need to have something ready for Henry when he comes back from holiday. I'll email you the model today and talk you through it. You can get cracking in earnest tomorrow.'

Wednesday, 22 July – 5.30 p.m.

Changed and ready, Laurie walked to Oxford Circus. There was no doubt that the Tube was the best way for her to get to Euston, but as she'd made her plans earlier in the day, she hadn't really thought about what it would involve. The familiar sight of crowds descending underground brought back an unbidden image of the man falling, but now he was Mum, pleading, with her hand stretched towards her. Laurie's palms started prickling; she could feel the blood thudding in her ears. She realised she was trembling; passers-by were looking at her with concern. It was all she could do stagger to the railings around the entrance and lean on them, breathing in great sobs of air.

Still grasping the railings, Laurie turned around. She had to pull herself together. She tried to concentrate on the familiar sights of Oxford Street: the mannequin wearing underwear whose scarlet hue clashed unapologetically with the pink *Sale* sign on the window in front of it; the pair of girls talking excitedly into their mobiles; a backpacker oblivious to the traffic jam of pedestrians behind him. Her breathing returned to normal, but her earlier confidence had gone. How long would it be before she could stomach the idea of going underground again? It was little more than a day since she had witnessed the accident. What else should she expect?

Laurie considered her options. She didn't fancy the idea of walking the best part of a mile in new shoes; footsore and sweaty was no way to begin a date. There were buses passing regularly, but the traffic on Oxford Street made them a lottery: a ten-minute journey could take half an hour. It went against the grain, but the thought of taking an Uber suddenly seemed awfully attractive.

'Hassan' was apparently three minutes away; the map on her phone showed him coming down Harley Street. Now he was waiting at the pick-up point she had suggested in Great Castle Street. She started walking towards it. Within a minute, however, Hassan had become mysteriously unavailable. Never mind, another driver could be there in five minutes, although the price had gone up by 20 per cent.

Laurie pursed her lips, and looked up to a see a solitary orange taxi light approaching from the west. Yes! She started towards it, already imagining the comfort of its wide leather seats, only for the cab to be snaffled by a trio of middle-aged women, laden with shopping. Behind it, however, was a 73 bus. In that moment, Laurie accepted her fate. She would go to Euston on the bus, and she would be late.

By the time Laurie arrived at Euston she had digested all that Twitter and Facebook had to say, before moving on to read every page of the free newspaper she found on her seat. She'd been grateful for the distraction as the bus inched along first Oxford Street and then Tottenham Court Road. Even so, she must have looked at the clock on her phone a hundred times in the course of the journey, cursing herself for her failure to get Paul's number. What were the chances he'd still be waiting, half an hour beyond the time she said she'd be there?

Running to the bike racks as fast as her dress and heels would allow, Laurie scanned every figure she saw for a sign of familiarity. He wasn't there. She stopped, the hope draining out of her. Now all the emotions she'd been keeping in check on the bus came to the fore. It was shame that she felt most deeply: shame that she hadn't been able to take the Tube; shame that she'd spent so much money on clothes for nothing; shame that she'd have to confess it all to Jess; shame at what she imagined she saw in the eyes of the passing commuters who saw her standing there, all dolled up with nowhere to go.

'You certainly know how to keep a man waiting.'

Laurie turned round. There was Paul, still dressed in the same blue suit: no lunchtime shopping sprees for him. How could she have missed him? She could feel the grin spreading over her face. It was all she could do not to hug him.

'Paul, I am so, so sorry. I will explain, but first give me your phone number. I'd like to make sure it never happens again.'

'Tell you what. Give me yours and I'll send you a text.' Paul got out his phone and keyed in the number she gave him. 'Right, shall we get something to eat? Have you ever eaten south Indian food? There are some great restaurants just round the corner from here.'

Ordinarily, Laurie would have objected to the way Paul took control, but today she was grateful for the chance to let someone else make the decisions. Within a few minutes he had led her to a place that he clearly knew well, though not to the extent that the waiters showed him any more than the usual deference. They squeezed into a corner table, elbows on Formica, knees touching. Around them uninhibited larger groups, including a couple of families, were shouting cheerfully at the waiters. The smell of curry hung in the air, but it was almost floral, nothing like the takeaways near Tufnell Park. Paul ordered them both beers and something else that Laurie didn't catch.

All this time Paul was solicitous, as if he could tell how wound up Laurie was, how close to the edge. He asked no questions and confined his own statements to generalities and directions. It was only when they were fully settled, each holding a glass of Cobra, that he allowed the conversation to move on. 'It's going to sound corny I know, and I'm sure it's the kind of thing you must hear all the time, but can I just say you look fabulous? That dress really suits you.'

'Really?' Laurie smoothed her hands down her thighs. 'Thank you. It's more than I deserve after the way I kept you waiting. I want to tell you why.'

Paul said nothing. Laurie liked that.

'I was all ready to get here on time. At six o'clock I was at Oxford Circus, and then I found I couldn't get on the Tube. It wasn't shut or anything. I just physically couldn't go underground.'

Paul took a swig from his glass. 'I could say that's no loss. I haven't been on the Tube for the best part of a decade, but I'm guessing that wouldn't be much comfort to you at the moment. Has it happened to you before?'

'No. And that's just it. I know why it happened as well. Yesterday morning I was on the Victoria line platform just here, and I saw a man fall under the train in front of me.'

Paul frowned in sympathy. 'God. That must have been terrible. Was he killed? Are you sure he fell?'

'I'm pretty sure he's dead. The train was still travelling quite fast when it hit him. I left my name as a witness but I haven't heard anything yet. And yes, he fell; I'm certain of it.'

Paul looked like he wanted to reach over to her. Laurie

wasn't sure how she would have responded if he had. In the end, he confined his reaction to a single wry comment: 'Well, that certainly puts my day in perspective.'

He turned out to be the manager of a gym. At least, that was his job title. As Paul talked about what he did, however, it became clear that, while he might wear a suit to and from work, he was, as much as anything, a personal trainer, booked for appointments by the gym's regular clients. So she was right in thinking he looked fit. God, it was good to meet someone whose first question wouldn't be 'What university did you go to?'

Their food arrived: *dhosas*. Paul made Laurie guess what they were made of. She got the main constituents of the spicy potato filling easily enough, but would never have realised that the wraps around them were made from lentils. She had to laugh when Paul described his own efforts to make them once: the gloopy mess of 'pulsating pulses' that he left standing for days as it fermented down to a batter, and the end result − scraps of burnt leather with no resemblance to anything edible. What she was eating now, however, was delicious, the crispiness of the pancake contrasting perfectly with the mouth-filling warmth of the potato: comfort food for vegetarians. Laurie felt a tingle of pleasure at the new experience.

Laurie looked across at the man in front of her. He ate neatly and methodically, finishing every mouthful before he spoke, keeping his elbows off the table and by his side. Mum would have liked that. Laurie stopped herself. Surely it was too early to be thinking along those lines? But he was kind as well as handsome; she could tell that already. She wanted to find out more about what lay beneath that suit.

Paul returned her gaze. Could he read her mind? What he said, however, was entirely serious. 'I've been thinking about what you said. How can you be certain that man fell? You hear about people jumping under trains all the time.'

'He was as close to me as you are now. He was about to speak to me when he lost his balance. The train came in at just the wrong time.'

'But he didn't actually say anything to you?'

'No. I think all he was going to do was tell me that I had a smudge on my nose. I can't help thinking about the whole chain of events that meant I was standing next to him with a dirty face, and that if one of them hadn't happened, he'd still be alive.'

'Hey,' said Paul sharply. 'Don't talk like that. If it hadn't been you, it would have been someone else. You can't blame yourself for something like that. It would drive you mad.'

Laurie wasn't sure about Paul's logic, but she appreciated his attempt to comfort her. Her reply, however, didn't come out like that. 'You sound like my dad.' Then she thought through the implications of what she had just said. 'Don't worry. It's a compliment.'

It was Paul's response that made Laurie certain that he, too, was thinking this might be the start of something. 'Hmm. Well, promise me that if you ever want to talk about it some more, you'll call me. I don't claim to have any great psychological insight, but this isn't the sort of thing you keep bottled up inside.'

Grateful that he had not attempted to draw any parallels with what happened to Mum, Laurie just nodded. She didn't trust herself to talk. Then Paul continued, 'there's something else you should know about me. I'm a dad already: got two kids, Aidan and Mia. Their mum and I are divorced. They live in Oxfordshire now.'

'Oh.' Laurie felt she should be asking something in response while she tried to process this information. 'How often do you see them?'

'Every other weekend and a bit during the school holidays. So I'm off tomorrow until Sunday night – taking them to my mum's.'

'Are they still quite small?'

'Six and four. We split up two years ago.'

Tiny! Laurie tried to imagine how she would have felt if Dad had moved out when she was two. She could feel her eyes starting to sting in sympathy. 'Oh Paul, I'm so sorry.'

Paul had gone a bit red. He looked down at his lap as he continued. 'It was my fault. I got too close to a client. Bethan always said one strike and you're out. So I was. Wish I could turn back the clock. I can't make up to the kids for what happened, but I'm trying to be there for them now.'

A series of images jostled for attention in Laurie's head: of Paul 'getting too close' to some gym-bunny, of an angry scene with his faceless wife, of children weeping for their father. She let the silence rest, not trusting herself to speak. Surely she should be feeling sympathy here for the wronged wife, not Paul?

There didn't seem much more to be said. Paul asked for the bill, and insisted on paying. It was still light outside. They walked back to the station, neither attempting to touch the other, talking of inconsequentialities – when the heatwave would break, whether it was a sign of global warming. Paul waited until the bus was slowing down to make one last admonishment. 'I meant what I said. Call me if you want to talk about that accident any more.'

The comfort Laurie derived from the idea confirmed what she already knew: she wanted to see him again. She turned to face him, ready to say goodbye. He was standing there. Did she imagine that his smile was slightly sad? That decided her. This time, when she leant towards him, it was for a proper kiss.

39

After the electricity of the morning, the feel of Paul's lips was everything Laurie had hoped. She wanted to linger, but pulled away before it developed into anything more. She wasn't ready for that yet. She had at least some composure as she turned and got on the bus.

Laurie went upstairs and took her favourite seat at the front of the upper deck. Her lips still tingled.. Staring out of the window, she tried to analyse her feelings for a man she'd known for little more than a day. Should she be put off by his confession of unfaithfulness? Somehow that seemed insignificant next to the news that he'd been married and had children. But that should have been no surprise either. He was at least ten years older than her. She could hardly expect that he would have been single all this time.

Jess was watching an ancient repeat of *Sex and the City* when Laurie came in, but she turned it off to look her up and down, raising her eyebrows as she did so. 'Nice outfit,' she said. 'I won't even try to guess how much it cost, but I trust it was worth it. You haven't texted me, by the way, but then you're hardly late enough for me to start worrying. How did it go?'

'It's a bit complicated,' Laurie had to admit. 'He's lovely, but he's got two kids, and he's not going to be around for the rest of the week. I'd like to see him again, I think. Fabulous body.' She flashed Jess a smile.

'Well if you fancy him that's one hurdle cleared. Just remember you can always dump him later. Kiss a lot of frogs before you find your prince. Send him a text now, to keep him warm. That's my advice.'

'Good idea.' Laurie got out her phone to find Paul's message so she could reply. There was nothing there: 'I don't understand. I saw him texting me.'

'Well, sometimes they take a while to get through.'

It didn't seem very likely, but Laurie was grateful for the explanation all the same. Suddenly she was too tired to engage in the usual back and forth. 'I don't know what's going on, but I do know I can't think straight. I'm going to bed.'

It was a still, hot night. Laurie kicked off the duvet and lay on her mattress in her second-hand t-shirt, thinking of Paul in spite of herself. She remembered the feel of his lips and imagined the touch of his fingertips. Wasn't she getting ahead of herself? The implication of the absent text was pretty clear; most probably they would never meet again.

So when Laurie eventually slept it was to dream, once again, of Mum, of trains and tunnels and outstretched hands.

Thursday, 23 July – 9 a.m.

Facebook listed eighty Paul Collingwoods. Of the half with photographs, however, none matched the man Laurie was looking for. Forty-odd others were visible only as stylised silhouettes, and at least twenty of those were potential London-dwellers. There was no way Laurie was going to send all of them a friend request, and without that any message would just get stuck in a spam filter.

The BT website was more helpful. There were seventeen Collingwoods with London telephone numbers; a surprisingly high proportion – eight – had the initial 'P', but only two of those lived in north London. Laurie noted the numbers. She would call them that evening, away from office eavesdroppers. Then she remembered; Paul had said he was going to be out of London for the rest of the week, taking his kids to his mum's. Ah well. Perhaps a few days of enforced separation would be no bad thing. If she still felt like tracking him down on Monday, she'd know it was serious. Right now, Monday seemed a long way off.

Laurie straightened in her seat. That had been an unproductive way to spend the first twenty minutes of her working day. It was time to get back to Michael's model. He had been at his desk since she arrived, in much the same position as when she had left the previous afternoon: hunched over his keyboard, face rendered even more pallid by the glow from his screen. Only the different pattern on his shirt provided any indication that he had not been there all night. He must be expecting her to get down to work now, to match him keystroke for keystroke as she methodically changed the variables and noted each set of results. It was such a boring and repetitive process – even Michael looked glassy-eyed – but there was no help for it. She settled down to work.

There was, Laurie had to admit, something faintly satisfying about the routine. It kept enough of her mind occupied to stop it wandering, but demanded nothing more in the way of intellectual effort. Enjoyment was too strong a word, but there was a sense of safety in the knowledge that she was doing exactly what Michael had asked her to do. So the ringing on her mobile, when it came, was a surprisingly unwelcome distraction. Neither Laurie nor her phone recognised the number. Might it be Paul? Laurie hardly dared hope as she pressed the green answer key.

But it was a woman's voice at the other end. 'Am I speaking to Miss Lauren Bateman? This is Sergeant Atkins, British Transport Police, Euston station. I understand you reported your name as a witness to an incident here on the morning of the twenty-first of July.'

'Yes, that's right.' Conscious that Michael had looked up from his computer, Laurie didn't feel like volunteering anything more.

'We'd like you to come in to make a statement, if that's convenient.' There was no interrogatory uplift to end the sentence. Its second half was there for form's sake only.

Laurie looked regretfully at her computer screen. Was it really half past three already? She must have worked through lunch without realising. Her sigh was entirely unintentional, but still audible at the other end of the line.

'I'm sorry if it's a bother to you, madam.' Sergeant Atkins's tone made it clear she wasn't sorry at all. 'But you will appreciate that there has been a fatality and we need to establish the circumstances surrounding it as expeditiously as possible.'

Laurie surrendered. 'Of course, when would you like me to come in?'

It seemed that the sergeant was hoping to complete her paperwork this evening. She made it clear that she was expecting Laurie before then: in fact, as soon as possible. Quite why she was calling now, rather than earlier in the day, or even yesterday, never became apparent. Laurie didn't dare ask, let alone suggest that she would have appreciated a little more notice. For all she knew, her evidence was necessary before they could release the body to the family.

Laurie noted where she'd got to in her progression through Michael's variables and rose from her seat. As if attached by an invisible cord, Michael's chin rose to face her. Laurie looked at him and sighed. 'I'm sorry about this. It's a bit of a long story, but I was a witness to an accident a couple of days ago and the police want me to make a statement. I'll be as quick as I can.'

As she changed out of her work clothes and cycled to Euston, Laurie tried to rationalise why she felt guilty at leaving Michael like that. It wasn't as if she had to work on his bloody model for him; it was way beyond her job description.

There was a man sitting behind the glass screen at Euston police station. He took Laurie's details, registered that she was

45

here to meet Sergeant Atkins, and motioned for her to sit in one of the three chairs that lined the flank wall.

Laurie chose the seat nearest the screen. There was no one else in the room, but if anyone arrived, she wanted to make sure she was at the front of any developing queue. The plastic squeaked slightly as she settled into it. Posters on the wall told her about Crimestoppers, about always reporting a suspicious or abandoned bag, about when to call 999 and when 111 was more appropriate. It all felt so different from the last time Laurie had spent any time in a police station. Then, boredom had been the least of her worries.

Laurie looked at her phone: no signal, no opportunity to divert herself in any way. For a moment she wished she had not deleted Candy Crush. Even the *Metro* would have been better than nothing.

A man and a woman came into the waiting room. Laurie prepared herself to interact, to acknowledge some fellow feeling as they joined her on the chairs, but they let themselves through, past the glass screen, without even looking at her.

Half past four: Laurie had been waiting for twenty minutes. Apparently Crimestoppers' specially trained agents will make sure your report contains no information that could identify you. Every time Laurie shifted, her chair squeaked in sympathy, its sound amplified by the smallness of the room. Should she go and ask the man behind the screen if it was OK to go out and get a paper? Laurie got as far as standing up, only to see that she was now alone. Presumably the man only appeared in response to a buzz on the outside door; at other times, he had better things to do.

It was another ten minutes before the door beside the glass screen opened, this time from the inside. A disembodied female voice said, 'Lauren Bateman.' Laurie got up and was almost at the door before she saw the speaker. 'I'm Sergeant Atkins.'

Laurie had never thought of herself as tall, so it was disconcerting to realise that her chin was level with the top of the policewoman's head. Didn't the police have some sort of minimum height requirement? Did the fact the sergeant wasn't in uniform mean she was CID? Laurie considered asking, but something about Atkins's manner – the way she had not yet made eye contact, the projected aura of having been interrupted on important business – discouraged any attempt at small talk. The magnanimous 'No problem', which Laurie had been prepared to issue in response to an apology for being kept waiting, proved to be entirely unnecessary.

Then all thoughts of social niceties ceased. Along the corridor a door opened to reveal a young man dressed in the standard t-shirt and shorts of a tourist. Without trying to analyse his looks, Laurie could see immediately that he was beautiful; there was no other word for it. Behind him a uniformed policeman had a grip on his elbow. The two of them stood there in the corridor, side on to Laurie, before the young man turned to the left and looked her full in the face. In that moment, he made his calculation. What occurred next seemed to happen unbearably slowly, although Laurie still had no time to cry out. In one move the man wrenched his elbow free from the guiding hand behind him, turned around, headbutted the policeman's nose with an audible crack, and kneed him hard in the groin. Then he sprinted towards Laurie, clearly aiming for the door she had just entered while it was still ajar.

The sergeant had her back to the corridor. The man dealt with her even before she realised there was a problem, pushing her over with ridiculous ease. Then he came to Laurie. The shove in her chest made her stagger back and out of his way. 'How dare he?' Instinctively, Laurie stuck out her foot, making the man stumble as he headed for the door.

'Bitch!' The man wheeled round and punched her hard in the stomach, a winding blow so painful she was sure he must have broken a rib. She crouched down, arms round her middle, desperate to breathe, unable to protect herself from the blows that would be sure to come.

None did. Instead Laurie was assaulted by an alarm so loud she had to put her hands over her ears. She opened her eyes in time to see Sergeant Atkins and another policeman running past her, heading on into the train station, presumably in pursuit of the man who had vanished.

The air seeped back into Laurie's lungs. The pain receded. She stood up, uncertain what to do next. Then the man she had originally seen manning the desk appeared in front of her. He must be fifty at least, Laurie realised, with enough of a paunch to mean he wouldn't be running anywhere very fast. Conversation was impossible, but he beckoned for Laurie to follow him further into the corridor. The policeman whose nose she had heard break was still there, sitting slumped against the wall. He must have been too wrapped up in his own concerns to notice what had happened to Laurie; now he eyed her over the bloodstained tissue pressed against his face. Her guide looked at him, clearly deciding what to do next. Then he opened the door beside him, the one from which Laurie had seen the two men emerge – was it really only a minute or so ago? – gestured for Laurie to go in, and closed the door behind her.

The alarm rang on, precluding any thought, dominating Laurie's consciousness.

And then it stopped. Now it was the silence that was overwhelming. Laurie shut her eyes and concentrated on getting her breathing back to normal. What had she been thinking? The only thing she knew about that man was that he was capable of extreme violence. And she had tried to trip him. It was only luck that his need to escape outweighed any desire for vengeance. Never fight if you can run. Isn't that what they'd drummed into them in those self-defence classes at school? She would remember it next time.

Her pulse slower now, Laurie looked around the room she had entered. It was windowless, with strip lights in the ceiling. Two chairs faced each other across a table. Laurie sat down in one, realising as she did so that it was fixed to the floor. So was the table. She looked up; a security camera seemed to be aimed at her face. Another realisation: there was no handle on this side of the door. If Laurie had not already used up her stocks of adrenaline, this might have been a time to panic, to succumb to claustrophobia. As it was, she could only greet her surroundings with recognition. She wasn't stuck in a nightmare. This was an interview room, entirely similar to the one she had occupied in Cambridge, the one where she had not so much been interviewed as lectured about the dangers of drugs and underage drinking. On that occasion the arresting officer had given the impression that he cared about her, even as she was processed through fingerprints and mugshot, and waited for Dad to come to retrieve her from the holding cell. She had only been fifteen of course, covering her fear with bravado.

So when Sergeant Atkins arrived about twenty minutes later, Laurie's residual shock at what had occurred was overlaid by a spirit of warmth towards the police. There was nervousness too, the sort she always felt in any encounter with a figure of authority. She had to suppress the urge to rise at the policewoman's entrance, remembering her old headmistress as she did so ('Stand up when I come into the room!').

49

The sergeant placed herself in the chair opposite Laurie's. They looked each other full in the face for the first time. Laurie saw a woman a few years older than herself: shoulder-length brown hair, no obvious make-up. The sergeant gave a little nod, as if of recognition (surely that mugshot had been destroyed?), examined her notebook, and began: 'You are Lauren Miranda Bateman?'

'Yes,' Laurie replied, and then, still eager to please: 'How is your colleague? You know I saw the assault. Would you like a statement about that too?' Laurie paused, wondering if she should mention that he'd hit her too. Was that relevant?

'I'll note your details on the file in case the investigating officer wishes to be in touch. In the meantime, I'd be grateful if we could focus on the reason you are here. On 21st the twenty-first of July you reported yourself as the witness to an incident on the Victoria line southbound platform here at Euston station. Is that correct?'

And so the interview began. At one level, it was relatively unremarkable. Throughout, Sergeant Atkins continued to be unfriendly, almost austere. Was Laurie just imagining that she had been weighed in the balance, and somehow found wanting? There was certainly no understanding that she might be distressed by the way a random encounter, sparked by friendliness, had ended in a death, no attempt to get to know Laurie herself. Rather, the policewoman's concern was simply to establish why Laurie was so sure the man's death was accidental. She took her through the sequence of events that led to him falling at least three times. Did Laurie really think he'd been trying to point out a smudge on her nose? The disbelief with which she treated Laurie's suggestion seemed to be rooted in scorn.

The final part of the interview provided some explana-tion for Sergeant Atkins's behaviour. Laurie had just said something like, 'I didn't move for a while, but then I came up to the surface as quickly as possible for some fresh air,' when she noticed the policewoman nodding. That was when Laurie realised: 'I suppose you've been able to see me on the platform video?'

Laurie blushed as she remembered her moment of panic, all consideration for others thrown aside as she barged through to the escalators. All she could say was, 'I'm not usually like that.'

And all Sergeant Atkins would say in return was, 'You'll appreciate that there are reasons why passengers are asked to make their way upstairs in an orderly manner.'

Even after the interview, the sergeant still had to transcribe Laurie's words onto a statement form for her signature. Converted into witness-speak, the result bore little relation to Laurie's own description, and made no attempt to convey her accompanying emotions, but it was, at least, an accurate summary of what she had seen. Several other forms established Laurie's personal details, from address to ethnic identity. One final admonition seemed particularly heavy-handed: 'If you are summonsed to attend the inquest then I must warn you that failure to do so will be an offence and the coroner can impose a fine or prison sentence.'

Laurie was sensible enough to realise that this would not be a good time to lose her temper. 'I understand,' she replied. 'Any idea when that might be?'

Sergeant Atkins's response was businesslike but surprising. 'My investigation is almost complete, but psychiatric reports generally take at least three months.'

'Psychiatric reports? Does that mean you think he killed himself? But I know it was an accident. I saw him fall.'

'Your statement will be passed to the coroner, together with the other evidence.'

The interview ended on that unsatisfactory note. In the corridor outside there was no sign that anything untoward had ever taken place. Laurie wondered if she should ask Sergeant Atkins about what had happened again. Had they caught the man? Why hadn't the sergeant at least asked how she was? Did she even know that she had been attacked as well? Laurie was still in two minds when they reached the door to the waiting room, and there the sergeant left her, with a handshake that was such a surprise, and so out of place, that it could only have come from a training manual.

Back in the station concourse, the evening rush hour was at its peak. Commuters hurried past Laurie, heading for the trains to take them north and out of London. No one gave her a second glance, but that was just as well. What would she have done if they had? How many of them had the capacity for the sort of violence she had just experienced? Where was the man? If he had escaped then he would surely be a long way from Euston by now, wouldn't he?

Laurie's route to her bike took her by the escalators going down to the ticket hall for the Underground. She must have passed them on her way to the interview without a second thought. Now she couldn't help shivering a little. Was it Euston station itself that was dangerous? The people around her did not seem to think so. Or was it just that the potential for horror existed everywhere?

None of these thoughts seemed so powerful outside in the evening sun. Laurie looked at her phone: seven o'clock. Perhaps she should return to work? She imagined Michael sitting there, tapping away, as desks slowly emptied around him. It wasn't as though he was able to authorise overtime, but he'd surely be pleasantly surprised to see her; the routine she had established during the afternoon would be a good return to normality. Laurie shook her head and smiled. The last thing she wanted now was to be stuck in an office. She wheeled her bike to Eversholt Street and headed for Tufnell Park.

Saturday, 25 July – 5 p.m.

Laurie tightened her knees and brought in her heels. Even now, after all these years, she still felt a thrill from the sense of latent power waiting for the call. Roxanne needed little encouragement; she picked up her pace to a trot. Laurie allowed the saddle to rise and fall beneath her, flexing her hips in rhythm as they rounded the corner into the main part of the field. It was empty; Laurie had timed it right; the cows were all inside for their evening milking. Twenty acres of pasture stretched out before her, sloping gently up towards the ridge: considerably yellower even in the two weeks since her last visit, but no worse riding country for all that.

One small squeeze behind the girth and Roxanne flowed into a canter. Laurie did little more than aim her towards the gate in the far corner, relaxing for a brief moment into the smoothness of the ride. But she wanted more than relaxation. Now, for the first time, she used the crop, flicking Roxanne's neck to urge her on up the hill, through a fast canter and then, as the slope levelled out, into a full-on gallop. With her knees bent, Laurie leaned forward, her torso almost parallel to Roxanne's neck as the horse strained for speed. The insistent beat of the hooves ran up Laurie's legs and into her body, drowning out the rhythm of her heart, so that it seemed the gallop itself was pumping the blood she could feel in her ears and fingertips.

They were approaching the gate. When Laurie had saddled Roxanne a few minutes earlier she'd had no intention of going for the jump, but now she sensed an added urgency to the horse's stride. It was as if Roxanne remembered their last disastrous attempt as well as she did, and was equally anxious to erase the memory. Laurie ignored the sudden twinge in her collarbone; she made no move to slow the horse down. Instead, it was Roxanne who paused, gathered her stride and, with no hint of refusal, leapt, smoothly and freely, over to the other side.

One more empty field beyond the gate allowed the gallop to continue. Then came the bridle path at the top of the ridge. Laurie was forced to slow down. She could never tire of that view: Glastonbury Tor, wobbling in the haze that rose up out of the Vale of Avalon. If the blackberries lining the hedgerows had been ripe, it would have been a perfect ride.

Returning, Laurie leaned back slightly in the saddle to compensate for the downhill gradient. She could see the cottage at the bottom of the hill. It wasn't much to look at really, certainly not the kind of place to interest weekenders. The loose box Dad had constructed against one side wall did nothing to improve its lines, nor did the way he'd turned most of the garden into a paddock, with the remainder set aside for vegetables. Well, Roxanne made all of that worthwhile.

Dad was waiting for her in the yard. 'Did I see you getting a monkey off your back just now?'

Laurie grinned in response. 'It was Roxanne more than me. I just let her do it.'

Dad tried to sound severe, although Laurie could tell he was as pleased as she was. 'I would have thought one broken collarbone would be enough. Anyway, she's getting too old for it, even if you're not.'

'Dad,' Laurie chided. 'That was years ago. You know I'd never have let her go for it if I wasn't sure she wouldn't refuse this time. Anyway, you're right. The monkey's off my back. Once was enough. I don't think I'll ever need to jump that gate again. And I've got the feeling Roxanne won't either.'

With that, Laurie swung her leg over, slipped off the saddle and gave the horse a little hug, before tying her to a ring set in the wall of the cottage. Roxanne nuzzled her pockets: she could smell the Polos in there somewhere. 'Of course you deserve one, my lovely girl,' Laurie whispered to her, slipping her first one mint and then another, before popping a third into her own mouth.

'And what about me?' Dad was watching them.

'There you go, the last one.' Laurie didn't mention the second tube in her other pocket. She undid Roxanne's girth and placed her saddle and bridle on the door of the loose box. She'd clean it later. For the time being, the horse was her main concern. The sweat had lathered on her neck, making Laurie conscious of the heat for the first time. Roxanne would be thirsty, but she needed to cool down first. Laurie used the hose to run water over her, going over her coat with the sweat scraper as she did so. Only then did she fetch a bucket of water and place it within easy reach of the horse's mouth, while she gave her a final rub-down with the towel, all the time whispering sweet nothings into her ear.

Meanwhile, Dad began mucking out the loose box, forking the dirty straw into a wheelbarrow and replacing it with fresh from the small stack that he kept under wraps just outside. 'I've been keeping her in here for the cool, would you believe? It's been that hot in the paddock. But you might as well put her out there when you're done, now the sun's a bit lower. Check her trough's full, won't you?'

Dad was in the kitchen by the time Laurie returned. It had become his natural habitat ever since Mum was ill, although he'd hardly ever cooked before. Now he treated food with the same care she imagined him once applying to his physics experiments, doing his best to recreate old favourites from Laurie's childhood. He looked up from the chopping board. 'Supper in about half an hour. I've taken your bag upstairs and run you a bath. Take a glass of wine with you.'

It was closer to an hour than thirty minutes before Laurie appeared for supper in the dressing gown that hung on the back of her bedroom door, her hair wrapped in a towel. Dad was sitting down, doing the crossword and listening to Radio 3. A rice salad stood on the table. This was a dish that Dad had reverse engineered soon after they moved down here, and then gone on to perfect, at least as far as Laurie was concerned. He'd kept the things that made it special in Mum's day – like the walnuts and fresh basil – but had improved the dressing, and added avocado. Being in the country helped, of course. Laurie could tell that these French beans were homegrown as soon as she bit into one, and she was sure the same went for the tomatoes, eggs and cucumber.

They ate for a while in companionable silence. When they did start to speak it was of nothing particularly important. Dad updated Laurie on his new sideline building henhouses for the rest of the village. She described her evening in West Hampstead the night before. Josh and Lizzie had gone out to a film, leaving Laurie in full 'godmum' role, from watching *In the Night Garden*, through supervising a bath where she could hardly see any water for all the toys, to reading Tessa the same bedtime story three times in a row. Laurie was glad to have something like that to tell Dad; it saved admitting to all the other evenings spent alone. He liked hearing about Lizzie, although expressed his usual shock at the idea that a girl he remembered coming round for play dates when they were both at Park Street Primary was now herself a mother.

'She's the only one I've kept in touch with, of course,' Laurie mused. 'And that's only because she made an effort when she came to uni in Bristol at the same time I was at college there.'

Dad was quiet. Laurie could tell he was replaying the old arguments in his mind: her accusations that he was ruining her life, running away, dragging her to the back of beyond; his own stock responses that it would be better for both of them. It was time to say something.

'You know I don't mind, don't you? Not any more. God knows what would have happened to me if we'd stayed in Cambridge.'

Dad suddenly got very interested in his salad. Silence returned for a minute or two.

'How about you?' Laurie burst out, seized by a sudden thought.

'What?'

'Do you regret coming here? I mean, you had a nice life there, didn't you?'

Dad shook his head and smiled. 'Laurie, we are both so much happier now. How could I regret that? You know I wasn't in great shape either. Mum being ill was bad enough. I hadn't published anything for three years. And then she was gone. I'd been so full of hope; she really did seem to be getting better, and then – nothing. You were all I had. The students scared me. So did the idea of making a grant appli-cation. I brought you here because I knew if you'd stayed in Cambridge you'd have only got worse, but it was for my sanity as much as yours.'

Laurie was stunned – and ashamed. Of course she wouldn't have noticed that Dad was struggling too just after Mum's accident. She was in no state to notice anything then, but it still shouldn't have taken her the best part of ten years to find out. She thought back to the Dad she remembered from her childhood: solving the Rubik's Cube in three days, as he brushed away Laurie's attempts to teach him all the tricks, installing his own boiler, either because he resented paying a plumber to do so, or because he only trusted himself to do it properly – probably both. He had always been able to do anything. He still could, couldn't he?

Dad changed the subject. 'So, tell me about your week.'

Laurie knew exactly what he was getting at. 'Well, I haven't been on the Tube again, and I've been having night-mares. I still can't get past the idea that if my bike hadn't been wonky, if I hadn't got a smudge on my nose, if I hadn't gone to that end of the platform, if I hadn't smiled back at him, for God's sake, then that man would still be alive.'

Dad made no response. The silence was long enough for Laurie to think about telling him more: about the thoughts she had been having just before the man smiled at her, about the way she couldn't stop thinking about him. Then Dad began, hesitantly, 'It's a while since we talked about Mum, isn't it? I guess this has made you think about her?'

'Dad. I'm always thinking about her.'

At this Dad looked Laurie straight in the eye and gave her a smile of such warmth, happiness even, that she felt ashamed again that he'd needed to hear her say something that should have been so obvious. Then he rescued her with a slight change of subject: 'Good. She deserves it. But I suppose I'm worried that this has made you think about how she died again.'

'Yeah' Laurie admitted, with a little sigh. 'You too?'

Dad nodded and Laurie carried on, 'I mean, I know she was in a car, not on the Tube, and I know it was ten years ago, but something's got a hold of my subconscious. I'm thinking about that man a lot, but I often feel as though she's the one I'm seeing in my dreams.'

'At least you know what happened to him – know it was an accident. With Mum, we've never quite known.' Dad sounded almost ruminative.

'You mean the open verdict?' Laurie asked. 'Well yes, but the awful thing is, I got the impression that the police were leaning that way with this man too – talking about psychiatric reports, that sort of thing. Even though I saw him fall.'

'Well, at least you could tell them what you saw. With Mum, I didn't have that certainty.'

'Dad!' Laurie exclaimed. 'You don't really think Mum killed herself, do you?'

Dad blinked, clearly taken aback by her vehemence: 'Laurie, I'm quite sure that Mum – the Mum we knew – would never have done anything to hurt us. And God knows we were both hurt by her death. But she was ill. The open verdict was the best we could have hoped for. As far as the police were concerned, there was very little doubt.'

Laurie lay in bed, eyes wide open, analysing the evening's conversation, regretting the way she had broken it off so quickly. Why didn't they talk like that more often? But it probably wouldn't do any good if they did. Mum was dead. Why rake up the past?

Laurie thought back to herself as a teenager, to the black pit she'd found herself in after Mum's death, to her attempts to self-medicate for grief with anything she could lay her hands on. The world would have found it so logical, wouldn't it, if she'd killed herself then, so soon after her mother had apparently done the same? Well, she hadn't. She was still around.

With her eyes shut now, Laurie thought about Mum – the periodic check that she could still remember her face, her hair, her smell – but newer images kept pushing themselves into her mind: that afternoon's ride, the glorious leap over the gate contrasting with the time she found herself launched out of Roxanne's saddle. Then it was no longer herself falling, but the man on the Victoria line platform, desperately grasping at the air.

Now there was a memory that wouldn't go away. Dad was right that at least she knew what had happened, could be absolutely certain it was an accident. Surely that was something she could fight for? Would anything convince the police?

In her mind's eye, Laurie began replaying the events leading up to the accident. There was the man, brought back to life by the magic of Laurie's memory, elegant, smiling in a way that Laurie found infectious. He leaned across to talk to her, pointing at his nose. Laurie remembered his hand as a fist from which only his index finger protruded. Why should that have made an impression? Isn't that the way people always point? Ah yes, he was holding something in his hand, something connected to a small brass disc.

Laurie knew what was coming next. She had to force herself to continue, to kill the memory she had just recreated. The tunnel roared; the crowd shifted. Somehow, the man was spun off-balance. How? Did Laurie's memory contain any clues? No. She was looking at his face – at that awful sequence of surprise, realisation and panic – and at his hand, stretched out towards her, his last hope of salvation.

Then Laurie remembered. The man's hand was open – supplicating, grasping at thin air, but also empty. It was the same hand that had been pointing at his nose a fraction of a second earlier. Laurie was sure of that. There had been something in it, and now there was nothing. Whatever it was, he could only have dropped it as he fell.

Sunday, 26 July – 9 a.m.

Dad was cooking breakfast when Laurie came down. It was all part of their usual routine. He would do the works: fried bread, tomatoes and sausages with scrambled eggs. She would tell him not to waste his time on something she'd never be able to finish; he would cook it, and she would eat it all. It was reassuring, the idea that they could go back to normal after their conversation last night. He looked round as she came in and put the eggs on to cook. Laurie sat down. Now was not the time to speak.

Two minutes later they were sitting opposite each other, their plates gently steaming.

'I'm sorry,' Dad began.

'No, I'm sorry,' Laurie interrupted. 'I shouldn't have run off like that. Quite apart from anything else, I must have left you with the washing-up.'

Dad smiled at the reference – they always had shared the same sense of humour – but he had more to say. 'Perhaps I shouldn't have brought up the subject.'

'It's OK. We had to talk about it some time. Are you really sure it wouldn't have done any good to challenge the verdict?'

Dad was silent, for long enough for Laurie to realise there was no good way for him to answer her question. It was time to change the subject. At this point, if she were following custom, she would be asking about the provenance of the food on her plate. Instead she tried something different. 'I've been thinking. I might get an earlier train back – the half eleven, if that's OK.'

'Oh, right.'

Laurie could hear the disappointment in Dad's voice. He deserved some sort of explanation. 'It's just that after talking to you last night I thought through what I saw of the accident a bit more. It made me realise something. I just want to check it out.'

Dad was as gentle as ever. 'Laurie, you know you don't owe this man anything.'

Laurie thought about the way the man's smile reconnected her with the world. She did owe him something, although she wasn't going to tell Dad that. 'It's for me as much as him. The police as good as told me they think he killed himself, while I know he didn't. You were told much the same about Mum. I just can't let it rest there.'

Dad stared at his plate long enough for Laurie to regret dragging Mum into the conversation yet again. Why did she do that? What could he be thinking? When he finally spoke, however, there was not a hint of reproach. 'Good for you. Half eleven still gives you time to give Roxanne another outing. I'll get going in the garden so you've got something to take home with you.'

Laurie sat on the train as it pulled out of Castle Cary. Experience had taught her to prepare for having more to carry from home than to it, especially now it was high summer. The large wheelie suitcase she had dragged empty from London now contained a dozen eggs (carefully packed in old cartons and wrapped in newspaper), six ripe tomatoes, three firm but muddy beetroot, a large bundle of runner beans, a bag of French beans, four sweetcorns, five leeks, about a pound of new potatoes, a large punnet of raspberries and a head of garlic.

That last item had apparently been an afterthought, shown to Laurie shortly before they left and popped into the suitcase 'in case you meet any vampires on the train'. Laurie was pretty sure that Dad was proud of his garlic's plumpness – it was a new thing for him to grow – and he was, in his shy way, calling her attention to it. Her pragmatic response included as much acknowledgement of his skill as she dared. 'It smells as gorgeous as it looks. I'd better wrap it up before it goes in with everything else.'

All of this was in accordance with the traditions Dad and Laurie had established in the year since she left home. Normality had returned. Nevertheless, things felt different for Laurie, at least, and she guessed they did for Dad too. As usual, he had insisted on bringing the suitcase onto the carriage before he got off to wave through the window. This time, as the train picked up speed and Laurie watched his figure gradually recede, she found herself wondering what he would do now. How did he spend his time when she wasn't around? The garden, Roxanne and chicken coops were all very well, not to mention the A-level tutoring, but Laurie couldn't shake off the idea that, a lot of the time, Dad must be lonely. The move to Somerset had served a purpose. She could see that now more than ever, but it had also circumscribed Dad's life in a way he could scarcely have imagined when he was a brilliant physicist with the academic world at his feet. And then what had it cost him to encourage her in the move to London, when Jess had produced that unexpected suggestion?

Laurie got her book out of her shoulder bag. This was an integral part of her plan for coping with her first journey underground since the accident. She needed something she hadn't read before but could be pretty sure she'd find absorbing. The bookshelf in Dad's bedroom had yielded the perfect title: *Sylvester*. Georgette Heyer had been Mum's favourite author, then Dad's and, in the last few years, as she'd grown up and out of the girl she'd once been, Laurie's too.

By the time the train arrived at Paddington, she was deep into her book. Sylvester, Duke of Salford, had started to realise that there was more to the mouse-like Phoebe than he had previously thought. Laurie had to wrench herself away from Georgian England to get off the train. She was at the door when a man approached her. In an instant she was back at Euston police station, witnessing a shocking descent into violence. She flinched, but before she could put her fear into practice in any other way, the man reached out a hand for her suitcase, took it off the train and put it down. He had only been trying to help. Recovering her poise, she imagined herself a Regency maiden and bestowed a suitably grateful smile, trying to ignore the pounding in her chest.

From where Laurie got off the train, it was a simple matter to pull her suitcase up the ramp to the footbridge over the lines coming into Paddington, walk across it to the ticket hall above the Hammersmith and City line, and descend to the eastbound platform. She had got herself back on the underground network, and apart from that one shaky moment she felt fine – in fact, pleased with herself. This far west, the Hammersmith and City line ran above ground; she had fooled her body into thinking she was only changing trains. Soon enough she was in a carriage, sitting down and engrossed once more in Phoebe's plight.

Laurie did not lose herself totally in her book. She was

aware of the train heading into a tunnel soon after it left Paddington, and of the succession of brick-lined stations that followed, but she felt as if she were an observer of the journey, much as she was of the conversations between Sylvester and Phoebe, not an actual participant. It was only on arrival in King's Cross that she took control once again, dragging her suitcase off the train, up a short flight of steps and along to the top of the escalator going down to the Victoria line.

Laurie had been worried that she could have trouble here. She might already be underground, but now she really did have to descend. She took out her book, opened it to the correct page, and held it in front of her face with her right hand while her left grasped the extendable handle of her suitcase; a few steps more and she was on the moving staircase, sinking rapidly.

The tines at the bottom of the escalator pushed the soles of Laurie's feet away from the flattening steps. She was six again, being told off by Mum for putting her toes at risk. She started to walk before she could cause a pile-up behind.

The advantage of doing this on a Sunday afternoon was that the Tube wasn't crowded. The few people there were walking casually, with no air of hurry about them. Even down on the platform, now only one stop away from the site of the accident, Laurie could maintain a sense of detachment, helped by the fact that a good portion of her brain was engrossed in Sylvester and Phoebe's journey on a snowy road from Marlborough to Newbury. Nevertheless, she was careful to stand well away from the tunnel entrance as she waited for the southbound train to arrive.

Laurie didn't even bother to sit down on the train that eventually came. It was a simple matter to stand holding the guardrail, still reading her book, propping up her suitcase between her hip and the side of the carriage. In less than a

69

minute, she felt the deceleration that indicated the train was arriving at its next stop, heard the difference in engine noise that announced it had emerged from the tunnel, and finally looked up from *Sylvester* to see the platform moving past and slowly coming to a stop. Laurie stowed her book, re-extended the handle of her suitcase and stepped out through the open doors. She was back on the Victoria line southbound platform at Euston station.

Now was the time for Laurie to focus. With her suitcase trundling behind her, she walked up the platform to the back of the train, moving against the flow of the few departing passengers. By the time the train pulled out, she was, as far as she could tell, in position, standing at the edge of the platform, right where she had been almost a week before.

There was no hint of the accident. Laurie knew not to expect one – certainly nothing in the vein of those sad bundles of flowers, poems and photographs that she occasionally came across by lamp posts in Tufnell Park. Still, she found it odd to think that no one else around her had the faintest idea that here was the scene of a tragedy. If she had been religious, this might have been the moment for a prayer. As it was, she thought back to the man and his smile. She was glad she could do this for him.

Laurie looked up at the platform indicator: three minutes until the next Brixton train. A quick scan of the track area would be a good place to start. To see right down into the pit Laurie had to lean slightly over the edge of the platform, while keeping as much height as possible. She was never going to put herself in any danger of overbalancing, but she was still surprised by how exposed she felt. It was just as well there were so few people around. If there had been any risk of being jostled she would not have been able to do it.

There was nothing to be seen – just crisp wrappers, a

discarded train ticket, a couple of rubber bands, nothing that might have been what Laurie hoped to find. She moved along the platform, looking along the pit from different angles, searching for anything that might catch her eye. Trying to be systematic, she kneeled down to examine the area between the platform edge and the nearest rail, ignoring the curious glances of waiting passengers. Then, alerted by the tunnel's roar, she looked back along the platform to see her three minutes were up: *Next train approaching*, the indicator was now flashing, with simulated urgency.

Laurie retreated to watch the engine emerge, all too conscious of the last time she had been on this platform. She thought back through her memory. There was no doubt. The man had something in his hand when she first saw him right beside her, and nothing when he was falling out across the track. He must have dropped it, whatever it was, during that last frantic pirouette. If so, he could have flung it just about anywhere, but far more likely away from the platform than towards it. How about that other rail – the one running along the back wall, furthest from the platform – the electric rail? Might something have got lodged behind that?

Now Laurie could hardly contain her impatience as she waited for the train to leave. When it finally did so, picking up speed with what was surely deliberate slowness, at least the section of track she was interested in was the first to clear. There was the rail, but seeing behind it was almost impossible. The best Laurie could do, after some experimentation, was to lean out from the platform as far as she dared and look back along the track. The obliqueness of the angle meant she was at least able to get a partial view of the area that had previously been hidden from her. She had to shift positions several times, each time devoting her gaze to a different portion of the track. Then, suddenly, she saw it, nestling against the white ceramic of one of the rail's brackets: a small patch of incongruous circular brass.

That was it! Laurie was certain. The only question was, what to do now? She did not even know what she had spotted. Why might a smartly dressed man have been grasping a circular piece of metal on a Tuesday morning at Euston Station? Was it some kind of token? A roulette chip? One thing was for sure, Laurie was in no position to retrieve the object. Even if she were brave enough to leap down between the rails during a gap between trains – and she wasn't – those ceramic mountings almost certainly meant the line was live; electrocution was a risk too far. Besides, she'd cause such a commotion that station staff would be bound to take an interest. She'd end up arrested and whatever it was that was lying there would be confiscated.

Somehow it was that last thought that Laurie found most distressing. This was her discovery. Eventually, of course, she would have to tell the police about it, but in the meantime it wouldn't do any harm, surely, if she tried to work out how someone might go about retrieving it?

Sunday, 26 July – 3 p.m.

The flat felt like more of a haven than ever. Laurie was glad to find it empty. If Jess had been around, she would never have been able to get on with the serious googling she now planned. She settled down to work on the old computer in her bedroom, the one she'd brought up from home two years before. It might be slow by comparison with the super-fast desktops at Fitzalan Capital, but at least it got the job done.

The most informative sites were those that opened with something like 'I'm not a trainspotter, but . . .' Within a few minutes Laurie had learnt that the fourth rail, nearest the wall, was indeed live, and so was the more central third rail that ran between the two running tracks. Beneath them, running the length of every platform, was a 'suicide pit': intended to allow trains to pass safely over anyone who jumped in front of them. How unlucky that man had been to fall at the exact time when the train was there to hit him. Mind you, electrocution alone could have killed him.

On the other hand, there were lots of photos of people walking the tunnels when the trains weren't running. There must be a time when the lines were turned off, but was it every night? Website led to website, each click drawing Laurie further in. Finally, a 'customer case study document' provided the answer. It was written by the company that had put in the Underground's new control system. One of its benefits, apparently, had been an improved response time, which meant that 'engineers working on the track during the night when the power is turned off (between 1.00 a.m. and 4.30.a.m.)' could start work earlier. It was only an intellectual exercise, Laurie told herself, but if anyone were to go on the track, there was the time window in which to do it: three and a half hours would surely be long enough.

Long enough for what? Euston must be close to impregnable. If someone was going to get onto that track, they would surely have to come to it from a less well-guarded station elsewhere, somewhere on the Victoria line, for example. That might be the obvious place to start, but there was no obvious access point: King's Cross to the north would be as bad as Euston, and Warren Street to the south not much better – cameras everywhere. But how about the Northern line? There was that funny little station, Mornington Crescent, just one stop away from Euston. It was a fantasy, Laurie knew as she clicked on another site, but might that offer a route underground?

Laurie continued her surfing, turning her attention to the Tube network itself. She could remember faintly unsettling moments when she'd been travelling on the Underground, staring out of the window to avoid catching anyone's eye, and the wall rushing by on the other side of the glass had suddenly disappeared, sometimes to reveal another train, whose passengers' looks of surprise mirrored her own, but more often onto an empty set of tracks. There must be intersections, and they raised the possibility of getting lost. The fantasy could quickly turn into a nightmare.

One website discussed the history of the different companies that were eventually amalgamated into the Northern line. It explained why both the Charing Cross and the City branches stopped in Euston, and why their platforms were so far apart. Then there was the series of deep-level tunnels, originally planned for an express route running from Belsize Park to Clapham South, converted to air raid shelters and bunkers during the war, and now abandoned or used for document storage. Laurie was starting to understand why 'London under London' exerted such a strong fascination over so many people.

Gradually, the pieces came together. All those underground junctions, it turned out, were in the City branch – the result of Euston's reconfiguration when the Victoria line was built. She liked the idea of the loop that meant that a train could transfer from the Piccadilly line at King's Cross to the Northern line at Euston, although it was never used now for passenger trains. Then there was the siding that apparently terminated at the end of the southbound platform at Euston. The Charing Cross branch, on the other hand, was clean and simple. It went straight from Mornington Crescent to Euston: a few hundred yards with no interchanges, perfectly doable. Emboldened by the sense that a solution, no matter how far-fetched, was emerging, Laurie decided to go for a little journey to make certain.

The street-level indicator at Tufnell Park showed that the next southbound train was going via Charing Cross. Armed with *Sylvester*, Laurie got in the lift and let herself be taken down. She raised her eyes from the page as the doors opened, but otherwise remained determinedly engrossed on the short walk down another flight of stairs onto, first, the platform and then, after a brief wait, the train.

For three stations, Laurie did not look up from her book. Only when the train pulled out from Mornington Crescent did she put it away and stare out of the window, allowing her eye to follow the cables that ran along the tunnel wall. There was something mesmeric about it. She had to concentrate just hard enough to focus, but not so hard that she took back control of her eyes. It was a relief when, after only a minute's travel, the train arrived in Euston. Laurie was dizzy, almost disoriented by the experience, but it had achieved what she wanted. She was sure that the cable continued unbroken from one station to the other. She crossed to the northbound platform and repeated the exercise, with the same result. One more round trip, looking out of the other set of windows, and Laurie was certain: there really was no intersection. If someone did walk down the line from Mornington Crescent to Euston, there was no chance they would lose their way in the dark.

Laurie broke the second of the two return journeys by checking the topology of Euston Underground station itself. She'd used it countless times, but always just following the signs, with no real consciousness of what she was doing. This time she forced herself to notice, properly, how everything fitted together: the way the line she'd used from Mornington Crescent was at one end of the station, the short flight of steps up from it to the main interchange level, the corridors leading to the two Victoria line/Northern line concourses – one southbound, the other northbound. She rode up and down the escalators that descended from the interchange level to the two concourses, and registered the way both were also served by a single spiral staircase coming down between them. Was she becoming obsessed by a fantasy? Well, at least it was getting her used to being on the Underground again, and that was no bad thing.

Back at Mornington Crescent everything was much simpler – just a platform level and a ticket office, with lifts and a staircase connecting the two. Laurie climbed to the top, the metal steps ringing beneath her feet, satisfied that she'd worked out the answer to her notional problem. It was surprising how good it made her feel.

Her phone was beeping. She had a voicemail: 'Hi Laurie. Just calling to check you're OK. Give me a call some time. It would be good to see you again. Bye . . . Oh, this is Paul, by the way, Paul Collingwood.'

Paul! Laurie found herself smiling at the sound of his voice. Simultaneously, she realised that was the first time she had thought about him all day. Of course, it was Sunday; he'd presumably be back in London now from seeing his kids. Yes, Laurie admitted to herself, she would like to see him again. All of a sudden that little brass disc started to feel less important. The message envelope had his number. Within seconds she could hear it ringing at the other end.

After such excitement, it was a little disappointing to go through to voicemail: 'Hello, this is Paul. I'm sorry I can't take your call just now, but if you leave a message after the tone, I'll get back to you.'

'Hi. It's Laurie. Just got your message. I'm back above ground now. It would be great to talk to you. Call me back.' Oh God, did that sound too eager? Should she have hung up without leaving a message, or at least called back once she'd had a chance to compose one that didn't make her sound like a breathless teenager? What if he didn't call back?

Knowing it was ridiculous, that she should be getting home, that if he hadn't answered now, then it was probably because he was too busy, or away from his phone, Laurie nevertheless stared at her handset, willing it to ring.

And it did! The screen announced a number with no name

attached. Laurie was pretty sure she recognised it as Paul's. She lifted the handset to her ear.

'Laurie, is that you in person? I was afraid we were destined to play phone tag all evening.'

'Paul!' Was that too breathless? Surely it couldn't hurt to let him know she was happy to hear from him. 'You know I haven't had your number until now?'

'I've just worked it out. I was wondering why you hadn't been in touch, so I looked back at that text I sent you on Tuesday and realised it hadn't delivered.'

'Well, I guess I've got your number now. How have you been?

'We had a lovely time, thanks. The kids always seem to relax when we're at my parents. How about you? Your message said something about being back above ground. Does that mean you've been on the Tube?'

Laurie could hardly keep the note of triumph out of her voice: 'It certainly does. I remembered something else about the accident, and I've been checking it out.'

'That sounds interesting. I don't suppose you're free now for a bite to eat?

Laurie was beyond playing it cool. 'I'm free. Where did you have in mind?'

Laurie liked the romance inherent in Paul's idea of meeting at the top of Parliament Hill. Eight o'clock? That sounded fine too. It was only after she'd hung up that Laurie realised it was already seven. She must have spent two hours underground, and she was in no fit state for that all-important second date.

Luckily, the trains were running smoothly when Laurie went back down. It took less than forty minutes to get back to the flat and take a shower. After towelling dry, she shrugged on the cotton dress she had bought in Bristol two summers ago, slipped her feet into sandals and put on a bit of lipstick; no time for anything fancier. Oh God, her hair was still wet. Two minutes with the hairdryer would have to do. Laurie tied it back in a ponytail and was out of the door at eight.

Five minutes later she was locking her bike to the railings by the café, and walking fast up the hill. If she could be less than ten minutes late, that wouldn't be too bad. The evening sunshine meant there were still crowds of people about: dog walkers, joggers, tennis players walking back from a game, even a few pushchairs. It was good to see these reminders of ordinary life, of people who might have lived in London for years without experiencing any of the horror she had witnessed in the last week; she really should come here more often.

When Laurie got to their rendezvous, she picked out Paul immediately, despite all the people milling around him. He was standing at the very top of the hill, looking out at the view of London stretched out before him. In profile, eyes scanning the horizon, he was as handsome as ever. It wasn't so much his looks, but his air of capability; nothing could faze him.

As if to confirm the thought, Paul turned round just as Laurie approached – no chance of him being caught una-wares. Why didn't she find it unnerving? Perhaps it was because he was so obviously happy to see her: smiling broadly as he leant forward to kiss her on the cheek. His skin felt a bit rough against hers. If Paul had dashed home to get ready, then his preparations had not included a shave. He let his hand rest on Laurie's waist for a fraction of second, long enough for her to feel it there. Then he spoke. 'I'm glad you could make it. On days like this, I sometimes think there's no better place to be. Just look at that view!'

Laurie looked. It was good to be up high, looking down

on the city after the hours she had spent underground. There was the Shard, the most immediately recognisable landmark, with St Paul's looking dumpy right in front of it; were they really that close? Another cluster to the left must be Canary Wharf, but it looked so near. Then, as Laurie got accustomed to the scale, she began to pick out other buildings to the west: Centrepoint, the Telecom Tower, some pylon on the far horizon.

Laurie felt a surge of pride in her adoptive city. It was just as beautiful, in its way, as the view towards Glastonbury from above Dad's house. Paul was right. It was amazing that she had lived around the corner for almost a year and had never been here before. Now she knew she would return often, dragging her friends with her, claiming ownership with her ability to point out the landmarks. She had to stop thinking of London as a dark place, full of violence. 'Where's the Eye?' she suddenly asked, curious.

'What?' Paul had been looking at her, she realised, not the view.

'The London Eye. You know, the big wheel by the Houses of Parliament. I'm surprised you can't see it from here.'

'I'm not sure. Perhaps it's behind that tree.' Paul gestured to the beech in full leaf that stood in the foreground and provided the view with its right-hand frame. 'Are you ready for your picnic?'

For the first time, Laurie noticed the M&S shopping bag at Paul's feet. He picked it up and they walked down the hill together, looking for a less crowded spot. As they did so, the Eye appeared from behind a tower block almost directly in front of them. The beech tree Paul had indicated turned out to be concealing Battersea Power Station. It was strange how the angles could play with your sense of perspective.

Paul led the way down to the slope above the running

track, high enough not to lose the view, and they sat straight down on the dry grass. Laurie watched while Paul extracted various pre-packed delicacies from the bag, realising how hungry she was as he did so. Breakfast seemed a long time ago. For a brief moment, she remembered the huge quantities of fresh vegetables sitting in the fridge back at the flat, then she consoled herself with the thought that they would still be there tomorrow, unwrapped a plastic fork and tucked in.

In the meantime, Paul was producing a bottle of Prosecco and two glasses, with something of the flourish that he had displayed when repairing Laurie's bicycle the first time they met. They sipped and ate as the shadows lengthened, admiring the sun's golden reflection on the buildings below.

At some point Laurie started to feel chilly. Goose bumps were appearing on her arms. Paul overrode her half-hearted objections – at least he had a long-sleeved shirt on – and draped his jacket over her shoulders – only linen, but it was better than nothing. They both lay down, heads beside each other, looking up at the darkening sky. Neither touched the other, but Laurie was sure Paul felt their proximity as much as she did.

The silence grew. It had been so easy to talk before. Where had that gone? Laurie couldn't help feeling that each was waiting for the other to cross some bridge, do something to break the growing tension. 'Do you—' she began, only for Paul also to start speaking. 'Laurie.—'

It felt good to laugh with him. 'You first,' said Paul, narrowly beating Laurie to it.

'Oh, I was only going to ask what you think when you see aeroplanes going overhead, whether it makes you want to travel? Whenever I see the trails high in the sky, I always wonder where they're going, wish I was on them, that sort of thing.'

'I know what you mean,' Paul replied. 'Just taking off

seems so tempting. Then I think no, I couldn't bear it if I never saw my kids again. They keep my feet firmly on the ground. I can't just up sticks, at least not while they're little.'

Silence fell again. Laurie tried to imagine the sense of responsibility that must come with being a parent. She thought of Dad and the way he worried about her while pretending to be unconcerned.

'Sorry,' said Paul, interrupting her reverie. 'Was that a bit pompous?'

'No, not at all,' Laurie replied, her voice trailing off. Then, 'Anyway, your turn.'

'What?'

'You were going to say something before we so rudely interrupted each other.'

'Oh, right,' Paul paused in a way that suggested he might be having second thoughts. He took a breath. 'Well, I was going to ask if I could kiss you.'

Laurie only had to turn her head for her lips to meet his. She could taste the Prosecco on his tongue, its tip pressing against hers. She felt his arms around her, pulling her towards him. The sheer joy of it took her by surprise; she had been on her own for far too long.

The silence was no longer awkward. Paul walked beside Laurie as she wheeled her bike back towards Tufnell Park. No need to be afraid of the gathering shadows with him beside her.

Back in the flat Paul sat on the sofa while Laurie fetched some glasses from the kitchen and returned to sit beside him. She never got around to pouring out the last of the Prosecco. Now Paul was kissing her on the lips, on the nose, on her eyelids and earlobes, smiling as he made her laugh, until Laurie stood up and led him into the bedroom.

Laurie lay with her head on Paul's shoulder, his arm

wrapped around her, hugging her close. She had been right to think of him as kind. A feeling of contentment enveloped her.

'So,' Paul said through a yawn, 'what was it you were going to tell me about the accident?'

The accident! The events of the last hour had pushed it out of Laurie's mind so much that it took her a moment to realise what he was talking about. It was an effort to refocus, but as she did, she thought again about how she had spent her afternoon, and her satisfaction at what she had discovered; she wanted to share that with Paul.

'Last night I remembered that the man had been holding something when he fell.'

Laurie finished. She'd told Paul about her experience with the police at Euston, how she'd cast her mind back to check it really was an accident and been brought up short by the detail of the empty hand. She'd described her journey into London that day and how she had got herself back underground. And now she'd just revealed that yes, she had spotted something on the Victoria line tracks at Euston.

'I'm impressed. So are you still sure it was an accident?'

'What? Yes I am. He wasn't jumping; I'm sure of it. He wouldn't have looked at me like that if he was. And if you're going to jump, you don't hold something in your hand, do you?'

'Don't you? What if it was the last thing given to him by the love of his life before she died? Or the last coin he possessed in the world? Do you have any idea what it might have been?'

'No, all I could really see on the tracks was a bit of brass.'

'So, have you told the police about it?'

'Not yet. Instead – and don't laugh – I spent my afternoon

working out how someone could get it for themselves when the electricity is turned off for the night.'

'What?'

'Just a fantasy, really. I reckon someone could fairly easily get onto the Victoria line at Euston by breaking into Mornington Crescent. Although quite how they'd do that I'm not sure. Anyway, it doesn't matter; I probably will tell the police eventually.'

'Do you think they'll take any notice?' Paul had turned over so that he was looking directly into Laurie's eyes.

'No,' Laurie sighed, 'but there's no real alternative, is there?'

Paul continued in his examination of Laurie's face, as if he were weighing whatever he was going to say next, wondering how she would react. 'Well, if you really think you could get us from Mornington Crescent to Euston, then I'm pretty sure I could get us into Mornington Crescent in the first place. That would be an adventure.'

Us! Laurie started to laugh at the craziness of the suggestion, while a tingle of excitement started to build in her stomach. The fear that went with it was exhilarating – thrilling, even. She would never have gone down there on her own, but with Paul? That was a different matter. It would, as he said, be an adventure. Her arms were still around his head; she pulled him towards her for a kiss to seal the deal. As she did so, she knew that if they really were going to do it, if her nerve was not to fail her, it would have to be tonight.

Monday, 27 July – 2 a.m.

Laurie was back outside Mornington Crescent station, locking up her bike. She put the keys in her running belt, next to the torch. She was wearing black – leggings and a long-sleeved t-shirt that zipped at the neck. Her shoes were dark, rubber-soled trainers.

Paul was already there, waiting by the entrance and dressed in a tracksuit he must have picked up at the gym. The Action Man look was spoilt, however, by the conspicuous pair of Marigold washing-up gloves that extended halfway up his forearms. From his pocket he produced another pair for Laurie. This was something they had agreed. As she herself had put it, 'Although I'm confident about the power being off, it would be a shame to be wrong.'

Paul was not carrying a torch, but Laurie knew he'd have one in another pocket. Instead he bore an evil-looking object that she might have mistaken for long-handled secateurs if she had not known what to expect. It was lucky, she reflected, that the safety equipment at Paul's gym included a pair of bolt-cutters, 'In case we need to cut the cables on a weight machine in a hurry.' For all its brevity, Paul's laconic statement had immediately evoked the image of a sweaty middle-aged executive screaming with pain from fingers trapped in a pulley.

Now he just said, 'You're punctual.'

Laurie accepted the compliment. He wasn't to know about the half hour she'd spent pacing about the flat after he'd left, wondering if she still had the courage to go through with this.

Paul continued, 'Can you keep watch and shield me a bit from view, while I deal with this?' He gestured at the pad-lock, which was all that secured the grille across the front of the station.

As if this was the most natural thing to be doing in the world, Laurie obeyed. She turned around. Fifty yards away, a man and woman noticeably the worse for drink were sup-porting each other as they walked down from Camden High Street. To the south, a couple of cars were waiting for the lights to turn green. In the distance, she could hear a police siren wail. It was miles away, she told herself. And in any case, they hadn't done anything wrong – yet.

From behind her back, Laurie heard a *snick*. 'That's it,' said Paul. 'Is the coast clear?'

The drunken couple was now weaving away from them. The traffic lights were still red. The sound of sirens was grow-ing fainter. 'For another ten seconds,' Laurie replied.

'Well, in that case ...' murmured Paul. As Laurie turned back towards him, he pulled open the gate and held it expect-antly. This was it: Laurie's last chance to refuse, to admit what a ridiculous wild goose chase this was. She looked at Paul, ready to speak, and then, somehow, did not. Everything about him inspired confidence; she had to show that her determination could match his. She stepped though the gap. Paul swiftly followed, then reshut the gate and hooked the broken padlock back through. By the time the cars passed,

86

they had both retreated into the shadows of the station, well hidden from the casual glance of any occupant.

The street lights outside made it easy to see around the ticket hall. Paul stowed the bolt-cutters in a corner and led the way, clambering over the barrier. From above, the stairway down looked like a pit of inky darkness, but as they descended the first flight and then turned along a corridor to the left, enough light filtered down from above for them to see the top of the main staircase, switchbacking down. Each grasped the brass handrail with a rubber-gloved hand and, with it as a guide, continued on down.

After two flights, Laurie heard rather than saw Paul stop. Even his gloves, she now realised, were invisible, but she could hear his whisper well enough: 'I think we could risk some light now.'

She fumbled for her torch, carefully rezipping her running belt: this would be neither the time nor the place to lose her keys. A beam sprang out from Paul, two steps below, almost simultaneously with hers. Laurie half expected to hear a shout, of surprise or alarm. Some of those websites had suggested there were communities that lived in the Tube system, evading authority in hidden tunnels. But no, the silence remained unbroken.

Paul carried on down, still leading the way, keeping his torch pointed on the steps in front of him. As Laurie did the same, she noticed his shoes reflecting back at her, eerie spots of brilliance amid the gloom: presumably a safety feature for night-time jogging. That gave her a thought. She stopped, brought her running belt round to the front, and aimed her torch at it. Yes – its go-faster stripes leapt back at her, mocking her other attempts at camouflage. Ah well. It probably wouldn't matter. She flipped the belt back round and hurried on after Paul.

It was only sixty-three steps down – not that Laurie was counting, but she remembered the sign at the top from the afternoon. A short walk in front of the lifts and a further set of steps brought them down to the divide between the platforms. Paul made to turn right for the southbound platform, but a hand on his arm from Laurie stopped him. 'Let's walk south on the northbound track. They have these battery-operated cleaning trains. If there happens to be one on the track, I'd rather see it coming than be surprised from behind.'

Left it was, then left again, walking along to the southern end of the platform. They both stood there, torches aimed down at the rails, as though that alone might confirm whether the electricity was really off. It should be, of course, Laurie knew that from her research, but now that they were down here, translating that confidence into action was unexpectedly difficult. She thought the problem through. 'I don't suppose you've got anything metal with you that you wouldn't mind throwing at the rails?'

No, now that Paul had stowed the bolt-cutters he was travelling as light as she was. Laurie thought of the zips on his leather jacket, then of her keys: what if the rail really was live? She could hardly risk losing them. The key ring on its own, however, now that was another matter.

Paul had the stronger fingers. Laurie aimed his torch at his hands while he slipped the three keys off the ring. Then he leaned out and held it above the middle rail, the one that, if the trains were running, would have been energised to 210 volts. From the side, Laurie confirmed his aim. It was good. The dropped ring hit the rail with a satisfying ping and bounced off it into the suicide pit underneath. There was no spark, no other sound.

That was good enough for Laurie. Sitting on the platform, she felt with her feet for the near running rail, stood up briefly and then used her left leg to lower herself down while her right foot reached for the floor beneath. It was a graceful, almost gymnastic, movement and she found herself hoping Paul had noticed. She reached down to find the key ring and stuffed it back in her running belt with the loose keys. Then she stepped back up and into the tunnel.

Paul, meanwhile, had switched his torch back on, but had not moved from the platform edge. Was he having second thoughts? Laurie could understand it if he were; she was having them herself. Then her mouth overruled her mind. 'Let's run it,' she whispered, bolstering her own courage as she did so.

Laurie ran on, her attention focused on the pool of light juddering in front of her. Every now and then she'd see the beam from Paul's torch as well, when the rhythm of his running brought it into her path. Outside these points of reference was only darkness. The sides of the tunnel were invisible. If it wasn't for the closeness that Laurie felt around her, she might have been in the open air. She had no idea how fast she was going. In her experience, the dark always increased perceived speed; she certainly wasn't out of breath; and she must have been going for what, three minutes, five? It was almost as if she'd entered a trance.

Whoa! Without any warning the light from her torch was shining on nothing. The ground had vanished. It could only be the beginning of the suicide pit at Euston. Laurie brought herself to a stop and aimed her beam around the walls. Yes. There, to the left, the wall disappeared too. They had arrived.

'Nice,' said Paul. He paused for breath. 'Let's get onto the platform.'

Laurie stepped onto the left-hand running rail, walked along it until she felt the wall open out, and clambered up. Soon Paul too stood beside her.

Laurie aimed her torch to the left. The flight of stairs going up to the interchange level was right next door to them, as she knew it would be. They were almost there. She whispered as much to Paul: 'It's probably best if you follow me now. We're changing onto the Victoria line – up, along and down again.'

Paul had no quarrel with that, although there was, perhaps, a hint of irony in his immediate rejoinder, 'Lead on, Macduff. I place myself entirely in your hands.'

The air felt slightly fresher at the top of the stairs, although they were still two levels below the train station. A faint glow shone down from the ticket hall above. Clearly it had some kind of low-level lighting throughout the night. Laurie started confidently for the passageway that went to the other lines, and then stopped, bemused.

The light from her torch had suddenly illuminated the bars of a concertina gate, pulled across to block the entrance to the passageway. It was secured by a padlock very similar to the one Paul had dealt with so efficiently at Mornington Crescent. Only now they didn't have the bolt-cutters. Laurie was ashamed of herself. How could she not have noticed the gate that afternoon? And of course it was necessary. At the very end of the day, only one line would be open; this gate would stop people heading for the wrong one after its last train. Laurie sighed.

Paul was beside her. He inspected the padlock. 'It's no good, I'm afraid. I guess we can come back tomorrow, and bring the cutters with us this time.'

Laurie loved the sheer matter-of-factness of Paul's offer to return, but she knew already she could never bring herself to do this again. Was there any alternative? From where they were standing, there only was one: to climb to the ticket hall up one of the two escalators beside them. Would it do any good? Laurie tried to remember what happened at the top.

The route down brought you to where they were standing now, but how did you get back up? Laurie remembered her own mad dash the previous Tuesday all too well. You ascended on escalators that started from above the Victoria line. They could circumvent the gate by going via the ticket hall.

There was no guarantee, of course, that other gates would not appear to block their path, but at least it was a possible plan. She put it to Paul, in a low but urgent whisper, excitement overcoming nervousness. His reaction, however, reduced her enthusiasm.

'I'm not sure it's a good idea. There may be people about. The moment we're up there, in the light, we'll probably be on camera.'

He was right about the cameras. The last thing Laurie wanted was to have this visit recorded for posterity, especially if there was any chance that Sergeant Atkins was on duty the next morning. They should have worn hats. As it was, Laurie would just have to improvise something with her top. She experimented with pulling it over her head, so that she was looking out through the neck-hole. The result was not comfortable, and could hardly have been stylish, but at least it obscured her face, and she would only have to keep it like that for the ten seconds they were in the light.

As for the possibility that there might be someone up there, Laurie doubted it, but to make sure, she and Paul stood in silence, straining their ears for any sounds of movement from above. All sorts of noises echoed up from the tunnels below: strange clanks and screeches, evidence of activity somewhere in the network. From above, however, there was not a sound.

Laurie counted a hundred breaths before she whispered, 'I'm off.' Then, without waiting for a reply, she started climbing. Halfway up, with the glow from above getting stronger, she turned off her torch and turned round to make sure Paul was doing the same. He too had just stopped, and was aiming his torch down into the gloom, but when Laurie touched his arm he switched it off and set off to follow her once again, with a whispered explanation: 'I thought I heard something.' Laurie sympathised with his nervousness, but said nothing in reply.

A few steps from the top, Laurie pulled her shirt over her head, and watched Paul follow suit, turning himself into some kind of headless hunchback. The action made the t-shirt he had on underneath his jacket ride up slightly, revealing the flatness of his gym-honed stomach.

Coming up into the ticket hall, Laurie gave a quick sweep round, turning her head as she looked out through the tunnel formed by her neck-hole. Although bright by comparison with the gloom they had left behind, the hall was deserted. A few yards in front of her were the barriers, waiting for her to flash an Oyster card. Beyond them, the red LEDs of the ticket machines glowed, sleepless despite the lack of custom. Compared with the hall's usual bustle, not to say air of barely controlled chaos, the quiet was eerie. It certainly left Laurie in no mood to tarry. She moved swiftly to the left, to the top of the other bank of escalators. Within seconds they were descending towards the Victoria line.

After a few steps Laurie stopped, let her shirt slide back into its normal position, and bent forward, undoing her ponytail as she did so. She gave her head a quick shake and then swept her hair back, gathering it up in one quick movement. That was better. She picked up her torch and continued on down.

By the time Laurie and Paul reached the bottom, their torches had become necessary once again. Laurie couldn't help remembering the panic that had gripped her a few days before. It was at this spot, between the two escalators, that she had started to calm down, forced to be patient by the immobility of the crowd. Now they were surrounded by emptiness, and by a sense of stillness that was almost more disconcerting than the lack of light.

If Paul noticed Laurie's hesitation he didn't let on. His torch picked out the top of the stairs, heading down deeper still. 'Is this the one we want?'

Laurie shook her head, realised he had no chance of seeing the gesture, and whispered, 'The escalators are easier. Follow me.' A short walk down a passage to the left brought them back on familiar ground, to the point where Laurie was repeating the journey she'd taken the morning of the accident, the one she'd replayed in her head the night before and the route she'd scouted out that afternoon: down the short escalator, right onto the Victoria line platform and, as well as she could judge it, opposite the point where the brass disc lay.

On this occasion, however, Laurie wasted no time trying to pick out the object from the platform. Instead, she aimed her torch at the near rail, so as to be sure of the footing, and stepped down onto it. A similar careful step brought her down into the pit. Then she felt for the central rail, and swung first one leg over it and then the other, bringing her next to the far two rails. Leaning over, she shone her torch onto the far side of the fourth rail.

For what seemed an age, Laurie was unable to find anything. She swept the back of the rail with her torch as the uncertainty rose within her. Had the disc already been picked up? Had it ever existed in the first place? What would Paul think if it turned out they had done this for nothing? Refusing to panic, she moved methodically along the tracks, carefully examining each white ceramic mounting that she passed. On the platform, Paul kept pace with her, aiming the beam from his own torch so it intersected with hers, and saying nothing.

It was the glint of metal that ended the search. Laurie had misjudged her distances in the dark. There was the disc, about ten metres from where she began, lying exactly in the position she had spotted it half a day before. And there attached to it, invisible from the platform but now reflecting back the light from her torch, was a key.

Laurie could hardly have hoped for more. Here was all the justification she required for this mad expedition – a genuine find. In a second she had reached out a rubber-gloved hand and plucked the key from its resting place. The brass disc, she now realised, was a fob. It bore the digits *869*.

'Have you found something?' Paul's voice came out of the darkness, making Laurie jump. He deserved to know. 'Yes. It looks like it might be a locker key.' Was it absurd for her to be feeling so delighted by her find?

Paul's reply was suitably appreciative but also a reminder that this was only a beginning. 'You are something else. Is there anything to say where it's from?'

'I don't think so: just a number. Let's have a closer look when we're back in the light.' With that, she carefully zipped the key into her running belt, stepped back over the middle rail, and graciously accepted Paul's outstretched hand to help her back onto the platform.

'Thanks for making me do this,' Laurie said simply. Then, like any couple out for an evening stroll, but still wearing their rubber gloves, they walked hand in hand along the platform and up the escalator they had just come down. In ten minutes they would be back at Mornington Crescent, mission accomplished. Laurie had faced her fears and triumphed.

Near the top of the second escalator, Laurie released Paul's hand. The CCTV cameras meant she had to hide her face. To soften the feeling of separation, she turned around and gave him a kiss, a reminder to them both of why they were there, before using the hand she had freed to pull the back of her t-shirt over her head. They were smiling at each other as they created their makeshift hoods. Laurie led the way up towards the barriers.

Then she saw the men.

Monday, 27 July – 3.05 a.m.

That casual moment with Paul felt like a distant memory, for all that it was only twenty minutes ago. Now, after her panicked flight, Laurie was deeper underground than ever. The lights ahead remained unwavering, waiting for Laurie to step towards them. She tried to put herself in the position of a night worker on the Tube. How would she react to a woman wandering in a tunnel? There must be procedures for dealing with trespassers on the line. Presumably they involved the police; would Sergeant Atkins somehow manage to be involved? Was prosecution inevitable? Fitzalan Capital would not be relaxed about something like that.

Still, better to end up back in front of Sergeant Atkins than with friends of the two thugs from earlier. Laurie felt the weight of her torch. Would it be any kind of weapon?

The light was growing stronger now, its source hidden only by the slight curve of the tunnel. Laurie held her breath and continued around the bend, blinking at the glare as she came out of the gloom. For a moment she was blinded, but her eyes adjusted so quickly that she realised the light itself was actually quite dim. It was wall-mounted, and looked like a permanent fixture — nothing to do with workers on the line, or with any kind of ambush. Beyond, Laurie realised, was another light, and beyond that another. In all, she counted six, regularly spaced along the left-hand wall, illuminating the track as it gently curved away.

Laurie looked around. She was as alone as she had ever been. That much was clear. More than that, the tunnel had opened out. It was as if she had arrived at a station, but this was like no Underground station that Laurie had been in before. To her right, where she would have expected a platform, there was only rubble and the occasional piece of rusting metal from long-defunct machines. There was no suicide pit in front of her: no need to worry here about crazies throwing themselves in front of trains. The whole area was covered in white paint, but it had flaked off in places to reveal the familiar red glaze of ancient tiling.

Of course! This must be a disused station. Laurie tried to think about the line between King's Cross and Angel. Above ground it was a fairly straightforward journey up the Pentonville Road. Could she remember any building that might mark the site of an old ticket hall? Wherever it was, that would surely be an exit.

Laurie looked along the right-hand wall. It didn't take long to spot where the platform entrance had once been. A false wall had been constructed out of some kind of chipboard to block the passageway, but there was a door set into it, at what must once have been platform level. Leading up to it was a short flight of steps with a tubular handrail.

The door was locked of course, but Laurie had not come this far to be frustrated by something like that. She was a hundred yards underground, goodness knows how far from the nearest person, out of sight of any security camera. Now was not the time for inhibitions. One of those pieces of metal would probably do the trick.

Laurie went searching and found the perfect tool. Long ago, presumably when they'd lost interest in shifting the rubble from the old platform, someone had abandoned a spade. Now the blade was so blunt that it could not have dug even the loosest soil, but it was still thin enough to be inserted between the door and its frame. Having done that, all Laurie had to do was lean against the spade's handle.

However strong the lock was, the frame had not been made to take that sort of treatment. It buckled; there was a splintering sound, and the door swung free. Still holding the spade, Laurie stepped through the doorway and looked around. She was not sure what to expect: the feeling that she had stepped back in time, perhaps, or at least a hint that this had once been a bustling station. What immediately struck her, however, was the smell: stale urine mixed with damp – familiar from so many other parts of the Tube network, but somehow magnified here, where there were no competing odours. This was no place for loitering.

Laurie was in a short corridor, painted the same dingy white as the tunnel she had just left behind. At the far end her torch picked out another false wall and door, presumably leading to the other platform. Halfway along on the left-hand side an ancient grille blocked access to a lift that had presumably seen no service in at least fifty years. But before that, only two steps away, was another opening and the clear beginning of a flight of stairs. This would be her route back to street level.

Laurie took the stairs carefully, following the torch beam as it led her upwards. Once it illuminated a large pile of what could only be human faeces, slightly shrunken but fresh enough to make her reflect that she might not be alone even now. She stepped around it and carried on up, glad of the spade she still carried.

At the top, a short landing ended in another locked door. Laurie was about to wield her spade once more when a buzz in her crotch made her yelp in surprise. She pulled out her phone. For the second time in twenty-four hours, her arrival at ground level had brought a message from Paul. This time it was a text – *Are you ok?* He must be back above ground too, and presumably fine. Laurie's mind lightened, relieved of a burden that until this moment, she had not even realised was there. This was no place, however, to be composing a response. She shoved the mobile back into her waistband and applied the spade to the door.

This door, however, opened outwards. Its frame was not susceptible to the crowbar treatment that Laurie had given its predecessor. There was nothing for her to get leverage against. She was locked in.

There was a time for science and there was a time for persistence. Laurie emptied the contents of her leggings onto the floor, placed her torch beside them, retreated to the top of the stairs, ran forwards, and put all her weight into a kick just below the door handle. The rubber soles in her trainers absorbed some of the impact, but she still felt it jarring through to her pelvis. Retreating back along the corridor, she repeated the manoeuvre. With heavy boots, she was sure, she would be out in an instant. At least her attacks didn't make too much noise: the thud of wood, not the clang of metal. It must be worth carrying on. If the worst came to the worst, she could always call Paul and try to direct him to the far side of the door; surely it wouldn't be too hard for him to break into a second Tube station.

That thought sustained Laurie as she continued with her running kicks. She imagined talking Paul through her whereabouts, gradually narrowing down his options until the only the door stood between them. It kept her mind occupied as she maintained her rhythm: retreat, run, jump, kick, retreat, run, jump, kick.

Then, without any warning, the lock gave way. Unable to adjust her stance mid-kick, Laurie found her legs moving away from her when they should have been meeting resistance. She came down heavily on her behind, squashing the hand with which she instinctively tried to break her fall. It left her wrist stinging, and she would have a juicy bruise on her bottom in the morning. At least there was nobody there to see her embarrassment. More to the point, she was through.

Sprawled on her back in the doorway, Laurie took a moment to get her bearings. She must have arrived in the old ticket hall. A distant street light visible through large arched windows on the other side of the room gave all the confirmation she needed that she was, finally, back at ground level. It did little, however, to illuminate the room itself. That reminded Laurie that her torch was still on the floor behind her. She picked herself up and went back to retrieve it, along with her other valuables.

Sweeping the torch's thin beam around the vaulted room, Laurie could see that it had become some kind of storage facility, piled floor to ceiling with office furniture. Desks that must have been the height of fashion in the 1970s jostled for space with filing cabinets and swivel chairs. Enough of the floor space was clear to allow Laurie to move around, but with only the light of the torch to guide her, she felt like she was in some kind of labyrinth, complete with dead ends and false turnings, as she gradually worked her way across to the wall with the windows.

Laurie was so focused on making it to what she thought of as the front of the building, where she was sure there would be an entrance, that she almost missed seeing the side door. Then two huge towers of stacking chairs caught her attention. They were about three feet apart, but by some quirk the chairs had settled as they stacked so that the two towers leaned towards each other, touching at the top, some distance above Laurie's head, to form a point. It was this Gothic arch that framed the door. What really caught Laurie's eye, however, was that the door seemed to have no lock. Instead, there were two large bolts, top and bottom. In a matter of seconds Laurie had worked them back and found her exit.

The air outside wasn't particularly cold. Even now, just before dawn, a balmy heat persisted from the evening before. But it was fresh. For the first time Laurie became aware of the foetid atmosphere she was leaving. At the beginning of the day, she'd needed the distraction of Georgette Heyer before she could even venture underground, and now she'd just spent hours there. It had been a remarkable effort of will, and now her body rebelled. An uncontrolled shiver spread from her heart to her head, followed by a tightness in her stomach and a sudden panicky need to squeeze the muscles in her buttocks. Bile rose up through her gullet, filling her mouth with a bitter, teeth-rotting aftertaste. Unexpectedly light-headed, she dropped onto her hands and knees and spat. She was terribly, terribly tired.

Something was wrong. Pentonville Road would still have traffic, even at this time, but here the air was still. Laurie could hear the usual background noise of a London night, but it was in the distance, as if she was in some sort of backstreet. Gingerly, she sat back on her haunches and looked around.

Laurie seemed to be in some sort of open area, but it wasn't a park; she was kneeling on concrete. To her right, she could make out the outlines of buildings, silhouetted against the night sky. There was a fence about twenty yards in front of her, and beyond that a road, dimly lit by the street light she had seen from inside the ticket hall. It was eerily silent, but a bus stop was a reminder of normality – that in daytime, at least, there would be vehicles. Laurie got to her feet, gave herself a moment to let the dizziness pass and stepped out towards the light.

It was all Laurie could do to stay awake on the 390 that, thankfully, arrived at the bus stop only moments after she did. As she got on, she looked across at the abandoned Tube station through which she had made her escape. It stood proudly alone in an area of what was little more than wasteland, its former purpose proclaimed by the arches and muddy-red tiles that she had seen on Underground stations across London.

The station's name was across the top of the arches: *York Road*. It was enough of a clue for Laurie to work out where she was: York Way, perhaps a mile from where she had expected to be. The realisation was chastening. How could she have gone so wrong? It brought home the madness of her decision to go underground in the first place. She could so easily have ended up lost and electrocuted. The only consolation was that she was close to home. The bus arrived at Tufnell Park in less than five minutes: any longer and she would surely have fallen asleep.

As Laurie came up her street she sensed, rather than saw, a shadow detach itself from a tree. She was about to turn round, or run, or something, except that she was really too tired to do anything. Then the shadow spoke. 'I'm sorry. I've got to get out of the habit of creeping up on you.'

'Paul!' Laurie leant her forehead on his chest, and as his arms wrapped around her, felt herself relax properly for the first time in hours. She tried to say that she was sorry she'd run away like that, that she'd been worried about him, that she'd got lost, that she was sorry (again) that she hadn't returned his phone message, but her words were so disjointed that nothing seemed to come out in the way she meant.

Eventually, Paul spoke again. 'Don't worry about it now. We're both safe. Let's get you to bed and we can talk in the morning. OK?' He stayed holding her until she nodded, then let her go.

Laurie approached the door. As she did so, she remembered where she'd put her house key. Paul was right behind her, and if she'd been any less tired she would have made something of it. As it was, however, she just reached down into the front of her leggings and drew out the key first time, flashing a nervous glance over her shoulder, but no more than that.

Through the door, Laurie was reassured by Paul's presence as they climbed the stairs to the flat. One more key and one more door: Paul hesitated on the threshold, but, tired as she was, Laurie at least had enough energy to pull him through after her.

Then he was kissing her, urgent. passionate kisses that travelled from her lips along her jawline and down the curve of her neck. He unzipped her collar and carried on down, gently pecking the swell of her breast above her bra. His hands cupped her buttocks, pulling her towards him. They were all over her.

Laurie tried to respond, to generate the same passion that she could feel in him. But she was tired: so, so tired. Her mouth still tasted of vomit. All she wanted was to brush her teeth and go to bed. She put her hands on his chest and let them rest there, gaining his attention so that she could say her piece. 'I'm sorry Paul. I don't think I'd be any good to you right now, but stay, please.' She led him into her bedroom and sat him on the bed, putting the stuff from her leggings on the table beside it. When she returned from the bathroom ten minutes later, he was already under the duvet and asleep. Laurie unwrapped the towel she'd put on after her shower and got in beside him. She just had time to think that she must be careful not to wake him, before she fell asleep herself.

Monday, 27 July – 9.40 a.m.

Laurie had not set her alarm. She was woken by Paul stroking her hair as he sat on the bed beside her. 'Hi you. I'm afraid I think we're late for work. I've just sent a text to say I won't be in today.'

Laurie liked the implication that Paul now had a free day; it would be good to spend it with him. She might as well use some of that holiday she had banked.

Paul was still wearing the t-shirt and boxer shorts that he'd fallen asleep in. The memory of his behaviour the night before flooded into her. Laurie smiled and pulled him towards her.

It was some time later that Paul said, through a lazy smile, 'That was lovely, but at the risk of seeming desperately unromantic, I feel I should point out that it's already past ten o'clock.'

Shit! Laurie grabbed her phone from the pile of stuff on her bedside table and punched in the number for work, hurriedly thinking of what she should say: that she'd been sick in the night, that she hadn't got back to sleep until four, that she thought it was best if she just took the day off and came in properly refreshed tomorrow. None of it was necessary. The office manager, Linda, was hardly going to make a fuss about the late request for a day off, especially with half the office already away. Laurie felt briefly guilty at the thought of Michael's face when he learnt that she wasn't coming in. Then she turned back to Paul. He lay on his side watching her. 'So where's the key?' he asked.

The key! The original reason for the whole expedition. Laurie was startled to realise that she hadn't thought about it since she woke up and was embarrassed to admit that, in the end, she'd had to abandon it. She could hardly blame Paul for the brief moment of irritation he displayed, quickly suppressed when she assured him that she should be able to find it again without another night-time expedition.

They compared notes about what had happened. Paul had been so busy following Laurie that he had hardly even seen the two men. When he lost her at the bottom of the stairs he had hidden in the shadows until they ran past him, each going in a different direction. Their shouts had soon made it clear that they had lost her, and he'd taken the chance to go back up to the top and retrace his steps to Mornington Crescent.

'So who do you think they were?' Laurie asked.

'I don't know. I thought at first perhaps they were official, but I don't think they behaved like they had an official reason to be there. Chancers? God knows. I think we were just unlucky.'

'Or lucky,' Laurie said reflectively. 'Did you hear them calling me an "unexpected bonus"?'

Paul fell silent. How would he have dealt with it if they had caught her? Laurie was glad that neither of them would ever have to find out. She changed the subject. 'So I haven't told you yet where I came out – some disused station north

108

of King's Cross. It was kind of weird. It all seems so unreal. Tell me I didn't dream everything.'

Paul recovered his poise: 'You didn't dream it. Let's find that key later to prove it.'

Paul made pancakes for breakfast. Although he tried to persuade Laurie to stay in bed, she insisted on getting up. Her excuse was that he wouldn't know where to find anything; in truth she just wanted to carry on watching him. She was not disappointed. He moved around Jess's kitchen with unshowy competence, producing perfect pancakes (flipped, not tossed) with very little effort. He even did his own washing-up, brushing aside Laurie's offer to help with something close to a statement of philosophy: 'I always like to finish what I've started.'

Laurie was thinking that afterwards they might return to bed, but Paul now had an air of purpose about him. The shower they shared was lovely but brief. Soon enough they were dressed, out of the house and back on their way to Tufnell Park. Paul had to buy a ticket – a reminder to Laurie of how rarely he used the Tube.

The first train was to Morden via Bank: they would hardly even have to walk at the other end. Within ten minutes they were at Euston. Hours earlier, Laurie had been running along this platform in pitch blackness, desperately avoiding pursuit. A few days before that, she had witnessed a man fall to his death in front of a train from another platform only twenty yards away. It was amazing how different it felt now, in the light, with Paul by her side. In a week or so, surely, she would be fine.

There was the grille through which Laurie had shoved the key. Even in the light, she noted with satisfaction, the louvred slats made it very hard to see through. She could hardly have picked a better hiding place. Paul stood beside her, shielding her from any cameras as she squatted down and ran her hand along the bottom gap, coming across the disc almost immediately. She had to work it a bit with her fingers to get it out before she was back on her feet beside Paul and they were both looking down at the key and its numbered tag, lying in the palm of her hand.

'So what do you think?' Paul asked.

Laurie thought that was pretty obvious. 'I thought it might be the key for a locker. There must be some here. That seems like the place to start.'

Paul nodded his agreement.

Up in the mainline station, Laurie looked around until she spotted the sign for left luggage. She beckoned for Paul to follow, but he was busy looking at his mobile phone. When he looked back up at her, she could see what he was about to say from the set of his mouth. 'I'm sorry. There's a bit of a crisis at work. The swimming pool isn't heating. They want me in there.'

'Come here then,' Laurie replied. She threw her arms around him and gave him a proper goodbye kiss, willing him to follow her lead, to recapture the memory of how they had spent the morning. Paul, however, kept his mouth tightly closed. Although he continued to hold her, he drew back his head and said with a smile, 'I've really got to go. Let me know how you get on, and we can speak again this evening.'

Laurie let her arms flop to her side. Paul stepped backwards, leant in for one more small kiss, and turned on his heel. She watched him until he turned round and waved on his way out of the station. Even his back view was sexy. Laurie had heard about men 'mentally undressing' women, but now she realised she was doing it herself. Of course it helped if you'd already seen the person concerned naked. She went to the left luggage area.

Even before Laurie got there it was pretty clear that this wasn't the place. There was a counter, a man standing behind it and behind him rows of metal racks, laden with suitcases and backpacks: not a locker in sight. 'None here,' the attendant replied to Laurie's question. 'Nor in any London station,' he added, almost as an afterthought.

Well, at least that last bit of knowledge saved Laurie a fruitless journey down the road to King's Cross. What next? She tried showing the man the key, to see if he had any ideas.

'Found it, have you?' He grunted. 'You should hand that in. The police are just down there.' He gestured to his left.

Laurie thanked the man and walked in the direction he pointed but continued straight past the police office and the unsatisfactory memories it contained. After all the effort she and Paul put in to retrieving the key on their own, surrendering it to the police was the last thing she wanted to do. Safely out of the luggage attendant's field of vision, she carried on out of the station through a side exit into a little parking area. Two London Northwestern employees and a policeman were standing there smoking, enjoying the easy camaraderie of a common vice. She couldn't ask them about the key, clearly.

Laurie walked back round to the front of the station and pondered her options. Where did people have lockers these days? Schools? Gyms? She thought of Paul. That must be worth checking, at least.

He answered his mobile almost immediately. 'Hi. That was quick. Any luck?'

'No, and apparently no London station has lockers. I was wondering about gyms.'

'Good idea,' Paul encouraged. 'Not ours, because we've moved on to combinations, but I'm pretty sure PureGym and Virgin are all still key-based. You could try them. Got to go. Bye.'

Hmm. How many gyms were there in London? At least she could rule out Paul's employer – except, of course, that Laurie didn't know where Paul worked. She called him back to find out, but this time the phone went straight through to voicemail. She didn't feel like leaving a message.

Perhaps she could limit her search by locality? Laurie opened the internet browser on her phone and started looking. It didn't take long to establish that there were half a dozen gyms within five minutes' walk of Euston. She called the first one on the list.

She'd found a locker key in the street, which she thought might be one of theirs. Did their lockers still have keys? They did? Perhaps she could describe the key she'd found?

It took only one conversation for Laurie to realise she wasn't likely to have much luck. At PureGym they did use keys in their lockers, but they were attached to wristbands so they could be worn while training; they didn't have brass tags. The same was true at Virgin Active, TriYoga and Gymbox. Presumably Paul was so used to dealing with combination locks that he hadn't thought through the implications of the alternative. She could tease him with it the next time they met.

Laurie might not have identified where the key came from, but she felt as if she had made progress. It wasn't just that she had eliminated both stations and gyms as possible candidates. In itself that didn't mean much. It was more that, instinctively, she felt she must be right to be looking for somewhere close to Euston. The man had the key in his hand as he stood on the Victoria line platform. He must have put something in the locker that morning and then walked to the Tube. If she wanted to find someone to recognise the key for her, then she could hardly do better than ask here, outside Euston station.

The people scurrying across Euston Square were no good. They were in a hurry, and conditioned by years of dealing with London beggars to avoid the eyes of approaching strangers. Laurie could sympathise; only a few months ago, while still new to London, she'd been scammed by a smartly dressed woman who'd 'been pickpocketed' and needed 'ten pounds for her fare'. She had to find people who could be a captive audience, where she could at least get to the stage of starting a conversation.

The bus station was the place, but even here Laurie found it surprisingly hard to get anyone's attention. She eventually succeeded with someone whom she could only think of as a little old lady: in her eighties, grasping an old-fashioned shopping trolley, on her way home from goodness knows what, and presumably glad of the chance of company.

'Hello dear. What's that? Found it did you say? In the street? Looks rather important, doesn't it? Someone will be missing that. They'll be grateful you're taking all this trouble, I'm sure. No, no idea, I'm afraid. I should take it to the police if I were you. I did once. Found a five-pound note on the pavement. That was forty years ago, mind, when five pounds was worth having. Took it to the police. They said if no one had claimed it after six weeks I could have it back. And you know what? No one did. I went back six weeks later and asked and there it still was. Bought my Cyril a nice fillet steak for his dinner. Told him I'd found it in the street. You should have seen his face! Oh, here's my bus, dear. I'd take it to the police if I were you.'

It was the man behind the little old lady who gave Laurie her breakthrough. Like the rest of the queue, he could hardly avoid overhearing their conversation and having his attention drawn to the key. Before he also got on the bus, he smiled at Laurie in a way that acknowledged their mutual amusement

113

at what they had just heard, and said, 'It could be from the British Library. They've got lockers in their basement with key fobs that look like that, and they're only just up the road.'

The British Library? Laurie thought back to the man who had dropped it, to his grey linen suit and air of understated elegance. Could she imagine him as an intellectual, rooting around bookshelves? Why not? Not every brainbox looked like Dad. Anyway, she had nothing better to go on, and she was sick of being told to take the key to the police. Perhaps she would do that after all if the British Library came up blank. She could always just say she'd found the key on the Tube and leave it at that, though she'd speak to Paul first, of course.

Laurie had been vaguely conscious of passing the British Library on the rare occasions she took the bus back to Tufnell Park, but she had never felt any reason to enter it before. Libraries belonged to the life she'd led before Mum died. She would be out place there, she knew.

Nevertheless, no one challenged her as she went through the gateway that opened off the Euston Road. That was hardly surprising, she soon realised, because it simply led onto a red-brick plaza. People milled about, some just enjoying the sunshine, some admiring the huge sculpture of a man squatting over a geometrical instrument, some walking purposefully to the buildings in the far corner. Laurie followed them, trying to look as if she knew where she was going.

The glass doors that led off the plaza bore signs saying that bag searches were in operation for security reasons, but even here Laurie was able to walk straight through, arriving in an atrium that, outwardly at least, was aimed at visitors as much as scholars: exhibition halls off to the left, a fabulous sculpture of a open book, large enough to act as a bench, immediately to the right and, straight ahead, escalators leading up to an enormous stack of books encased in glass. Perhaps this wouldn't be such a bad place to spend her unexpected day off after all. Playing the tourist could wait, however; Laurie's business was downstairs.

It was easy to spot the way down, just to the right of a large information desk. Laurie took it and followed the signs to the locker area, glancing at a nondescript painting of some bookshelves as she did so. Then she stopped, disoriented by what she had just seen. As she walked, the bookshelves in the painting appeared to bend round and follow her progress. Despite the urgency of her mission, she had to take a closer look. Only when she was right by the picture could she could work out what was going on. It was painted in relief, rising to peaks that corresponded to the ends of the bookshelves in a way that played around with perspective. Laurie stepped back and stood still; once again she was looking at an apparently ordinary painting. It was the best optical illusion she had ever seen. She walked on to her destination, gently exhilarated by the way she had just been surprised.

There were a few other people in the locker room when Laurie arrived. All were busy by open doors, stuffing laptops and writing materials into clear plastic bags. Once again, Laurie got the feeling that she didn't belong here, but the few tags that she could see hanging from the keys in unoccupied lockers certainly looked like the one she held in her hand, and she could see from the signs at the end of each aisle that the numbering ran up beyond 900. Laurie tried to look casual as she headed for locker 869.

There it was. The keyhole beckoned invitingly. Laurie was about to try her key in it when she saw the door was already open, and the locker empty. Was that it then? The end of all this madness? Why didn't she feel more disappointed?

Somehow her developing relationship with Paul put everything into perspective. Why did she still care about whatever some nameless man had left behind at the British Library before falling under a train?

But she had seen him die; she had in some way been responsible for his death. She did care. She owed it to him. Had the locker been forced open? Was that what happened when you abandoned a locker for a week at the British Library? It was hard to imagine any of the academics around her as thieves, but then anyone could walk in off the street; she just had.

Laurie looked around. There in the ceiling right above her was a glass hemisphere; behind that, she was sure, was a camera. Anybody who did try to jemmy a locker would be taking an enormous risk. Besides, Laurie considered, the British Library probably wasn't that keen on the idea of stuff being left in lockers overnight. In fact, now she looked, there was a typewritten sign on the wall saying exactly that. So, what would happen to the contents of lockers if they'd been emptied by staff rather than a thief?

The security guard on duty was pleasant enough. He listened with concern to Laurie's story of sudden illness, of how she'd been unable to get back to her locker for a week, and of how she'd found it empty on her return this morning; had they been the ones to empty it?

'We don't record the locker numbers.' The guard replied as he pulled out a file, 'but anything found should be in here. What have you lost?'

Laurie thought her answer sounded eminently reasonable. 'A cycle pannier and my bike helmet.'

The guard flicked through the pages and ran a pen down a column of writing. 'I can't see anything. What date did you say it was?'

'Last Tuesday, the twenty-first.'

'Hmm.' The guard showed the page to Laurie. 'Nothing handed in that day at all. Are you sure you left it in the locker? I'd better get you to fill out a form.'

Dutifully, Laurie filled out the form the guard printed off for her, comforting herself with the thought that the details of her fictitious loss would be filed and forgotten as soon as she walked out of the office. For real believability, she supposed, she would now be complaining, perhaps even shouting, about the slackness that allowed this to occur, but she did not have the heart for that sort of acting. Instead, she managed a rueful smile, and a muttered, 'I'll be more careful next time,' which at least elicited a sympathetic raise of the eyebrows from the guard as she left.

Outside the office Laurie's eye was caught once more by the trompe l'oeil that she had found so fascinating a few minutes earlier. Even though the rational part of her brain knew exactly how the painting worked, the bookshelves still seemed to twist round and follow her.

The real problem, of course, was what to tell Paul. On the one hand Laurie was pleased that she had identified the key's home so quickly. On the other, she couldn't quite shake off the feeling of disappointment that the knowledge had led nowhere. How would Paul react? Would he lift her out of herself? Laurie thought she knew him well enough to hope so. She got as far as calling to tell him the news, but decided not to leave a message on his voicemail. It could wait for the evening.

In the meantime, how should she use the remainder of the day? Those exhibition halls were surprisingly tempting, but an afternoon spent in them wouldn't get her anywhere nearer finding out why that man had a key to the British Library.

There must be some way she could find out more about him. Laurie remembered his stylishness, the suit that set him apart from the other commuters on that platform. She didn't even know his name. Surely it wouldn't be too hard to find out.

First, however, she might as well get her bike back. Enjoying the sun, Laurie walked back up from the British Library to Mornington Crescent, cutting through an odd little warren of streets and shabby housing estates to get there.

Even at its southern end, away from the markets, Camden High Street was buzzing. It was all so different from how she had found it the night before, making the whole episode feel even more dreamlike. The security grille at the station itself was concertinaed back in its usual open position, with no sign of the bolt-cutters that Paul had hidden behind it at the start of their adventure. Presumably he'd picked them up on his way back out. She'd have to ask him what he'd done with them the next time they met.

The bike was where Laurie had locked it the night before, and she was home in ten minutes. The next hour, however, was not so satisfying. For all her skills as an internet surfer, Laurie could not discover anything about the man she had seen fall. There was no site that listed forthcoming inquests, and no news story about a man under a train. Every query she could think of would suggest hundreds of thousands of web-sites, but none appeared remotely relevant. By two o'clock she was ready to admit defeat.

Well, there was something else Laurie could usefully do with her time, she supposed. The task she was doing for Michael was so repetitive; surely there was some way of getting the computer to do it for her? She couldn't actually work on the model at home, of course – that was strictly against Fitzalan policy – but she could at least do what she'd never dare waste time on in the office, and find out a little more about Excel's capabilities. This was exactly the sort of thing the internet was good at.

Six o'clock. When would Paul phone? Perhaps he'd be able to come round for supper. In any case, Laurie had to start doing something with all those vegetables. Soup seemed like the best answer. How about beetroot, leek and tomato? And perhaps corn on the cob to go with it. Would Paul object to a meal with no meat in it? No, of course not. Their first date had been at a vegetarian restaurant. Come to think of it, she'd never actually seen him eat meat. There'd been that sushi last night, of course. Might he be a fish-eating vegetarian? She'd have to ask him what he liked.

Jess made her presence felt the moment she walked through the door. 'Something smells good. Is it for me?'

Laurie sighed; seven o'clock already, and Paul still hadn't phoned.

Tuesday, 28 July – 8.30 a.m.

It was only when she arrived at the office that Laurie allowed herself to acknowledge her disappointment. There had been no sign of Paul on the cycle ride in. What were the odds of them meeting again like that? It presumably wouldn't be too hard to engineer. That junction between Eversholt Street and the Euston Road – the one where they'd met for a second time the week before – would be the best place. Would it be reasonable for Laurie to wait there? Or was she turning into a crazy mad stalker-woman? What was stopping her from just calling him?

Michael was already at his desk, looking, if it were possible, even paler than he had before the weekend. He hardly glanced at Laurie, but had an air of panic about him, that of someone in no mood to have an assistant suggest a different way of doing things. It was probably best if she just showed him.

So Laurie forgot about Paul, about keys, about men under trains, and concentrated on work – on using her brain, as Dad would put it. When was the last time she'd done more than just the minimum required to get by? Before Mum died, of course. That was when she'd stopped bothering. Despite herself, and the undemanding life she had been leading, very deliberately, over the last few years, Laurie had to admit there was something quite satisfying about it.

'You know that's the second time in a week you've worked through your lunch break?'

Laurie raised her eyes, embarrassed, to see Linda standing beside her. It was true, Laurie realised. She'd never noticed any of the other assistants doing the same. Was she breaking some sort of unwritten rule? 'It's just ...' she began, then stopped, defeated. If she had transgressed, then anything she said would make it worse. Besides, if that was the time, she might have missed a call from Paul. She got out her mobile – nothing – then looked up to realise Linda was still there. Now she was being rude; Laurie could feel herself beginning to blush.

Linda, however, was smiling. 'Don't worry. I only came to give you this.'

'This' was a retrospective holiday form for the previous day. Linda handed it over with some words of advice. 'You should have just called in sick. Less paperwork, as long as it's for no more than three days. No one's going to mind. It's not like you're going to make a habit of it.'

'Thanks.'

Laurie took the form and would have turned back to her computer, but Linda clearly had more to say. 'In fact, I haven't had lunch yet. Do you fancy joining me?'

Laurie looked across at Michael, who continued to ignore her in the way he had all morning, then back up at Linda. 'Sure,' she replied. 'That would be fun.'

Over a pizza, Laurie learnt about Linda's life, about how things were a bit easier now the kids were at school. She got the train in at seven-thirty, but Steve was able to drop them off at breakfast club before going to his own job for the council. Then they went into homework club after school. That ended at six-thirty, so she always left the office at half five on the dot so she could be there to pick them up. If her train was delayed she had to call Steve; then he had to make up the time another day. She missed out on overtime, of course, and Laurie didn't need to be told that was where the real money was, but she was still earning more than enough from the job to justify the commute. She'd been there five years by now – only six people in the office had been there longer.

'But the kids aren't at school now, are they? How do you manage?'

'Tell me about it: six weeks. It's lovely to see more of them, and they need the break, poor loves, but it's murder organising it all. My mum helps out a bit. Steve and I each take some time off separately. Then we're all having one week off together in Spain. I can't wait.'

'So how did you meet Steve?' Laurie hoped the question wasn't crossing an unacceptable line towards overfamiliarity.

'Salsa classes!' Linda laughed. 'You know, if I was single now I'd probably try internet dating, but ten years ago I don't think I'd even heard of it. I was working for BarCap then, team assistant in corporate finance, earning good money. I could do the overtime then, of course. Most evenings I wasn't getting home until after nine. I still lived with Mum and Dad. Anyway, I wasn't meeting anyone. The boys in the bank weren't interested. Or they were, but only in one thing, if you know what I mean. I soon realised that was a mug's game; stopped before I got a reputation. So I went to salsa classes to meet people. First lesson – there was Steve. He's never been much cop at dancing, I'll tell you that for free. He was there for the same reason. We got chatting. One thing led to another. Never went back for the second lesson. Never even paid for the course, either.' Linda laughed again. 'So, you got a boyfriend, partner, whatever?'

'No ... well, perhaps. That is to say, I don't know.' Laurie could feel the heat prickling her scalp as her reply petered out. It was her own fault, she knew, for bringing up the subject.

Linda, however, was contrite, if only briefly. 'I'm sorry – personal question, none of my business. I think it's good the way you keep yourself to yourself at the office. I wasn't a woman of mystery at your age, I can tell you.'

Laurie looked at Linda. Was she teasing her? Should she just play along? There was no sign of guile in the friendly, if speculative, look the older woman was giving her.

'It's just, well, I don't make friends easily, or haven't done since I moved to London. I go back to Somerset to see my Dad most weekends. Perhaps I should try salsa classes.' Laurie smiled, happy to have taken the edge off her confession with a joke.

'It's a big place.' Linda nodded. 'Not that I've ever lived here, of course. I'd certainly never dare cycle. It's pretty impressive the way you seem to know your way around. How long have you been here? Less than a year?'

Laurie nodded.

'Well, sounds to me like you've got nothing to worry about. Besides – and I'm not prying – if you have got a boyfriend, that's as good as way as any to get your social life going. You don't need salsa classes. Call him up! Take him clubbing!'

Back in the office, Laurie thought about what Linda had said. Should she phone Paul there and then? The idea was deeply appealing: she'd better think about it first. Besides, Michael was still opposite her, tapping away. However much he might be avoiding her eye at the moment, he'd still hardly be able to avoid overhearing her. Anyway, she was just starting to get somewhere with her Excel macros. In a couple of hours, with a following wind, she might have something to show him.

Friday, 31 July – 6 p.m.

'Right,' said Michael. 'I've just emailed the model to Henry, so it will be in his inbox when he lands. I imagine he'll want to talk to us about it on Monday. In the meantime, we've done all we can. Thanks for your help, Laurie. I really appreciate it. Now, I'm going home. I suggest you do the same. It's been a long week.'

Laurie stopped fiddling around with the sensitivity tables on their spreadsheet – that was how she'd come to think of it over the past few days – and checked the clock on her computer: just coming up to six-thirty. She looked up in time to see Michael give a final wave from the door of the office. She'd never been here to see him do that before. The desks around her were practically deserted. There was no point in hanging around. But what should she do?

Jess was unlikely to be at the flat this evening; Laurie remembered their brief encounter in the hallway earlier in the week: long enough for Jess to give her a hug, explain that she'd met this 'amazing man' at an exhibition opening and ask if everything was OK, but not long enough for Laurie to answer the question. Jess had been carrying a holdall; she obviously wasn't planning on returning any time soon. Josh and Lizzie were going out with some other couples from their NCT group. They'd already been excited at the prospect when Laurie saw them a week ago. On any previous Friday the obvious answer would have been to go home; Dad wouldn't mind the late notice. Today, however, there was no doubt about what she wanted: to see Paul.

Well, now Laurie could do what she'd been promising herself all week. She would call him, and this time, she would leave a message.

Even after hearing it so many times during the week, Laurie still found her heart racing at the sound of Paul's voice as he told her he wasn't there. Nevertheless, she did not let it put her off what she had prepared herself to say. 'Hi Paul. It's Laurie. Hope you've had a good week. My news is that I've found the locker for that key. Give me a call. I'll tell you about it.'

It was nearly seven by the time Laurie got home. She always took the ride more slowly on the way back and this time she'd been even less inclined to push herself than usual, as she kept an ear out for a telephone call that might summon her back to town. She dumped her pannier and checked the phone. No, she hadn't missed a beep. Her message really had produced no response – at least, not yet. It was pointless hanging around waiting for a call that might never arrive: time for an evening run.

Was it the memory of Paul that led Laurie's feet towards the Heath? It seemed natural to take a right and jog in that direction. Coming in by the tennis courts, Laurie lengthened her stride and set off northwards, powering past dog walkers and reeling in other runners. For a while she kept pace with an illegal cyclist before darting off between two ponds. It was all new to her and she liked the idea of being an explorer, of losing herself in a city of millions. Crossing a road, she arrived in a part of the Heath that she had no idea even existed. Only the backs of houses, visible through the trees, and the omnipresent background roar of traffic were an indication that she was not in some piece of ancient woodland. A pond, green with duckweed, exuded stillness. The evening sun slanted down through the canopy.

Laurie had found the solitude she sought, but it was accompanied by a pronounced sense of menace. She remembered the stories she had heard about what happened at twilight in some parts of the Heath; the back of her neck prickled with fear. Was that a human shadow she could see? The trees themselves seemed to form a tunnel, stopping the light, bringing back memories of the Underground. Laurie picked up her speed and ran on, crossing back to the main section of the Heath. Here she rejoined a thoroughfare, level enough for sprinting and with a slight downhill gradient that flattered her tiring muscles. It took her down an avenue of beech and oak, over a viaduct, past rabbits startled in the middle of their evening feed and back to a field where a group of frisbee throwers defied the lengthening shadows. Now she slowed back down to a jog, sucking in breaths that had somehow seemed unnecessary while she was pushing her legs to their limit. One more gentle trot to the brow of the hill, and she could coast down, back towards the ponds and the comfort of the crowds.

Laurie was just turning into her street when a shout rang out – 'Oi!' How could one word contain so much aggression? Back on edge, Laurie began to walk faster, hoping the shout wasn't directed at her. The light had almost gone. This was no time to attract unwelcome attention.

'Oi!' There it was again. 'Do you see what your fucking dog's just done?' Laurie began to relax. It was nothing to do with her. She stole a glance across the road at the source of the voice.

The man looked about fifty, dressed in a filthy t-shirt and nylon trousers whose shine spoke of years of wear. He was shouting at a woman who was so well turned out, the contrast was almost comical: their only point of commonality was that they might have been the same age. Her hair had that just-set look and her summer coat was a beautiful swirl of colours, including an emerald green picked out by her sandals and handbag. Now, however, she was doing her best to be inconspicuous; head down, she ignored both the shouts and the Border terrier trotting off the lead behind her.

'Oi!' cried the man again. 'Fucking pile of fucking ess-aitch-one-tee right in the middle of the fucking pavement. You going to clear it up, or what?'

The woman's answer came through a quickening of her step. What would the man do now? Chase after her? Pull her back? Intercept the dog and kidnap it until she performed her civic duty? The possibility of violence hung in the air. The man turned and caught Laurie's eye; she looked away quickly, unwilling to get involved. Then, with a heavy sigh and much muttering to himself, he pulled a small green bag out of his pocket, and, with one surprisingly dextrous movement, used it to pick up the pile that the terrier had left behind and deposit it in a nearby bin.

This was not, after all, a violent man. The very fact he had one of those bags marked him out as a dog owner, angry with his less-responsible counterpart for giving their kind a bad name. Laurie felt slightly ashamed of the unworthiness of her suspicion, based on – what? – grubby clothes and an aggressive tone of voice. But even that wasn't true, she real-ised. It was just that he swore a lot.

130

Within two minutes, Laurie was back inside her front door. It was nearly ten. She knew she should have a shower, but it was all she could do to brush her teeth, strip off clothes from which the sweat had dried, and crawl into an empty bed.

Saturday, 1 August – 10 a.m.

One advantage of Jess not being around was that it gave Laurie licence to wallow in the bath without any sense that she was getting in her cousin's way. She'd just topped up with hot water for the third time when she heard the doorbell.

'Shit!' Laurie lay in the bath, willing whoever it was to go away.

Another ring. Most likely it was Jess, having forgotten her keys. Laurie rose out of the water, wrapped a towel around herself to catch the worst of the drips and went through to the hallway, leaving a trail of footprints behind her. More in hope than expectation, she put the entryphone to her ear: silence. The line was dead as it had ever been. Jess still hadn't got around to fixing it. Well, this would be an opportunity to remind her.

Laurie was about to press the button to release the latch below when a draught caught the back of her wet neck. The shiver made her pause: she didn't know this was Jess; perhaps it was time to be sensible. She went back into the living room and stuck her head out of the window to view the street below before calling, 'Jess?'

A figure in a cycle helmet stepped back from the front door and looked up at her. No, this was not Jess. It was Paul. He held a paper bag in his right hand. 'I'm sorry. I should have called first, but I got your message and thought I'd just come round. Fancy a croissant?'

Only Laurie's head was visible. Paul couldn't know she was wearing no more than a towel, could he? Why did she suddenly feel so exposed? She took a moment to reply. 'Yes, you should have called first. And I'm not sure croissants really make up for it. But thanks for coming. Give me a minute and I'll buzz you in.'

Laurie made the coffee. She had left Paul waiting outside while she pulled on some clothes, but she was still acutely conscious of his eyes on her from where he sat at the kitchen table. She was proud of her milk-frothing talents. They were wasted on the espresso-drinking Paul, but choosing a cappuccino for herself at least meant she had something to keep herself occupied while she concentrated on small talk. 'I've realised I still don't know where you live. Is it near here?'

'Not far, I suppose,' Paul replied. 'Out beyond Finsbury Park. Not as nice as round here – one effect of the divorce, I'm afraid.'

Ah yes, that opened up lots of possibilities. Laurie seized on one of them gratefully as she brought the coffees over and sat opposite him. 'So how are the kids? Have you seen any more of them?'

'No, last week was my lot for a while. One telephone call a couple of days ago and that's all. It's been a bit crazy at work. You remember how I had to run off on Monday?'

Laurie could only nod. Of course she remembered!

'Well,' Paul continued, 'there was a flood at the gym. I

134

spent the whole week moving equipment, sourcing replacements, dealing with clients, writing insurance reports. It's been mad.'

Paul drank his coffee while he spoke. Elegant though they were, his hands were large enough to make the cup look tiny, like something that wouldn't be out of place in a doll's house. Laurie ripped open the paper bag that sat on the table between them. 'Let's see what you've brought.'

'Well, I thought it was too early for brownies, but I did get a pain au chocolat in case that's your thing. My favourite is the almond croissant, but they're really filling. I'll split that with you if you like. Then there's the plain croissant as a sort of fallback.'

They agreed to share the almond croissant. Paul got a knife and halved it with such accuracy that his 'I'll divide, you choose' was entirely unnecessary. He clearly knew where to buy his pastries; it was delicious.

'So how's your week been?' Paul was speaking again. 'You said something in your message about finding out where that key came from?'

'Yes,' Laurie began. Then she stopped. There was a flake of pastry at the corner of Paul's mouth. He hadn't noticed it. Rather than point it out, she leaned forward to brush it away with her thumb, her hand lingering at his jawline, feeling the contrast between the softness of his lips and the faint roughness of the skin around his mouth. Paul smiled, brought up his hand to hold hers, pulled her towards him and kissed her.

Laurie thrust her tongue between Paul's lips and gripped him tightly. She made no objection as he lifted her up, cradled her in his arms and carried her through to the bed next door. There was a brief moment of separation while each tore off their shirt and fumbled with their trousers. Then they came together again, skin on skin, her arms around his neck, tasting his sweat.

Later, they lay on their sides underneath the duvet, facing each other, barely an inch between their bodies. Paul was the first to speak. 'Penny for your thoughts?'

'So do you always carry condoms with you?'

'Yes, but not because I'm always having sex. It's just – well – one less thing to think about, I suppose. Do you mind?'

'No of course not. It's thoughtful.'

'Anyway, thanks for not being annoyed with me for not calling this week.'

'Who says I'm not annoyed?' countered Laurie. 'It's too late for you to find out what I'd do if I wasn't.'

'Well, either way, you're also wonderful. Anyway, tell me about the key.'

'Later.' Laurie said firmly, rolling over to face him and smiling.

Laurie let Paul go ahead of her. The towpath was really too narrow for two to cycle abreast safely, and although she was the nominal leader of the expedition – showing Paul a part of London he'd never seen before – it was not as though he could take a wrong turning. She liked watching him from behind, weaving around oncoming traffic, overtaking surprised pedestrians, his legs pumping with easy economy. In a couple of bridges she would take over, lead him on to the British Library, show him the match with the key she'd slipped into her pannier, share both her triumph and disappointment. It was still only three o'clock; a weekend together stretched out before them. What would they do that evening? Would Jess have returned? Laurie hoped not; she liked the idea of being back in the flat, alone with Paul.

They were approaching Granary Square now; there would

be crowds there, gathered around the development at the old gasholders, no doubt about it. Here, however, for a short stretch, they were alone. Paul had stopped. He smiled and pointed to a family of moorhens – three smaller ones following what could only be their mother – crossing the path in front of them. Laurie pulled up beside him, ready to breathe in the joy of it all.

Why did she answer her mobile? She was to ask herself that question many times over the next few hours. And each time she could only come up with the same half-hearted attempt at self-consolation: they'd have tracked me down eventually.

'Hello Laurie, it's Michael.' The weariness that washed down the line was unmistakable. 'I'm in the office. Henry wants to make a few tweaks to the model. He's authorised your overtime. Do you think you could come in?'

'What, now?'

'I'm afraid so.' And then, by way of explanation: 'He wants to take it to investment committee on Monday.'

The investment committee? That was a sign Henry liked it, wasn't it? Laurie looked over to Paul, waiting with every appearance of patience. She could say no, she was busy, but something was stirring within her, something she hadn't felt for a while. Was it ambition? This was her chance to show off in front of Henry. And she couldn't ignore the overtime either. 'OK,' she heard herself replying, 'I can be there in about half an hour.'

'Great. See you then.'

On impulse, Laurie didn't put the phone away immediately. Instead she used it to take a picture of Paul leaning on his bike, the sun full on his face. He started when he heard the click of the camera, put up a hand like a celebrity avoiding the paparazzi. Then she broke the news. 'I'm sorry. It seems like we're fated. I've got to go into the office. I'll call you when I get the chance. Are you around for the rest of the weekend?'

Paul looked rather put out. 'Yes, well, if I'm not you can always leave me a message. You still haven't told me what you found with that key. What do they want you for anyway? Is this normal? Do they pay you enough?'

That last question was a bit odd. Was Laurie's pay any of Paul's business? Was he implying she wasn't important enough to be needed at the weekend? Somehow it made the parting easier.

'I'm sorry,' she repeated. 'I'll call you tonight.' Then she turned her bicycle round and headed back west. Following the gentle curve, she looked back to see Paul still where she had left him, holding his bike, apparently lost in indecision. He responded to her wave with his own half-hearted salute. Then she set off again. A wind seemed to have come out of nowhere, channelled into her face as she rode into the gloom under every bridge.

Saturday, 1 August – 1 p.m.

Laurie had never thought of Michael as young before, but now, seeing him dressed in something other than a suit, she realised he couldn't be much older than she was. Not that casual clothes did much more for him than that. The short sleeves of the polo shirt, in particular, emphasised the scrawniness of his arms. The contrast with Paul was all too striking.

He was happy to see her. That much was clear from his greeting. 'Laurie, hi. Thanks for coming so quickly. Henry called me this morning wanting to make a few changes to the model. I've done them but now I can't get your macros to run. He's coming in later this afternoon.'

So it began. They worked together for four hours until Henry arrived, dressed in chinos and a polo shirt remarkably similar to Michael's. Was it some sort of uniform? Laurie was briefly glad that she'd worn a dress for her bike ride with Paul, not her usual Lycra. Unlike Michael, however, Henry had a tan. It extended up his arms and stopped on a line with the shirtsleeve, under which pale luminescent skin became visible when he reached over for the sheaf of papers that Michael was offering him. The two of them went into Henry's office.

139

Laurie could see them through the glass screen, bent over the papers on the desk, Henry talking, and Michael replying. Once they both looked across to her. Laurie immediately bent back to her computer, embarrassed at being caught out in relative idleness. It had reverted to her usual screensaver: the picture she had taken of Dad and Roxanne before coming up to London. On impulse, she replaced it with the one she'd just taken of Paul. That was making some sort of statement, she realised. Well, why not?

Henry's office door opened. He was speaking. 'OK. Why don't you model it for weekly trades as well as daily. I just get the feeling you won't lose too much, and it will be so much simpler to run. Good stuff. I'll be back in a couple of hours, once the children are in bed.'

Laurie risked a glance up from her computer and immediately caught Henry's eye. He was looking at her quizzically: 'Michael tells me you've been very helpful. Good stuff.' Then he was gone.

When Henry returned, it was with a couple more orders expressed as questions, but also with a suggestion that it was time they ate. It was Laurie's job of course, first to phone in the order to the Gates of Peking, and then to pop round the corner to pick it up.

The food wasn't ready yet. Laurie accepted the offer of a Diet Coke while she waited at the bar. There were two other women there, perched on high stools but both looking impossibly elegant. One got off her stool as Laurie approached and sashayed off to the other side of the room, hips wiggling beneath the silk of her dress, feet perfectly poised on heels that would have left marks in a softer floor. Laurie watched her, fascinated, and then looked away to realise that the other woman was watching her in turn, a look of amusement – or was it scorn? – playing about her face. Laurie was glad to take receipt of two heavy carrier bags shortly afterwards and escape.

There was an awful lot of food for three people. They ate together in one of the conference rooms, Henry and Michael shovelling from their plates to their mouths, wielding chopsticks like they were born to it, while Laurie, struggling with the unfamiliar implements, was significantly slower. That was probably just as well, even though it had been twelve hours since that croissant. How did Michael manage to stay so thin?

Henry eventually broke the silence. 'Right. I'm going to start writing the executive summary. We can fill in the blanks tomorrow. It's good you're here, Laurie. I should be able to give you some dictation in an hour or so.

'An hour or so', turned out to be two and a half, largely spent in discussion with Michael, who emerged to start working furiously at his computer while Henry spoke into a Dictaphone. He soon handed Laurie a tape with two commands, apparently meant for Michael: 'Use that as a rough outline. Let's meet again at ten tomorrow.' Then he addressed himself to Laurie directly. 'Do you think you could call me a cab, and book one for tomorrow morning as well?' Five minutes later, he left the office.

Michael looked at Laurie: 'I'm afraid that if Henry's here at ten, we'll have to be here by eight. Not much sleep tonight.'

It was nearly three when Laurie got home. She'd had a good chat with her cab driver about Arsenal's prospects in the coming season, and he gave her a cheery good night before waiting to make sure she got in safely. Within five minutes she was in bed.

Sunday, 2 August – 6.30 a.m.

Laurie cursed the diligence with which she'd set the alarm. The cab wasn't even due for an hour. She used the time to shower and breakfast. Jess had clearly been home – her bag was dumped in the hall and there were books lying around the sitting room – but there was no sign of her now. Well, tidying up would give Laurie something else to do before the taxi arrived.

It was her own fault really. She saw the cab waiting by the kerb and headed straight for it. Laurie would never have crossed a road without checking for traffic, and, as she reflected afterwards, much the same could be said of London pavements. The runner ran straight into her, knocking her bag off her shoulder and sending its contents flying. But he shrugged off her apologies with a mumble before setting off again, head down in his hood, at a speed that Laurie recognised as something more energetic than mere jogging; perhaps she wasn't entirely to blame after all.

The cab driver certainly didn't think so. 'Came out of nowhere, he did. Are you OK?'

'Yes.' Laurie replied. 'Just surprised more than anything.' It was true, she realised. The shock had left her faintly breathless. She needed to calm back down again. 'If you don't mind, I think I'll just close my eyes for a moment. You know where I'm going?'

'Here we are, then.' Woken by the cabbie, Laurie was confused for a moment. She felt drained rather than refreshed, as though her nap had been long enough to remind her of how tired she was, but nothing more. Today, she realised, would be a coffee day.

Michael was just settling down at his desk when she walked in. 'Morning. I've been thinking. It might help if we presented some of our results graphically. Is that something you could look at?'

Well, it beat trying to decipher Henry's dictation. Laurie googled onto the Excel manual and got to work.

There was no doubt that Michael's idea was a good one, but it inevitably meant they had a bit of a panic getting everything ready for Henry's arrival. In the end, they kept the tables in the presentation, where they had been before, with the graphs as an appendix. It looked good; Laurie was pleased with the role she'd played in its creation.

This time, when Henry took the presentation into his office, Michael suggested that Laurie come too: 'She's really helped a lot,' he insisted. 'She's done stuff with Excel that – well – it's really impressive.'

So Laurie was there to hear Henry say 'Good stuff!' several times as he read through the reworked document, but she did not contribute much to the subsequent conversation, leaving Michael to answer the machine-gun fire of questions. Finally Henry said, 'Right, I'm just going to make a few changes. Why don't you both take the chance for a bit of fresh air. Come back at twelve.'

Michael looked at his watch as they returned to their desks. 'That gives us an hour. I'm going to head to the gym. I'll eat there, and I'd suggest you grab something too. We're likely to be busy when we get back.'

The sun outside was an instant, aching reminder of how many better ways there were for Laurie to spend her weekend. Why on earth did the investment committee sit on a Monday? Was that something she could ask Michael? He probably didn't know either.

Laurie walked the couple of hundred yards to Berkeley Square. It was beautiful, she supposed. She loved the way the trees seemed taller than the surrounding buildings – green tufts over London's rooftops, visible to any passing bird. But it also felt alien, part of a world where Laurie had no place. No one real lived here. Even Henry, who could surely afford Mayfair if he wanted it, needed a cab to get home.

Lunch was all very well, but before eating she would call Paul. She couldn't wait to hear his voice. He'd be wondering what on earth had happened to her. She reached for her handbag.

The phone wasn't there, at least, not in its usual pocket. Laurie peered inside: keys, purse, Kleenex, lipstick, compact, a couple of tampons, but no phone. With a gathering sense of panic she tipped the contents onto the ground, checked the bag was empty and then refilled it item by item. With the exception of her Oyster card, she could add nothing to the original list.

Laurie thought frantically. Could she have left it at the flat? No. She'd got it out as she was coming down the stairs to get in the cab. She'd been looking for a message from Paul but then had that collision with the runner. Of course! Why hadn't she checked then that nothing was missing? Christ, it was easy to be wise after the event. Might it still be lying on

145

the pavement? She couldn't go back to look for it now. In any case, now she thought of it, that man had run off awfully fast. Shit!

Laurie scanned her memory but came quickly to the realisation that there was no chance Paul's number was lodged anywhere within it. She'd never even had to dial it. The number only existed on her mobile. How had she left things with him? Surely he'd phone when he didn't hear from her? What good would that be if she couldn't receive his calls? She had to get a replacement handset – and SIM card – as soon as possible. And that was only one of several calls she'd have to make. Lunch forgotten, Laurie headed back to the office.

Once at her desk, Laurie started off by calling her own number, only to go straight through to voicemail. That was no help. Next Jess: if she was at the flat then she'd certainly be happy to step outside and look for the handset. That was a number Laurie knew by heart, but calling it had a similar result: 'Hi. Thanks for calling. Leave a message; you know you want to.' Laurie obeyed, telling her what had happened and asking her to call back at the office. Then she tried the flat's landline, and ended up shouting into the answermachine – 'Jess, it's me. If you're there, please pick up' – but with no response.

Next Dad: he just needed to be told so he didn't worry, although that was a fairly vain hope. It was with some difficulty that Laurie persuaded him that no, she hadn't been mugged, that she certainly hadn't been hurt, and that there was really no point in reporting the loss to the police. The handset had a resale value of £20 at best. It was, Laurie agreed, just as well she'd never got around to acquiring an iPhone.

Finally O_2: it might be Sunday, but their lost phones hotline was able to reassure her that no, the robber had not spent the last two hours calling South America. In fact, the phone hadn't been used at all. Laurie started to worry again; perhaps she really had just mislaid it? Another search of her bag and of the space around her desk yielded no dividends, however. So Laurie bit the bullet and cancelled both handset and SIM card, ordering replacements that should arrive at work by 2 p.m. on Tuesday.

Michael was back by the time she finished that last call. He'd clearly had a shower, but the flush on his face and sweat on his forehead showed that his body had not yet cooled down from whatever workout he'd put it through. He carried a McDonald's bag – rather sheepishly, Laurie thought, although just the thought of chips made her stomach rumble. She wasn't sure whether to be disappointed or relieved when he opened the bag to draw out a drink container and a salad.

'You know those contain as many calories as a Big Mac?'

'Yes.' Michael produced one of his rare smiles. 'And I don't care.'

That was the extent of their small talk for the rest of the afternoon. Just as Michael was chasing the last scrap of lettuce around the plastic container, Henry came out of his office. He bore their presentation, and even from a distance, Laurie could see that it was covered with scrawls.

It was midnight before Henry finally declared himself satisfied with a, 'Good stuff. Eight o'clock tomorrow, then.'

Laurie was glad of the taxi home, but too tired to chat to the driver. God, her bed was welcoming.

Monday, 3 August , – 7 a.m.

Now there was no doubt that Jess was back. That much was clear to Laurie the moment the alarm woke her. Unfortunately, the moans that Laurie could hear through the wall indicated that her flatmate would be otherwise engaged for some time, and not much good as any sort of companion to Laurie for the next few weeks at least. It was just as well she had met Paul – not that she could do anything until after her phone arrived tomorrow. In the meantime, and with her bike still at the office, she would have to get the Tube into work: no time to lie in bed thinking nice thoughts. Reluctantly, Laurie hauled herself into the shower. As she left the flat, muffled noises through Jess's bedroom door indicated that she and – what was his name? Nigel? – were still going strong. The man clearly had stamina.

Getting into the lift at Tufnell Park reminded Laurie that she still hadn't finished *Sylvester*. Where had she left it? Dad wouldn't be pleased if it was lost. The Tube journey itself was as unpleasant as ever – a good reminder of why she'd taken up cycling. Well, she should get away in time to cycle back this evening.

149

It was five past eight when Laurie got to her desk, but Michael was already in Henry's office. He looked up from the document they were reading together – presumably the presentation – and caught Laurie's eye, but made no indication that she should join them.

The investment committee met at eight-thirty, an immoveable fortnightly ritual even in the middle of the summer holidays. It was held in the conference room where the three of them had eaten Chinese two evenings before. Henry and Michael went into the meeting together, along with the four other partners of Fitzalan Capital who were still in the office. After about thirty minutes, Michael emerged. He came over. 'I think it went well, but it's hard to tell; they're always so poker-faced.'

'What happens now?' Laurie wondered, aware that this was the first time she'd felt any sort of interest in what went on behind those walls.

'They discuss it. Decide whether or not to give it the go-ahead. We were the only agenda item today, so it shouldn't take long.'

Michael was right. The meeting broke up only ten minutes later. Henry beckoned Michael, who looked at Laurie questioningly, his eyebrows raised. Was that an invitation to follow him into Henry's office? Laurie remembered how useless she'd felt the last time she'd tagged along and shook her head. Michael didn't press the point and in any case didn't take long to return. He was smiling, but seemed curiously flat as he passed on what Henry had just told him: 'Two hundred million, with a review after the first quarter.'

'Is that good?' It sounded it, but Michael's manner somehow introduced an element of doubt.

'It's the maximum they'll do as a first investment. So yes. I'm just a bit tired, that's all. Henry's sent me home for the day. He wants to see you now.' Michael was shutting down his computer as he spoke, preparing to leave. Now that he had said it, Laurie could see that Michael had a washed-out look to him, as if he'd been surviving on adrenaline alone for the last few days. It was interesting that Henry had spotted it too. Did she look the same, after her weekend in the office? Would Henry be telling her to go home as well?

Henry looked up from his desk as Laurie came in, but it was not to scrutinise her complexion for signs of pallor. 'Laurie. Thanks for your help yesterday. Have you got my diary with you? Let's go through the rest of the week.'

Monday, 3 August – 5.30 p.m.

Laurie left the office and looked towards her bike, still chained to the railings where she had left it two days before. In almost any other part of London, she reflected, it would have lost its front wheel by now. There were some benefits to working in Mayfair, for all its soullessness. Was she up to riding it home? It was either that or the Tube. Yes, it was time to get back in the saddle. It didn't matter that she was in her work clothes; the dress would cope with the journey, as long as she sat on it so it didn't flap all over the place. She'd just have to take it slowly.

In the end, Laurie found the ride invigorating. The streets had their summer-holiday emptiness and there was enough of a breeze to temper the sun. She arrived back at the flat with a sense of freshness, of new possibilities, for all the way her dress stuck to her back. London didn't have to be a place of violence, did it?

The atmosphere behind the front door was stuffy: hot, still and humid, as if Jess had left the central heating on .Laurie walked through the hall to the sitting room, intending to check the thermostat and let in some air. Then she became conscious of something else: an acrid, almost tomcatty smell. She checked the bathroom. No, Jess hadn't failed to flush. Perhaps it was coming from the kitchen.

Going through the sitting room to get there, Laurie realised that it was exactly as she had left it that morning. There was no sign Jess had been in the kitchen either: no plates waiting to be washed up, the milk in the fridge still unopened. The smell had to be coming from somewhere else.

Laurie came to Jess's door. Could she hear any sound from within? Might Nigel still be in there with her? She knocked, hesitantly at first, and then with more purpose. Was that humming she heard? Moaning? Surely the two of them couldn't have spent the whole day in there? Laurie knocked again.

'Hmm hmm.' There was a strange insistency to the double grunt, but it didn't have the rhythm of ecstasy. 'HMM HMM,' it came again. Laurie reached a decision. If all was well, so to speak, she could simply close the door again and hope they hadn't noticed her. What was the worst that could happen? She opened the door gently and prepared to look inside.

Even before she saw anything, Laurie knew she'd done the right thing. The smell of urine that attacked her as she opened the door was enough to make her gag. And the heat! Prickles of sweat started up on her forehead and between her shoulder blades. She wanted to hold her breath, to get out and shut the door – anything to escape. As it was, she couldn't help making for the window as her first action, throwing it open to let in some cool, fresh air.

The curtains, however, Laurie left drawn. Jess's window was overlooked by others across the street. She didn't want there to be any chance others might see through to Jess's bed, to the sight that had met her eyes on entry, which she could even now barely acknowledge.

154

Jess lay on the bed. Apart from her pants she was, essentially, naked. Her dress had been torn down the middle and was now rucked under her, held in place only at the shoulders, where it tangled with her bra, which had been cut open at the front. Her head was not visible; an Emma Hope shoe bag enveloped it, tied loosely under the chin. Jess's arms were extended beyond her head, as if Laurie had caught her mid-stretch. Except that these arms were going nowhere. Something was looped through the headboard, tying Jess's hands together, keeping her whole body in place.

'HMMM, HMMMM!' Jess was still saying.

'It's me,' Laurie replied. She approached the bed. Now she could see the full horror. Jess had been locked to the bed with a pair of handcuffs. All the way up to the base of her thumbs, her lower arms were raw and bloody. The hands themselves looked puffy and lifeless. The smell of dried urine was almost overpowering.

Laurie steeled herself. Now was no time to retch. Jess needed help. She should be talking to her, reassuring her.

'Don't worry,' Laurie said, 'I'll just get this bag off your head.' The drawstring had been tied off in an incongruous bow. Despite her trembling hands, Laurie had no problem in loosening the knot and slipping the makeshift hood up over Jess's head.

Now she could see the reason for the strange sounds Jess was making. A wide piece of plastic tape was wrapped around her chin from ear to ear, covering her mouth. It turned her into some strange object, deprived of voice and expression. Without the use of her hands Jess had no chance of removing it. Laurie reached for the tape, ready to peel it off as gently as possible, to restore her cousin to humanity, but with a jerk of the head Jess made it clear this was not what she wanted. Her eyes, bloodshot and watery within an otherwise papery, dehydrated face, shot to the side and then came back to stare at Laurie, willing her to understand her meaning

'Huh, hmm, hmm huhhh.' Once again Jess's eyes shot to the side. Laurie attempted to follow her gaze. What was she trying to say?

'The bedside drawer? You want me to look in the bedside drawer?

Jess nodded as vigorously as her contorted position would allow, then slumped into inactivity, exhausted by the effort to make herself understood.

The dildo was hardly a surprise. Laurie knew Jess well enough for that, but that certainly wasn't what she wanted. What else was in there? Two boxes of condoms, one still in its plastic cellophane wrapper, a packet of disposable sterilising wipes, a tube of KY jelly. Perhaps Jess thought that would make her wrists slippery enough to remove the handcuffs? Laurie picked it up, doubtfully, revealing one other item – a small silver key, the kind that might, in fact, fit a pair of handcuffs.

If Jess knew the key was there, then presumably the handcuffs were hers. Until that moment, Laurie had been assuming that her next act would be to phone the police, or perhaps an ambulance. Now she saw that things were slightly more complicated than that. Still, questions could wait. She fitted the key in the handcuffs and released first Jess's right hand, and then her left. Both arms remained in place, as if their owner did not yet believe they were free. As gently as she could, Laurie cradled each and returned it to a more natural position by Jess's side. 'Now,' she said, 'how about that tape?'

Again Jess shook her head, but not with the urgency that saw off Laurie's previous attempt. Her eyes remained shut; tears crept out from beneath their lids. She lay there for a moment, her feelings unfathomable, then, with slow deliberation, rolled onto her side. Laurie had some idea of the relief this brought when she saw Jess's back. Were those pressure sores? And was that general redness a nappy rash? The renewed smell of urine that rose up from the mattress certainly seemed to suggest it.

Jess lay there, hunched in a foetal position, her hands by her mouth, picking away at the tape. Laurie moved to help, but once again she was shrugged away. For whatever reason, this was something Jess had to do for herself. Finally, however, she got a corner of her mouth free. Laurie could hear the air whistling in and out as her cousin gathered her strength. Finally, a painful whisper emerged. 'I think I'm going to need your help getting to the bathroom.'

By half past seven, Jess was tucked up in Laurie's bed; there was no other place for her. The mattress in her own room would clearly have to be thrown away, and she had firmly rejected Laurie's alternative suggestion of a visit to hospital. Her first act on getting into the bath run by Laurie had been to roll over and hold her face underwater, loosening the glue on the tape over her mouth so that it eventually peeled off relatively easily. The skin beneath was white – almost translucent – and her lips so chapped and flaking that Laurie immediately understood why she had been so anxious to remove the tape carefully.

Since then, Jess had drunk five glasses of water, sip by careful sip, and had eaten the best part of a banana with painful slowness, but had uttered hardly a word other than the occasional command. Laurie had performed the role of nurse to the best of her ability – removing the ragged dress, carefully soaping Jess's aching arms, helping her into and out of the bath and dressing her in the old pyjamas she found at the bottom of her chest of drawers. For most of the time, however, Laurie simply held her hand, or – more accurately – allowed her own hand to be held. Apart from her brief absences in the kitchen, the only time Jess let her out of her sight was when – after the third glass of water – Laurie had helped her out of the bath to sit on the loo. She had crawled out of the bathroom some minutes later, shutting the door behind her with an emphasis that both belied her general feebleness and made it clear Laurie was not to go back in. Now she snoozed, still gripping Laurie's hand.

Laurie sat there, uncertain what to do next. Every time she thought of moving her hand, Jess's grasp tightened. The only way to get comfortable was to lie down beside her. Instinctively protective, Laurie used her free arm to hug Jess. Only then was her hand relinquished, as one comfort was exchanged for another. So, finally, they fell asleep in each others' arms.

Monday, 3 August – 10.30 p.m.

Laurie woke up to realise first that she was alone in the bed, and second that it was dark. Surely she should be the one who was up and about, while Jess slept? That must be her moving about in the kitchen. Laurie swung her feet onto the floor, and went to investigate.

Jess was sitting at the table, eating ice cream straight from the tub. Her wrists bore bruises that would take days to fade but had lost the puffiness Laurie had found so shocking earlier, and her voice, when she spoke, was close to normal. 'I suddenly thought what the fuck am I doing in bed? I've just spent the best part of two days there, for God's sake. That's the last place I want to be.'

'Two days?' Laurie didn't even try to keep the shock from her voice. 'But I've been here.'

Now it was Jess's turn to look surprised. 'I've been on that bed since lunchtime on Saturday. This morning was the first time I could hear you in the flat. I thought you must have been at your dad's.'

'I got stuck at work.' Laurie paused before continuing. 'Do you want to talk about it?'

'Not much to tell, or not much that I care to remember. I came in about one. Nigel's gone back to Australia, so I'd been saying goodbye. There was a man in your bedroom. I assumed he was with you, though I can't say I thought much of your taste. He reminded me of one of those Mitchell brothers off *EastEnders*. Anyway, I stepped into your doorway. I was about to speak when I was banged over the top of the head. Woke up like you found me.' She shuddered – an involuntary shiver that for a moment revealed the terror within – and then fell silent.

Laurie reached across for her cousin's hand. 'Jess—' she began, but what to say next?

Shooting Laurie a look, Jess went on, 'They ripped my dress; one of them ... felt me ...'

Laurie's mind raced in the pause that followed. Should she be doing more to comfort her? Encouraging her to speak? Let the trauma out? But it was Jess who eventually filled the silence. 'They stayed for quite a while longer. I could hear them moving around the flat. I kept thinking they were going to come back ... It's as if they just wanted to see me like that ... for me to realise how vulnerable I was. Then they left. I thought it's OK. You'd be home soon. Then it got uncomfortable. It was a relief when I fell asleep.'

If that was as much as Jess wanted to tell, Laurie was not going to press her. She gave the hand she was already holding a squeeze. 'What can I do now? Are you sure you won't go to hospital? I could call a taxi. Have you called the police?'

Jess removed her hand, in a way that spoke of determination, to signal that she was no invalid, rather than a desire to put distance between them. 'I'm not going to hospital. That's for ill people and I'm not ill. And if I did they'd want to know what happened. I don't particularly feel like talking about it at the moment, so I don't want to get the police involved either. It's not as though I've got any insurance for whatever they've taken.'

Jess paused, and Laurie waited. Was she supposed to argue with her now? To try to persuade her to do the right thing? What was the right thing? Surely Jess would know? She'd lived in London for years. Now was clearly not the time to ask her about those handcuffs.

'Well, OK, if you're sure.' Laurie looked at Jess to check but could detect no hint of uncertainty. 'Are you missing much?'

'I haven't looked yet, but we should probably both do that, and we'd better track down a locksmith sooner rather than later. I don't want them coming back.' Jess's voice cracked a bit as she spoke. Once again Laurie wondered if she should be arguing with her, and once again she decided to let it rest.

Now that she was alert to the possibility, Laurie could see that someone had gone through her drawers. The idea of an alien hand in there, rooting through her clothes, was more upsetting than she had anticipated, but she only seemed to be missing her laptop. No real surprise there; it was the only thing she possessed with any kind of resale value – not that they'd get much for it. At least all her photos and stuff were stored in the cloud.

Jess was still moving slowly and took longer to search. She had lost more: not just her laptop but also her iPad and phone. Overall she seemed more relieved than anything, when a moment's panicked search showed they hadn't found her nice jewellery. 'I knew I was right to keep it all jumbled up together!'

Despite everything, Laurie had to smile at a glimpse of the Jess she knew.

Without a computer, they were reduced to calling 118118 for a twenty-four-hour locksmith. He arrived within thirty minutes, and was finished half an hour later, even allowing for the long visit to the bathroom that Jess later swore was a staple of every workman's visit: 'It's like dogs marking their territory.' Along the way he'd given Jess a lecture about the uselessness of the lock he was replacing: 'You might as well hang out a welcome sign to villains.' And she had reluctantly agreed to an upgrade.

Changing the mattress, however, was beyond the power of money to solve at that time of night. So Laurie and Jess slept head-to-toe like two nine-year-olds on a sleepover.

Tuesday 4 August, 7.30 a.m.

The alarm had no effect on Jess. When Laurie left she was still lying there, head slightly askew, mouth open, snoring gently, suddenly looking ten years younger.

Michael, by contrast, appeared to have derived little benefit from his day off. Perhaps the rings under his eyes were slightly less pronounced? He certainly seemed to have got stuck back into work: a slew of forms that left him no time to talk to Laurie, although he did look up and smile when she sat down. Every now and then he'd go into Henry's office with a question, or to ask for a signature. As for Laurie, a Dictaphone tape left on her desk told her that Henry had been busy since yesterday afternoon, and that now she would be too.

It was lunchtime before Laurie remembered her mobile phone. She called down to reception: yes, a package had arrived this morning. At last! Who needed to eat, anyway? This would be a much better use of her free time.

Eagerly, Laurie returned to her desk, assembled all the disparate parts – SIM, battery and handset – and plugged in the charger, waiting for the phone to fire up properly. It gave her an idea for a modern version of the old saying: 'A watched phone never finds its network.' At any rate, it seemed an age before it started waking up, with various beeps and buzzes to indicate texts received and voicemail messages waiting for her attention.

The three texts were all from O_2. In order, they commiserated over the loss of Laurie's last phone and suggested that next time she insure her handset for the bargain price of £4.99 a month, welcomed her to her new payment plan, and told her she now had 300 minutes of speech, 3,000 texts and 1GB of data, with the next update to take place in one month's time.

And there were only two voicemails. On Monday, Dad had called to ask how she was. His messages were always short; this was no exception, but there was an evident note of concern to the enquiry. Laurie had been neglecting him. She would have to put that right. In the meantime, she moved on quickly to the second message: 'Hi. It's Paul. Bit worried that you haven't been in touch yet. Hope I haven't offended you. If I have then I'm sorry, but do call me anyway.'

That was it! Eagerly, Laurie accessed the message envelope to get the number. 'This message was received . . . today at . . . eight . . . thirty-one, from . . . a private number.' Only an automated voice could have delivered such devastating news with so little emotion, let alone sympathy.

What? No number? How was she going to get hold of him now? What if he never called again?

At that moment, her new handset burst into life. Dad! From the moment he started to speak, Laurie realised she was in trouble.

'Lauren Miranda Bateman. You certainly know how to wind up your loving parent.'

'Dad! I'm sorry. It's just things are frantic at work. I've only just got my new phone and heard your message.'

'It shouldn't need hearing a message to work out that your Pa might be getting a bit worried. All I get is a call to say your phone's been stolen and then total silence. For all I knew you'd been stolen too.'

'Dad, I can't really talk right now, but it has only been two days.'

'Two days in which it turns out you've had a break-in.' Dad paused for a moment, as if waiting for a response, before continuing. 'I thought that might shut you up. I called Jess just to check you were OK, and she let the cat out of the bag. Don't be too hard on her. She was trying to explain why you hadn't called yesterday.' There was a note of amusement in his voice: Dad knew how annoyed Laurie would be at the idea of him checking up on her.

'OK,' Laurie surrendered. 'What did she tell you?'

'That you've been burgled and both lost your laptops.'

'Yeah, well. That's London for you.' Laurie hoped she sounded suitably world-weary.

Dad wasn't going to be fooled. 'London or not, you don't have your phone stolen and flat broken into within forty-eight hours unless something's going on. I'm coming down this evening.'

Dad! Come to London? The thought left Laurie struggling for words. The best she could come up with, after a pause that Dad could have hardly failed to notice, was, 'But who's going to look after Roxanne?'

'I'll sort something out. You matter more. I'll be with you around seven. Love you.' Dad hung up.

Talk about an overreaction! One little coincidence and Dad turned into a Victorian patriarch. He hadn't been this emphatic with her since he dragged her down from Cambridge to Somerset. If only she had remembered to call him first thing this morning. Then he would never have spoken to Jess and things would have been fine. It was just as well she'd never told Jess about her trip underground the week before. Imagine if he'd heard about that! As it was, Laurie faced the problem of keeping Dad entertained in London for however long he chose to stay. It couldn't be for long, could it, not in high summer? In the meantime, however, any prospect of meeting Paul again receded into the distance.

Meet Paul? Could she even call him? If she hadn't lost her laptop, of course, she could have found his number there; it synced with her phone automatically whenever they were in Bluetooth range.

Hang on! Surely that meant it would have backed up into the cloud with all her other data?

Her heart pumping with excitement, Laurie logged on to her Gmail account to check. Yes: there was the contacts.pst file, but she'd need a computer with Outlook to open it. With any luck, Dad wouldn't have left home yet. She caught him just in time. 'Yes, I was bringing it anyway. See you later, darling. Bye.'

And now to phone Jess and ask why on earth she'd told Dad about the break-in, not to mention ensure they were singing from the same hymn sheet when it came to describing what had happened over the weekend: there really was no point in letting Dad become any more agitated than he already was.

The moment Laurie spoke, Jess launched into her apology. 'I'm sorry. I had no idea David would go off the deep end like that. He's always seemed quite relaxed about things to me. I was just trying to explain why you hadn't called him last night. I guess he was just already worried and the idea that we'd had a break-in didn't help.'

'What did you tell him about it?'

166

'Just that we'd been burgled, that they'd taken the obvious stuff, but nothing that couldn't be replaced.'

'Did he ask if you'd called the police?'

'Yes, but he didn't seem that bothered once I'd told him we didn't have any insurance.'

'That doesn't sound like Dad. Though I'm sure you're not complaining. You're obviously better at calming him down than I am. How about the mattress and everything else? Have you sorted all of that?'

Now Jess sounded pleased with herself. 'New mattress bought at John Lewis this morning, brought back in a taxi. Sheets etc washed and dry. And if by "everything else" you mean the contents of my bedside table, well let's just say they've been edited slightly. I'm not sure I could bear to look at some of them again.'

'Jess—' Laurie began, and then stopped. Anything she'd say could only sound either censorious or prurient. 'Jess, are you sure you're OK?'

'I've been better, to be honest, but I'll be all right. It's been good for me doing all this stuff. Actually I'm quite glad David's coming down. I'm not sure I can face work tomorrow, but it will be good to have company.'

Was Jess really all right? Should Laurie be doing something more to help her? Dad, would know of course, but if she asked him then she'd have to tell him what had happened, and there was no way she was doing that. There was something very calculating about the idea of tying someone up, stripping them and then leaving them, with no apparent care for whether they would ever be found. What kind of a person did something like that?

On the desk in front of her, Laurie's computer went back into hibernation. There was Paul looking back at her and it made her feel so happy. This evening, she would be speaking to him. More than that, Laurie realised. This was the only photo on the phone that would not have been backed up onto her computer, but, quite by chance, she had saved this one too. It only took a moment to send a copy to her Gmail address, access it from her new handset, and set it as the background image on that too.

It was with the feeling of a job well done that Laurie returned to Henry's dictation. She could already see that she'd be leaving the office after Dad was due to arrive at the flat. As ever, the overtime could only come in useful.

Tuesday, 4 August – 7.30 p.m.

The real benefit of a visit from Dad became apparent the moment Laurie walked through the door. It was amazing how delicious fried onions could smell. He was cooking one of his special omelettes using entirely homegrown ingredients, and had only been waiting for Laurie's arrival to add the eggs to the pan. Within minutes, they were sitting down with Jess around the little kitchen table in a threesome that was immediately very comfortable.

Jess certainly seemed to have benefited from having Dad around, unless it was all a front she was putting on for his benefit. Of course they'd always got on well; that was why Jess had kept in touch after Mum's death, and why she'd invited Laurie to come to live with her. In any case, it was good to see someone else enjoying the dry way in which Dad told his stories of village doings. Afterwards, he let 'you girls' clear up, while he did the crossword. Guiltily, Laurie noticed that he'd already emptied the fridge: no chance of hiding from him that she'd never used half the provisions he'd sent down with her ten days earlier.

Only then could Laurie snatch a few moments with Dad's

laptop. There was her user account, its password unchanged for five years. Laurie logged on, entered the Wi–Fi code, logged onto Gmail and downloaded the contacts file she'd spotted that afternoon, saving it onto her account as 'old laptop'. Then she started up Outlook and opened the file. Yes! There were all her old contacts and there was Paul, filed under 'P'; she'd never got around to adding his surname. Laurie keyed the number into her new handset.

'I'm just popping out for a walk.' Laurie might as well have been talking to an empty room for the reaction she got. Dad nodded vaguely while Jess didn't even look up from her own newly acquired iPhone.

Laurie was dialling Paul's number as she walked down the stairs. He picked up after three rings: 'Laurie?'

Laurie could hear the uncertainty in his voice, and her heart skipped: 'Paul. It's great to hear your voice. I'm so sorry you haven't been able to get me, but I lost my phone. And then, would you believe it? My computer was stolen.'

Laurie added a little laugh to this last statement, as if to emphasise the triviality of the occurrence, but it was clear she wasn't fooling Paul in the slightest.

'Stolen? What, like you were mugged? Are you OK?'

On this point at least, Laurie could be reassuring. 'Oh no, nothing like that. We just had a break–in. The computer was all I had that was worth stealing; my flatmate lost a bit more. Anyway, it took me a while to track down your number, but I eventually found it in the cloud, so to speak.'

Laurie paused to give Paul a chance to reply, but she heard him take a couple of breaths before he did: 'The cloud? You mean you've got everything backed up?'

'Yes, Dad set it up for me on my Gmail account when I came to London. Anyway, I was wondering if you wanted to meet up soon?'

170

'Laurie, it would be great to see you, but I'm afraid this is a kids week again. During the holidays we alternate. Can I call you back next Monday, when I'm a free agent?'

Laurie tried to keep the disappointment out of her voice. In any case, she reminded herself, she'd probably be tied up most of the week with Dad. 'Oh, OK, I'll call you next Monday. See you soon. Bye.' Determined to keep it casual, Laurie disconnected without waiting to hear Paul's reply.

All in all, it had not been a terribly satisfactory conversation. And it would be days before she could have another go. What was she thinking of? Laurie was walking round the block, brooding, when a ping announced the arrival of a text from Paul: *Text me when you get the chance. Px.*

Hmm, only one x? Laurie laughed at herself for what she recognised was a different kind of worry. Still, she could show him: *Xoxoxoxoxoxox.* When had she last done that? On a get-well card for Mum? Laurie found she could entertain the thought without wincing. It was good to be childish occasionally.

Back in the flat, Dad was sitting alone, waiting for her. 'So tell me what's been going on since we last saw each other.'

Laurie didn't tell him everything – it was just as well Jess wasn't there to catch her eye when she skated over some of the details – but she told him enough: about finding the key (which she described as being close to the platform; again there was no point in worrying Dad unnecessarily with the details of her night underground), about how the locker it fitted at the British Library was empty, about work, about the jogger who crashed into her two mornings before, about the break-in. She said nothing, of course, about going to the police, but was half-expecting Dad not to let her off the subject as lightly as he had Jess. Instead, he asked an entirely unrelated question. 'What do you know about the man that fell under the train?'

'Nothing except what the key told me: that he liked to hang out at the British Library. I don't even know his name. I've tried looking on the internet, but that got me nowhere. Why do you ask?'

'I need something to do while you're at work; thought I might have a go at following that up, since you seem to have lost interest.'

Laurie was vaguely irritated, partly by the perception Dad had shown in guessing that she had lost interest, and partly by the implication that he thought he could succeed where she had failed. She decided to let some of her feelings show. 'I've always thought I was pretty good at finding things out. I'd hate for you to waste your time.'

'I have to admit, darling, that you saying that only spurs me on even more. Let's just say I recognise the challenge you have just issued, and accept.'

Laurie had to laugh. She watched Dad as he rooted around in the kitbag he'd brought up from Somerset, eventually bringing out a much-patched air mattress that she remembered from family camping holidays. Somehow the sight brought home the realisation that had been building all evening: despite all the annoyances, it was good to have him here.

Wednesday, 5 August – 7.30 a.m.

So many of Laurie's childhood memories involved Dad urging her awake, carrying her downstairs, practically forcing food into her mouth as he tried to get her ready for school, it was strange having to tiptoe round him in the morning. She could hardly remember seeing him asleep before. All of a sudden, she felt unexpectedly grown-up, flashing forward to a future when she really would be the one in charge, the one looking after him. She took extra care to shut the door to the flat as quietly as possible.

At the office, things had settled back into the usual routine. Michael was his usual monosyllabic self, head down as he got on with implementing the trading strategy she'd helped him model. And Henry was – well – the same as he'd always been, entirely capable of generating enough work to keep a person busy with mundane tasks requiring little or no thought. A few weeks ago, Laurie had really believed that she preferred it this way: a job that she could leave behind each day, a life unhampered by ambition. Now, however, she had to admit she was bored.

So it felt like a welcome break when Henry came over

to Laurie's desk and asked if she could 'come in for a word'. Unusually, the glass partition that separated his office from the rest of the floor was opaque. Clearly, this was 'a word' that required some privacy. Nevertheless, Laurie was taken aback when she entered the office to find Tom Spencer there too. As Fitzalan's director of administration, he was nominally Laurie's boss, although she had worked out within a few days of arrival that it was the partners like Henry who really ran the show.

Tom didn't waste time on niceties. 'I'll get straight to the point, Laurie. You know the rule that we send no files out of the office.' He didn't wait for her nod. As far as he was concerned this was a straightforward case. 'Well, our email records show that a large attachment was sent from your terminal to your Gmail address at two thirty-four yesterday afternoon. I assume you're not going to say it wasn't you? We can always check the CCTV footage.'

Laurie shook her head and looked at Henry. He was avoiding her eye.

'In that case you are suspended without pay while we investigate the security breach. I will accompany you to your desk while you collect your things. I'd remind you that you remain under a duty of confidentiality under the terms of the employment contract you signed when you joined us. If you attempt to discuss your case with anyone outside this room then we will regard it as a breach of contract and pursue you for it.'

Laurie could feel herself flushing with the shock. She was to be treated like some sort of criminal? Where was the justice in that? When she finally spoke, it came out almost as a shout. 'But it was only a photograph!'

This time she did catch Henry's eye, but she could detect no response or answering empathy. An air of disdain hung about him. Mentally, he was already moving on.

174

Laurie was angry now. She deserved better treatment than this. She raised her voice, conscious that she could probably be heard outside, but too far gone to care, 'Henry, I've just worked all weekend for you. The least you can do is talk to me.'

But it was Tom who replied. 'You'll be paid any overtime due to you.' Then he stood up, and took hold of Laurie's elbow, attempting to steer her out of Henry's office. Shaking herself free with a muttered, 'Watch it, you pervert,' Laurie stalked over to her desk, gathered her phone and cycling bag and left the office, followed by Tom and what felt like a hundred pairs of eyes.

Laurie stood in the street, dressed in her cycling gear, holding her bicycle. Her immediate anger had just about subsided, to be replaced with low-level resentment at the injustice of it all. Even that was hard to maintain as she stood in the summer sun, acknowledging the pleasure that came from being outside in the middle of the day. What was she going to do now? Phone the agency? Not for a day or so, at least. The flat would harldy be a refuge at the moment – she couldn't face having to explain what had happened to Dad - but London was no place to cycle round aimlessly without a destination. She had got as far as wheeling her bike in the direction of Oxford Street, looking for a stand where she could pick up a copy of *Time Out*, when she remembered the hour she'd spent in the British Library. She'd felt at home there. How hard would it be to get a reader's card and have access to all the world's knowledge, or at least such of it as had been published in Britain since 1852 or whenever it was?

In just over ten minutes Laurie had arrived at the Euston Road entrance. Once there, she followed signs to bike racks that were so full that she could only stand there, uncertain of what to do. It was another cyclist who unconsciously led the way, wheeling his bike up and round the back of the permanent racks to a set of temporary stands close to the main entrance, where some space at least remained. The two of them locked up their bikes next door to each other and walked into the library together, never exchanging a glance or a word.

Laurie was feeling more confident than she had on her first visit. No one here knew her background. Here she could be the Laurie who'd been predicted a set of straight A stars for GCSEs, who had imagined herself following her father and mother to Cambridge, not the Laurie for whom school had suddenly ceased to hold any interest, who had been heading for God knew what kind of future before her father removed her to Somerset. The feeling bore her on and past the information desk, into the office for reader registration.

Laurie had prepared herself for some kind of grilling: why she wanted access to the library's collections, where else she had tried, what were her qualifications? So, remembering something she'd heard Michael say to Henry, she volunteered that she was researching interest-rate movements and the effect on the yield curve. The man who interviewed her might have been impressed, or might just have been in a hurry. At any rate, his only comment was, 'So you'll be wanting the Business and IT Centre, then.' All he demanded from Laurie was some ID. Her driving licence – the one real qualification she had to show for the Somerset years but almost irrelevant in London – was good enough for that. Two minutes later, she had her newly minted reader's card, complete with photograph, valid for one month. The whole experience had been uplifting: confirmation that she had some worth, some rights, despite the way she had been kicked out of the office only an hour before. Laurie had a spring in her step as she went to leave her things in the locker room, which even the need to queue for a locker did little to dispel.

That brief conversation in reader registration had decided Laurie on one thing: she would not be basing herself in the Business and IT Centre. She could just imagine what that was like: full of people like Michael huddled over computer screens. But where should she go? Rare Books and Music? She wasn't sure she was ready for that yet. Most of the people her age were heading for a door marked *Humanities I*; she followed them.

Well, there certainly wasn't a party going on inside. Even here, Laurie realised, laptops were almost essential. The room was vast. There must have been two hundred people, each with their own desk, but she could hear only a few low voices, and those came from the enquiry desk in front of her. It made Laurie ache to see it; if she hadn't fucked things up so badly after Mum died, would she have ended up somewhere like this? Then she noticed something else: a tension under-lying the overall air of studiousness. Heads had risen at her entrance; some eyes attempted to meet hers; others seemed almost too determined not to break away from the page. The sense of being on show, of judgements being formed, was both flattering and unnerving. Laurie did her best to ignore it. She found an unoccupied computer terminal and started to surf her way around the library catalogue. The complete works of Georgette Heyer were there and at her disposal; which ones hadn't she read? Two minutes later, she found herself looking up, keen to check out the Reading Room's latest arrival.

Wednesday, 5 August – 7.45 p.m.

Laurie felt a nudge on her shoulder. 'The Reading Room is closing now.' She looked up from her book, surprised. She'd been vaguely conscious of announcements, but had taken little notice of them since the arrival of the books she'd ordered. *Sylvester* had long since been finished; now she was deep into *The Masqueraders*.

Laurie joined the queue to return her books – yes, could she keep just the one on reserve please? – and then another to leave the Reading Room, waiting for security to check the belongings of those in front of her. She glanced up at the clock: almost eight already! Dad would be waiting for her. She was dreading the inevitable explanations. How would he behave? He'd be on her side of course, but she couldn't bear the thought of sympathy. Perhaps now was a good time to try Paul? The moment she got out of the Reading Room, Laurie pulled out her phone to call him. No luck: there were the usual four rings and then the call went through to voicemail. Should she send him a text? Somehow she couldn't face it.

A few last stragglers were leaving the locker room when she got down there. Rows of lockers stood agape, their doors open. She dug her key out of her pocket to remind herself of the number: 592. It was one of only two or three that remained shut. As Laurie collected her things two security guards appeared. They started moving down the rows of lockers, checking they were empty and removing the occasional pound left behind in the door by a forgetful reader.

'What do you do about the locked ones?' Laurie asked.

'We empty them.' one of the guards replied, a large woman, whose open friendliness was in marked contrast to the taciturnity of her colleague. 'We can't leave them because they might be a bomb!' This was with a laugh that invited Laurie to share in her opinion of the ridiculousness of the idea.

Laurie couldn't help smiling back. 'At least you get the pound, I suppose.'

'Goes in the collection box,' the guard replied. Then, as if unwilling to let the conversation end there, she added, 'The funny thing is, often enough the lockers themselves are empty.'

'What?' Laurie asked. 'You mean people take the keys home with them, even when they've left nothing behind?'

'Yes. Caught one of them at it once. Asked him what he thought he was doing. He said it was worth losing a pound just to make sure he had a locker the next morning. Gave him a piece of my mind, I can tell you.'

Laurie grinned in response, gave a wave and went on her way, but inside she was delighted at the turn the conversation had taken. It might not be the solution to why the man under the train had a British Library key, but it was a plausible explanation at least: one less thing for her to worry about. It balanced out, to a surprising degree, the sick feeling that came from having been as good as sacked earlier in the day. She felt unexpectedly happy as she unlocked her bike and started the uphill ride back towards Tufnell Park.

*

Laurie could hear laughter when she came into the flat. She followed the sound into the kitchen. Dad and Jess were in the middle of some sort of chopping race. Dad had clearly been passing on his technique – the one that involved pivoting off the end of the blade; Laurie remembered him doing the same with her years ago. Jess seemed to have mastered the speed aspect, but not the quality; the slices of courgette on her chopping board had thicknesses ranging from a millimetre to an inch. Laurie felt vaguely affronted at seeing them together like this, but suppressed the urge to make an acerbic comment about the danger of playing with knives.

In any case, they stopped as soon as they noticed her in the doorway. Dad had a broad smile on his face. 'Hello darling. Stir-fry tonight, if that suits you. There's some wine in the fridge. We're celebrating my triumph.'

The bottle of Gewürztraminer had just enough for a glass left in it. Laurie helped herself and sat down. Dad and Jess didn't seem to need her help. And it didn't seem the right time to bring up the subject of where she'd spent the day, either. She took the opening implied by Dad's remark. 'Your triumph?'

Dad looked up from the counter, where he was now re-slicing Jess's courgette into uniformly thin pieces, and smiled. 'The man you saw fall was William Pennington. He was sixty years old and he lived in Watford. Are you impressed?'

William Pennington? It was good to put a name to the face. Yes, Laurie thought, he looked like a William. That's how she would think of him now. Mr Pennington was too formal for someone you had seen die; and Billy or Will just weren't right. In the meantime, Dad was waiting for a response; she just had to oblige. 'Go on, then. Tell me how you found out.'

'I don't suppose you've ever read the *Camden New Journal*?'

Laurie must have looked suitably blank. 'It's your local paper. There are piles of it sitting in the hall downstairs. I thought they might be the sort of people that knew, or at least be able to point me in the right direction. So I went down to their office. It's in Camden itself, right by the bus stop. Spoke to a nice man there; he seemed quite pleased to be asked a proper news question. That used to be how you started in the newspapers – on a local before moving on to the nationals. Wouldn't surprise me if he just never moved on. Anyway, he's a proper old-style investigative journalist, with a filing system to match. Took him five minutes to find your man, in a report that his inquest was adjourned, pending psychiatric reports. He said that meant he was a jumper.'

Laurie sighed. Her evidence had made no difference at all. 'But I saw him fall. I told that policewoman.'

'Apparently, there's less than one accidental death a year on the Underground. Whenever it looks like someone just fell, they turn out to have been a jumper.'

'But I saw it.' Laurie could only repeat herself. It was so frustrating.

'Are you really sure? Even if he didn't jump, how about if he was pushed?'

'Dad – you're ridiculous. How likely is that?'

'Well, apparently even that is more likely than him just falling. So anyway, I thought I might pop up to Watford tomorrow to visit Mrs Pennington. See if she can shed any light.'

'Dad! You can't just drop in on her two weeks after her husband's died. You'd be like some tabloid doorstepper, intruding on her grief.'

'Well, she didn't seem too distraught when I spoke to her a couple of hours ago. In fact, she seemed quite glad at the idea that I was taking an interest.'

'You didn't call her! What were you thinking?'

'I'd prefer to have written, of course. That's what you should do after a death, but we haven't got time for that.'

'So he was married,' Laurie mused. 'I guess there's no reason why he shouldn't have been. I'll come with you, if that's OK.'

Through all this exchange, Jess had been chopping. She had clearly been listening, however, as her first contribution to the conversation made clear. 'Things still quiet at work?'

Ah well. They would have to be told at some point. 'I'm afraid that looks like it's not going to be a problem.' Laurie settled down to explain her day.

It was Jess who was most voluble in response, expressing the mixture of sympathy and horror that Laurie required, but also coming through with the necessary consolation. 'You know you'll have no problem getting another job, don't you?' Dad, by contrast, was much quieter. Only the way he seized on that last remark – 'Yes, I'm sure that's right' – betrayed his worry.

Jess picked up Dad's tone too, and made an immediate move to lighten the mood. 'Tell you what. How about watching an episode of *University Challenge*? I've got several on TiVo that I promise I've never watched. A nice bit of competitive question-answering will take your mind off things.'

Dad was clearly nonplussed, but Laurie had to smile. 'I know you'll beat me, but you may have bitten off more than you can chew, challenging Dad too. When I was little I thought he knew everything. I'm not so sure even now that I was wrong.' Then she turned to him in explanation. 'It's one of Jess's little obsessions. Humour her. If you know the answer, shout it out, but it only counts if you start speaking before anyone on screen buzzes.'

So after supper, Jess scrolled through the TiVo menu system and the *University Challenge* theme tune started to play.

'Goodness, I thought this went off air years ago,' Dad began, before his tone changed to one of disbelief. 'Jeremy Paxman?'

'Yes,' Jess sounded amused. 'He took over from Bamber Gascoigne when it switched to BBC.'

Then the questions began. As Laurie had predicted, Jess knew far more than her. She'd explained why the first time they'd played together. 'Benefits of a classical education, I suppose, plus the general knowledge that comes with age.' Laurie scored a couple of points from mental arithmetic and a lucky guess based on something half remembered from Mum's Mrs Gaskell period, but that was it. Jess seemed to be cruising for an easy victory. And then Dad got going. By the end of the first episode he was beginning to give Jess a good run for her money. During the second he seemed to know the answer to almost every question. Jess admitted defeat gracefully, but she still wanted a rematch. Dad was keen too – Laurie couldn't remember the last time she'd seen him so fired up – but she at least had played enough. She left them to it.

Jess had been right to suggest it, though. The whole experience had been fun – especially the way Dad had taken to it. It left Laurie sufficiently buoyant to dig out her CV there and then, to start thinking how she could tart it up for the agency. Then she went online to check the best route to Watford: no surprise that it turned out to be a train from Euston. Her emails took a while to download. How could she have accumulated 139 in two days? It was message 53 that was the problem. It clearly had a large attachment; it seemed an age before the computer starting ticking fast again, through 54, 55, 56 and onwards. Laurie, meanwhile, experienced a moment of shock when she realised that the message responsible for the hold-up was from herself. There it was: the email that had caused all the trouble. No harm in forwarding it back to Henry, she supposed, as evidence that she had done nothing wrong.

Dad and Jess were still watching television, shouting at the screen, when Laurie went to bed.

Thursday 6 August – 10 a.m.

Laurie and Dad walked to Tufnell Park station together. They'd both dressed up for the occasion. She wore her Zara dress, looking for all the world as if she was on her way to work. He had emerged from the bathroom as smart as she remembered seeing him for a long time, in a brown linen suit that was so unrumpled it could only be new. He had looked embarrassed when Laurie raised her eyebrows at it. 'I thought old clothes weren't quite right for a grieving widow. Jess took me shopping. Do you like it?'

Laurie had given her yes almost without thinking, but now, stealing a glance at him as they walked side by side, she was struck by how good Dad really looked. He'd never lost his figure, of course: one of the benefits, she supposed, of the country lifestyle. She slipped her arm through his and gave him a kiss on the cheek.

The Northern line was as hot and stuffy as ever. Dad's suit started to lose its crispness. Later, sitting opposite Laurie on the empty train out from Euston, he produced a tie from his pocket and whipped it into a schoolboy knot with the practised ease of one who did this every morning. Presumably it was the kind of skill that, once learnt, was never forgotten. The tie itself was new to Laurie – relatively sober, square cut, with muted greens and blues in horizontal stripes. It made him instantly elegant, but not flash. In fact, it suited Dad perfectly. Laurie wondered if that was new too, but any questions were forestalled by the emergence of yesterday's crossword from another pocket. She settled down to look out of the window.

It was only when the train pulled in to Watford Junction that Dad made any attempt to initiate conversation. 'I thought we'd play it by ear a bit with Mrs Pennington. All I've said to her so far is that you were on the platform with him. I don't know which of us should take the lead in the conversation – it depends a bit on what state she's in.'

'So she really doesn't know anything about us?' Laurie could only admire Dad's chutzpah. 'How do you know she won't throw us out the moment we arrive?'

'I don't, I suppose, but there's nothing to lose by trying, is there?'

Dad had clearly memorised the route. They walked past houses separated from the road by driveways and weed-free lawns. A couple of children ran by on some nameless errand. The sound of their laughter seemed to hang in the still air long after they had gone. With no wind, the heat was getting oppressive. The space between Laurie's shoulder blades began to prickle. She imagined the net curtains twitching as they walked past.

'Dad,' Laurie suddenly asked, 'why are you doing this?'

Dad stopped walking and looked at her. 'What do you mean?'

'You know what I mean. You never leave home, especially in the summer. You hate London. Yet all of a sudden here you are, turned into Sherlock Holmes. And please don't tell me it's just because you're worried about me. That might account for you coming to stay – just – but not for all this.' Laurie gestured at the suburban idyll around them.

'Well, perhaps it's time for me to get out a bit more.'

'Dad!' Laurie warned. She wouldn't let him get away with an answer like that.

'OK.' Dad paused. 'Do you remember us watching *True Grit* on telly when you were young? John Wayne western. It was one of Mum's favourite films.'

Laurie did remember. She nodded.

'Well, there's a great line in it when the old guide played by Wayne looks at the girl who has refused to be left behind. I think she forces her horse to swim a river. Anyway, he looks at her and says, "She reminds me of me." That's what I thought when you insisted on going back to London to follow up what you'd remembered about William Pennington. Then I thought about it some more – once you'd gone – and I realised that might not be how you see me. It's certainly not how I've behaved over the past few years. Anyway, I guess what I'm saying is, you might be seeing a bit more of me in London from now on.'

Laurie pondered this reply as they walked, surprised at how good it made her feel. Any form of Dad was great, but one that had a bit of the old dynamism? That would be wonderful.

All the houses on Chestnut Avenue were detached, solid-looking constructions of dull brick: places for bringing up a family in middle-class comfort. There was even an old-style telephone box on the corner. Number thirty-seven seemed to have undergone fewer redesigns than its neighbours: the garage had not been extended; its bay window was still glazed with what looked like the original little leaded diamonds; and the front door was a relatively plain slab of wood, with no added porch. Dad rang the bell. During the pause that followed, he straightened his tie and ran a hand over his hair. Laurie felt an odd nervousness. What were they doing here? What must they look like? Then they heard a bolt being shot back and the door opened to reveal a woman wearing jeans and a striped cotton shirt rolled up to her elbows. Her grey hair was slightly at odds with a face that seemed to belong to a younger woman: relatively unlined, but with a mobility that said Botox was not the reason. She could have been any age between forty and sixty. The woman looked at them enquiringly.

'Mrs Pennington?' Dad began, and on receiving a confirmatory nod, continued, 'I'm David Bateman, and this is my daughter Laurie. I spoke to you on the phone yesterday.'

'Yes.' The woman's voice was surprisingly strong and deep. Laurie looked at her with renewed interest. Mrs Pennington, however, was looking beyond them.

Laurie turned round to follow her gaze. On the other side of the road a car was just pulling away, reflecting back the sun from tinted windows that could only be necessary on a day like today. Presumably the glare had caught Mrs Pennington's attention; perhaps she thought that was their taxi? No harm in putting her straight on that: 'We came up on the train.'

'Of course. You'd better come in. I hope you don't mind my gardening clothes.' Mrs Pennington stood back from the door to let them pass and fingered the top button of her shirt. Muscles flexed in her forearms as she did so, giving her a slightly masculine air, for all the prettiness in her face. She noticed Laurie's glance, but seemed to misinterpret it, admitting, 'It's an old shirt of my husband's.' That was all it took. Without warning, she emitted a strange keening cry, a precursor to great convulsive sobs that shuddered through her body and tears that streamed down a suddenly contorted face.

Dad took charge, ushering Laurie and the grieving woman into a cork-floored conservatory, while he went into the kitchen and prepared tea. Uncertainly, Laurie sat beside Mrs Pennington on a rattan sofa, holding her hand as the sobs subsided. She didn't know what to say. How did you soothe a complete stranger, someone old enough to be your mother? In the end, she stayed silent; her presence alone seemed comfort enough.

When Mrs Pennington eventually spoke again, it was with a measured tone. She had regained control. 'We never had children: never felt the need, really. I had my yoga - I teach it, you know – that and the garden. He had his work and his old Sunbeam.' Her voice really was powerful, like a singer's, but there was a crack to it. She paused. Laurie glanced across. Mrs Pennington was composing herself again, and seemed in no hurry to withdraw her hand. 'You guessed about the shirt didn't you? Was it the buttons? It still has his smell, you see. Is that silly?'

Laurie shook her head and Mrs Pennington continued. 'Now it turns out he'd lost his job in June. He never even told me, just carried on getting up in the morning, putting on his suit, going into work. I mean, why would he have done that?'

Laurie didn't try to respond.

'And now he goes and throws himself under a train. Of all the unnatural things to do. I just don't understand it. We could have worked things out. With his pension and my classes we had more than enough to live on. I thought I knew him. It feels like I've been living with a stranger all these years.'

Now Laurie did feel the need to speak. 'He didn't throw himself under a train. I was there. I saw him fall.'

'You were there? Of course you were. How did he look?'

'Fine, happy even. He smiled at me. I think he was about to tell me I had a smudge on my nose. He had a lovely suit on.'

191

'I bought him that – wasn't really his usual style, to tell the truth. I think he probably wore it because he was travelling down with me.'

Then, without Laurie even needing to ask the question that she was struggling to form, Mrs Pennington went on. 'I don't go into London much. When I do I like . . . liked . . . to travel with William. We'd take the train down together. I got on the Northern line; I was going to the Chinese exhibition at the British Museum. He went onto the Victoria line like he always did. That was the last time I saw him – at the bottom of the escalator between the two platforms.'

There was a faint uplift in Mrs Pennington's voice as she made that last statement; it gave her voice, deep as it was, an almost brittle timbre. Laurie could tell that, having already broken down once, she was desperate not to do so again. Instinctively, she made no move to comfort the older woman. Instead, she left her to breathe, to regain some measure of composure in her own time, before she herself went on, repeating her earlier assertion. 'He didn't kill himself; he fell. I'm sure; I was right by him. I saw it.' Then she stopped, only too aware of what she meant by 'it', and of what her words might mean to the dead man's widow.

Mrs Pennington, however, was looking her straight in the eye. 'I wish I could believe you. But there's no doubt what the police think, although they haven't said it to my face. I got the impression they see it all the time: people made redundant who can't bear to tell their wives. The inquest may return an open verdict, but that will just be window dressing.'

Immediately Laurie thought of Mum. Dad had effectively said the same verdict was just window dressing there too. What wouldn't she give for someone to tell her they knew it was an accident? Well, she could do that for Mrs Pennington, at least. 'I saw him fall. The platform was crowded. He was leaning across to talk to me. He lost his balance.' Even as she spoke, the memory of the accident and her feeling about Mum overwhelmed her. Now she was the one crying. Why would no one believe her?

'It's true, you know.' Dad had come through from the kitchen and was standing in the doorway. 'At least, that's what Laurie said when she called me straight afterwards. She was certain then, and it looks like she was the only real witness. She's not the sort of person to make it up.'

Mrs Pennington breathed in and shut her eyes. When she opened them again there was a new sense of calmness about her, almost an acceptance of what was to come. Now she was the one who reached out for Laurie's hand. 'I think we'd better have that cup of tea, don't you?'

The conservatory was no place for a heart to heart, so they sat around the kitchen table. This was the business end of the house, where everything important happened. Laurie could look across at Mrs Pennington – or Margaret, as she soon learnt to call her – while she said what she had come to say. Dad sat between them, at the head of the table. He had heard the story before, of course, and was content to sit in silence as Laurie relived that morning once again. It was at his prompting, however, that Laurie went on to describe her interview with Sergeant Atkins. It struck a chord.

'Well, it seems you and I have had a similar experience with the ghastly Atkins. Not that she was rude to me, of course, but I got the feeling when we met that she was reading from a script for dealing with the widows of suicides. She was certainly in no mood to listen to me. She quoted some statistic that there was less than one fatal accident a year on the Underground, dripping with concern while she did so. I have to say that I've never felt so patronised in my life. It gave me an awful foretaste of what it will be like when I'm old.' There was a short pause, before she added, 'She certainly didn't mention any witness.'

'Do you think there's some sort of bias that means accidents are more likely to be registered as suicides?' Laurie asked. 'Like a vicious circle: less than one person dies by accident on the Tube each year; so therefore the assumption with any death is that it's the result of a deliberate action; so therefore the statistics show less than one accidental death a year.'

A small silence greeted this remark, long enough for Laurie to feel faintly embarrassed at having made it. Perhaps now wasn't the time to search for patterns; for Mrs Pennington this was all too personal. It was Dad who brought it back to the specific. 'Would you like to talk about your husband?'

Mrs Pennington was oblique in her reply. 'Sergeant Atkins seemed to assume that just because he'd spent forty-odd years with the same company then he must have found it too hard to take when he lost his job. I don't know. We'd had some bad news too, of course. At least he'd told me that.'

'Bad news?' Dad asked gently.

'Just the week before: an old colleague of William's who hanged himself. No wife or children. He left some sort of a note, but he wasn't found for a while. Sergeant Atkins seemed to think it might have been the last straw.'

'Old colleagues? Were they particularly close?'

'I don't know. They'd certainly known each other for a long time. Roger arrived at Sanderson's only a couple of years after William. He was the finance director – something like that. William was head of sales. It's a firm of recruitment consultants: William joined it straight out of school, when it was just a man and a dog. It specialised in IT. William always said that computers were the future. For a long time it seemed he was right.' Margaret tailed off, lost in remembrance.

'Go on.' Encouraged Dad.

'Well, William always said it was the millennium bug that did it – just not in the way they'd all expected. That was the boom time, you see. There weren't enough programmers to go round. Recruitment firms could write their own ticket. Sanderson's expanded to cope with the demand. Then, of course, it all hit a brick wall. New Year's Day, 2000: the world didn't come to an end; all those programmers were suddenly surplus to requirements.'

'Why was it called Sanderson's?' Laurie queried.

'Peter Sanderson started it. He's been dead for a few years now, and he'd already handed it on to Dominic, in any case.' Margaret's tone of voice changed as she said the name.

'Who was in charge in 2000?'

'That was Dominic already.' Margaret pursed her lips. 'He wasn't even thirty; had to make all these people redundant. William was rather impressed by his decisiveness, then started to worry that he was enjoying it. Anyway, between them, they kept the company going, but it's a lot smaller than it was.'

'So why would he have made William redundant now?'

'You'd have to ask Dominic that, but I don't suppose you'd get a straight answer. He wrote to me after William died, to express his sympathy. Didn't say sorry, though. Called it "early retirement". I shredded the letter. There always was something a bit odd about that man.'

'Was William close to retirement?'

'Not for a few years. He was only sixty, you know. He'd certainly said nothing to me about wanting to stop work.'

Laurie would have left it there. They'd come back to where they started. It was pointless to probe further. She wanted to be somewhere else, away from a suburban house in mourning. All of a sudden, she thought of Paul; she savoured the moment, imagining what they might do the next time they met.

Catching Dad's eye, Laurie felt herself blush. Could he read her mind? Then she realised he was speaking, asking something: did Mrs Pennington have any idea what her husband had been doing when she thought he'd been going to work?

It was to hide her embarrassment as much as anything that made Laurie leap in: 'Might he have been going to the British Library? Only I found one of their locker keys near where he fell.'

Mrs Pennington looked faintly startled, then reminiscent. 'He used to say that it held the answer to every question. I don't think I've ever seen him more excited than when he got the letter approving his request for a reader's card. She paused for just long enough for Laurie to remember her own feelings the day before, and then continued. 'That was a few years ago now. He had this idea to write a book about whether there were still descendants of Alexander the Great living in Central Asia.' She gave a short laugh and shook her head. 'Well, it gave him something to do on Saturdays. Then he had to make half his team at Sanderson's redundant and work later in the evening. Come the weekend, the last thing he wanted to do was head back into the city to read about Afghanistan. I assumed he'd forgotten all about it.'

Alexander the Great and Afghanistan! The idea was crazy, but wonderful too. How would you go about establishing that? And William Pennington had been as excited as Laurie was at the receipt of a BL card. She remembered his smile and his suit; OK, he might have been wearing it as a decoy, to let his wife carry on believing he was going into work, but that didn't make it any less elegant. This was a man she would have liked to know. 'I imagine,' Laurie said, 'that it wouldn't be hard to find out if he had been going into the library. They must keep some sort of record of everyone's requests.'

*

196

The police still had Mr Pennington's wallet, along with the other personal effects recovered from his body. Laurie toyed with the idea of suggesting that Dad impersonate the dead man. Surely it wouldn't be too hard to get the library to issue him a new card if he went in with the correct passport and something like a utility bill? They'd never check the photograph that carefully, surely? But she soon gave up the notion. How would she go about even suggesting such a thing to Margaret? In any case, a new card would still be useless without her husband's password. That, at least, was a point she could make. 'Even if we had his card, we'd need his password too, of course.'

'I can probably help you there at least,' Margaret replied. 'William kept a list of all his passwords in a drawer in his desk.' She disappeared for a moment before re-emerging with a sheet of A4. 'Now, William was rather cryptic when he wrote these down. What sort of thing do you think I should be looking for?'

Laurie noticed the 'I' and made no attempt to look over Margaret's shoulder while she scanned the list. Instead, she brought out her own library card. There was a code above the expiry date, just to the right of her photograph. 'Some sort of membership number? Mine has six digits.'

'Ah yes. Here we are. Three-six-four-five-one-one.' Laurie resisted the urge to note it down. 'And then against it he's typed "d-n-i-l-g". That will be the password.' Margaret stopped, folded up the piece of paper and put it down. She smiled at Laurie, but she seemed to have nothing more to say.

Laurie considered this. Dnilg? Could that be a password? Didn't they have to be at least six characters long? How many more questions could she ask? Then Dad stood up. 'Margaret, you've been really kind to us. Now, unless you'd like us to stay, I think we'd better go. We've been pestering you for long enough.'

He had called it right. Mrs Pennington made no attempt to prevent them leaving. Within a couple of minutes they were outside the house, walking back towards Watford Junction.

'Thanks for backing me up about him falling,' Laurie said.

'Well, in the end it didn't seem right to ask if he might have been pushed. In the meantime, I'm keeping an open mind on the subject for your sake.'

Laurie was wondering whether it was worth restating her certainty, when Dad changed tack 'I wonder if she'll ever think all that through.'

'What do you mean?'

'Well, the British Library is only a five-minute walk from Euston station.'

'So?' Laurie replied without thinking. Then the implication hit her. 'I see what you mean. Why would he have got on the Tube to get there?'

'I'm awfully afraid that it was only because his wife was with him. I thought we'd better leave before she reached the same conclusion.'

'Right,' said Laurie. 'It seems a shame, though, just as we were beginning to make some progress.'

'Oh, I think we'd learnt about as much as we could in a first visit.'

'Hmm.' Laurie's acquiescence was definitely half-hearted. 'You know, I'm not sure about that password she found for us. I set one up yesterday. They have to be at least six letters long. What she told us only has five.'

'Yes,' Dad couldn't keep a note of triumph out of his voice, 'but when you heard "d-n-i-l-g" I heard "d-nil-g". Margaret said he was cryptic. That was just his way of writing "dog".'

Laurie could think of all sorts of retorts to this flight of fancy, but limited herself to a single, not entirely dismissive, 'So?'

'So there's a dog's bowl on the floor in the kitchen. It's got a name on it: Freddy. There are your six letters.'

Thursday, 6 August – 4 p.m.

It was touching, Dad's level of excitement, as they sat down at his computer. He insisted on being there while Laurie navigated her way round the British Library website until she found *Log in as a Reader Pass holder*. Did she only imagine his hum of approval when she typed in *364511*? There could be little doubt that her facility with numbers came from him. If by any chance she had forgotten the digits read out by Mrs Pennington, she was sure he would have been able to fill the gap. Now for the password. She tried *freddy* first, all lower case. No joy there: the red error message at the top of the screen made that clear. *Freddy* had the same result.

'Try moving the upper-case letter along the word.' Dad suggested. *fReddy*, *frEddy*, *freDdy*, *fredDy* and *freddY* were all equally unsuccessful. Just for the hell of it, Laurie tried *dnilg*: useless.

'The trouble is' Laurie said, 'that even if you're right about "freddy", he could have manipulated it in any one of a number of ways that only he would know.'

'No,' Dad replied with surprising certainty, 'because

then he would have had to remember it. It's got to be something simple.'

'What if he had another dog, one that died, or a cuddly toy when he was a child?

'They're all possibilities.' Dad admitted. He seemed deflated, or at least lost in thought.

Laurie tried logging on as herself. It was marvellously simple. She could, she realised, order any book she wanted from the comfort of the computer in her bedroom and find it waiting for her in the Reading Room by the time she'd cycled down. More to the point, there was the button at the top of the page: *My Reading Room requests*. She clicked on it, re-entered her details and got straight through to a page with three tabs: *Current requests* and *Unsuccessful requests* were both empty, but *Older requests* showed, all too clearly, the previous day's activity. Behind her, Dad murmured, 'Nothing wrong with a bit of Georgette Heyer for soothing the soul.'

Laurie shut down the page and stood up. 'I'm going out for a walk,' she declared. 'Just to clear my head.' She had to get away from Dad for a while. It was lovely spending the day with him, but he knew her too well. Besides, this would be her first chance to phone Paul all day: perhaps in five minutes she would be speaking to him!

'Hi, this is Paul. I'm sorry I can't take your call right now, but if you leave a message I'll get back to you.'

That was Paul's voice all right, but no substitute for talking to the real thing. Laurie tried hard to sound positive after the beep. 'Hi, it's Laurie. Give me a call when you can. I'd love to talk to you.' His gym might be underground, she reflected. That would explain why her calls kept going straight through to voicemail. She carried on walking.

Turning the corner, Laurie suddenly remembered the

argument she'd witnessed there a few days before. What had brought that to mind? The man had been so free with his swear words. Well, used one swear word a lot, but then been curiously reluctant to say the word 'shit'. How had he said it? 'Ess-aitch-one-tee'. Laurie liked it, the idea that you denatured a word by replacing its vowel with a digit. That was, now she thought of it, what Dad said William Pennington had done with the word dog – just replaced the 'o' with '0' when storing the clue to his password. You could do it with every vowel really: 'A' would be '4'; 'E' would be '3'. Laurie never got on to thinking about 'U'. She'd had an idea. It was time to return home.

fr3ddy: that was it! Laurie was logged on to the British Library website as someone else. Was she doing something wrong? Should she be feeling this excited? Who cared? With Dad watching, she clicked on the link for *My Reading Room requests* and re-entered the user number and password. Just as it had been for her, the *Current requests* page was empty. She clicked on the tab for *Older requests*, entered a date range for the whole year, and there, in front of her, was the complete record of what William Pennington had been reading.

Titles like *The Greek Kingdom of Bactria from Alexander to Eucratides the Great* and *A History of the Moghuls of Central Asia* leapt out at her. What was it Margaret had said her husband was interested in – that there might be descendants of Alexander the Great in Afghanistan? Well, no inconsistency there: William Pennington was taking his research seriously. Dad pointed out the date against the first titles on the list. 'Looks like he ordered these the day before he died. That doesn't strike me as the action of a man about to kill himself.'

'No,' Laurie agreed, 'but I don't know if the police would see it that way. I guess if we look at his unsuccessful requests we can see if he'd ordered books for the following days.' She clicked on the appropriate tab, and entered the same dates in the search boxes. Only three books were listed, and all had been requested months before William Pennington's death.

'Ah well,' said Dad. 'No reason why he had to order books in advance, I suppose.'

Laurie was quiet for a while, looking at the titles of the three books he had never got around to reading. Two clearly continued with the theme of Central Asia, but it was the third title that caught her eye: *Pension Fund Deficits and the Minimum Funding Requirement.* Was that just an aberration, the only time William Pennington had strayed into this particular topic? No: a quick check within *Older requests* showed that he had ordered a number of similar titles at around the same time, and had at least got as far as picking those ones up from the issue desk. In fact, she realised, those had been the first books he had ordered that year, almost as if it was the desire to learn more about pensions that had brought him back to the British Library. What was he trying to find out?

Friday, 7 August – 8.30 a.m.

'You two might as well be brick walls for all the reward I get from talking to you! I know mornings are meant to be difficult for the young, but it's hardly the crack of dawn.'

Laurie looked up from her plate with a start. Her mind had been wandering, it was true: to Paul and when he'd call, to work, and whether she would ever be returning there, to Margaret, mourning the husband she was no longer sure she knew, and then to William Pennington himself, and his odd library requests. All in all, she reckoned, she had a good excuse for not being particularly talkative. She was about to say something to that effect when she realised Dad wasn't really talking about her.

Laurie had been conscious of Jess shuffling into breakfast a few minutes earlier, but it was only now, following Dad's gaze, that she took proper note of her appearance. She looked terrible; there was no other word for it. Her skin had a waxy pastiness to it that belied the sun outside. Deep rings under her eyes made her look old in a way Laurie had never seen before. She sat there, hunched over a plate that hadn't been touched, just gathering her dressing gown around her shoulders, staring into space. Ordinarily, Laurie would have supposed she had a hangover, but she knew Jess had turned in early the night before. At the time she'd muttered something about needing to be up early for work. That was a point. Laurie might not have an office to go to, but Jess certainly did. What was going on?

Jess looked up and met Laurie's eyes, then shifted her attention to Dad, as if she'd just realised that he'd been speaking to her. 'I'm sorry,' she murmured in a voice so low they had to strain to hear it. 'I don't feel very well today.' With that, she pushed herself up from her place, turned around and went back into her bedroom, shutting the door behind her in a way that made it clear she did not want to be followed.

Laurie watched her go, remembering what she had found behind that bedroom door. She felt herself colouring up. Had it really only been this week? If anyone had a right to be down it was Jess. Laurie had been a bad cousin to her. But she'd seemed so well before.

'I wonder,' started Dad. 'I wonder if perhaps you'd both like to come back with me this evening? I'm not the kind of evangelist who believes country air is the cure for all ills, but it seemed to do you some good last time you came down.'

This evening? Was it Friday already? It was amazing how quickly Laurie had lost track of the days without the office routine to remind her. Anyway, what about Dad's offer? She smiled at him. 'Good idea; you know how Jess loves it down there. What time were you planning to leave?'

'Soon after lunch. I'd like to beat the rush hour if possible. I told the Shillings I'd be back in time for supper.'

'Fine. I just thought I'd spend one more morning at the BL, if that's OK. I want to take a look at some of those books William Pennington ordered, see if I can get inside his brain. I guess you could come too, if you wangled yourself a reader's card. I imagine twenty years as a lecturer at Cambridge must count for something.'

'You imagine correctly. I was visiting the BL before you were born.' It could have been a put-down, but Dad had made the remark in a false-old-man voice that made it clear he was joking, and that the joke was on him, not his daughter. 'Not that I've got my card with me.' He continued, more normally. 'And I'm sure it will be out of date. The last time I went, it was still in the British Museum. No, you go without me. Just try to get back before three.'

Friday, 7 August – 4 p.m.

'I'm sorry,' Laurie hoped she sounded suitably contrite. 'I had no idea UK pensions regulations could be so fascinating.'

Laurie had never actually heard someone snort before, but that was the only possible description for Dad's response. She looked at the clock. Had he and Jess really been sitting there waiting for her all this time? Laurie remembered the bags she'd passed in the hall and groaned to herself. 'Look, I really am sorry. I'll just be five minutes packing my stuff.'

Laurie sat in the back of Dad's old Fiesta, feeling like a naughty child ignored by its parents. Her efforts to make conversation had been rewarded with answers whose shortness left her in no doubt that she remained in disgrace. Dad gave all his concentration to the road, as if split-second reactions might be required, although they were currently travelling at a speed no faster than a brisk walk. That was Laurie's fault too, she knew. This was all traffic that had built up in the last hour or so; if they had left when Dad wanted, they would have been well clear of London by now. As for Jess, her ostentatious thanks when Dad carried her luggage and held the front passenger door open for her had been evidence of some kind of recovery from her morning blues. Now, however, she seemed to be asleep.

Left alone with her thoughts, Laurie thought about what she had found out that day: specifically, about pension-fund deficits and the employer's responsibility to cover them. She really hadn't been lying when she said she found it fascinating. It reminded her a bit of the work she'd been doing with Michael. But what was the source of William Pennington's interest?

A plane passed overhead, so close that its undercarriage seemed in danger of clipping the trees that lined the motorway. Without Laurie noticing, they had got as far as Heathrow already. The road was still busy, but at least it was free flowing. They stood a chance of making it home for supper. Perhaps that was why the atmosphere in the car seemed slightly warmer. Dad and Jess had turned on the radio, and were listening to the news. Laurie leaned forward to listen along with them, sticking her head between the two front seats. Dad glanced across at her, and then, with his eyes back on the road, said, 'So, tell me what you found out.'

The edge to Dad's voice told Laurie that she was not yet entirely forgiven, but she also knew he would not have asked at all if he wasn't interested, so she took the question at face value. 'Pensions. I'm trying to work out why William Pennington suddenly got interested in them a couple of months ago.'

'Planning his retirement? That sort of thing?'

'The sort of books he was reading were more detailed than that. They were more like what somebody in charge of a pension fund would read. Makes me wonder if he was thinking about going in that direction himself.'

Jess laughed, and that was a good sign in itself. 'Listen to

210

the two of you, nattering on about pensions. Anybody would think you were a pair of OAPs, the way you're going on.'

'Sorry Jess,' Laurie was smiling herself now, as she injected a note of fake pomposity into her voice, 'but it's never too early to start planning these things, and Dad here isn't so far off his free bus pass himself.'

'Thank you for that darling, but there's life in me yet.'

Laurie was going to reply, but Jess beat her to it. Her 'Anybody can see that,' somehow left no room for a rejoinder.

Saturday, 8 August

The weather was so beautiful it could hardly fail to be uplifting. Laurie took Jess out for a ride on Roxanne, leading her round the lanes. Jess seemed to enjoy herself – she was certainly grateful at the end of the ride – but was hardly talkative. It gave Laurie the chance to carry on puzzling over the mystery of William Pennington's reading habits.

Lunch was heavy on eggs and tomatoes: neither had ceased production while Dad had been in London. In the afternoon he dragooned both the girls – as he continued to insist on calling them – into helping out in the garden, where his brief absence had apparently allowed an unprecedented burgeoning of the weed population. It was hard, sweaty work, but Jess, in particular, seemed to flourish under Dad's instructions. By the end she was taking a proprietorial pride in the alternating rows of onions and lettuces that emerged from a small thicket of chickweed.

The evening was spent watering. Laurie had thought little of it when Dad mentioned it earlier in the day, but she had forgotten about the hosepipe ban. She and Jess worked in relay, carrying buckets to Dad as he waited by various plants that seemed to require inordinate quantities of water. 'It would be much worse if I hadn't made sure everything was well mulched before I left,' was Dad's only response when Laurie questioned whether it was really necessary to pour this much liquid into the ground.

It wasn't clear how he had found the time, but Dad turned out to have been making bread in the course of the afternoon. It went perfectly with the leek and potato soup he retrieved from the freezer and served cold. They all had seconds, and would have gone on if there had been more. Instead, Dad broke the remains of the loaf into three chunks, which they used to mop their bowls clean. None of them was in a hurry to move afterwards. Laurie let her mind wander off again, secure in the knowledge that neither Dad nor Jess would think her rude for failing to make small talk, but keeping half an ear on them as they continued the conversation they had begun at dinner.

'Well,' Jess was saying, 'I suppose if you can cook like that then you're entitled to be a bit of a slave driver. Where did you learn?'

'Being a slave driver comes naturally. But if you mean who taught me to cook, then I suppose the answer is Fran.' Dad's voice tailed off for a moment, before continuing, in a more reminiscent vein. 'I don't know if you remember, but the kitchen was always her domain. I came back from work around seven, and every day she'd serve me a delicious meal. God knows how she managed it. Don't forget she was working too. I guess I – we – just took it for granted, until she was ill.'

'Go on,' Jess encouraged.

'Well this was before she was really ill, if you see what I mean. She had to go into hospital for something else: a hyster-ectomy, actually. She was meant to be out in a few days. I can't remember how long it was meant to be, but she'd prepared for it: meals for every day she was going to be away. Put them in the freezer with strict instructions about what to defrost and when. I'd arranged my teaching load so I could pick Laurie up from school, then we'd eat that day's meal together.'

'I remember that,' Laurie interrupted. 'It was great, felt like a real adventure.'

'Yes.' Dad was smiling, but his eyes were sad. 'You were ten, I think. I rather loved it too. Anyway, the day before Fran was due to come home there was a complication. Nothing serious – in fact, she eventually found it funny. They'd used a balloon to keep everything in place while her tummy healed, and they suddenly realised that it had burst. Apparently it had never happened before. She had to stay in hospital for another day. It threw out all her plans. She was more worried about that than anything else. What would we eat? I had to promise that I'd cook – spaghetti bolognaise. She gave me detailed instructions about softening the onions and grating the carrot, and how the meat had to be properly browned before I added the tomatoes. I still follow them today, really.'

'And so do I,' said Laurie. 'I think spag bol was the first thing you taught me how to cook, too.'

'Yes, well you always loved it. Anyway, I was rather surprised, but I found I really enjoyed it: the satisfaction of a job well done, I suppose. Fran came home and took over again, of course, but when she got really ill . . . well, it was something I could do. She seemed to like it when I used her recipes, but I would always experiment a bit too.'

'So you've never used recipes from books?'

There was a note of incredulity to Jess's question, which Dad could hardly fail to pick up. 'Oh, I'm not dogmatic about it. Sometimes you need a book. And now we've got the internet as well, of course.'

215

Dad stopped with a look on his face that spoke volumes. Laurie reached across and held his hand. He looked across to her with a start, as if he had forgotten she was there, and smiled again.

Sunday, 9 August – 10 a.m.

If Mrs Pennington was surprised to hear Laurie's voice at the other end of the telephone, her voice did little to betray it. 'No, not at all,' she said, when Laurie apologised for disturbing her. 'I was just on my way to church, but I don't need to leave just yet.'

Laurie responded to the invitation to speak before the moment was lost. 'Oh good,' she started. 'In fact, I think we're about to do the same ourselves.' It was true. Dad and Jess had come into the hall while she was on the phone, and were getting ready to go out. 'I just had a very quick question. Do you think you'd be able to tell me the date when your husband left Sanderson's?'

'Well, I'm not sure exactly, but now that I've looked at our bank statements I can see that he stopped receiving a salary in June.'

That figured. It was what Laurie had already deduced from William Pennington's library records: he'd started reading about Central Asia again on 1 July. The next question was the crucial one. 'And I don't suppose you know what notice period he was on?'

'Would you believe it was only six weeks? I asked him about it when they were making all those redundancies a few years ago. I said surely we needed more security. He said that now was hardly the time to be pushing for something like that.' Mrs Pennington sniffed so deeply that Laurie had an immediate vision of her nostrils flaring. 'It never was the time, of course. Would that be all?'

Laurie was halfway through nodding before she realised Mrs Pennington couldn't see her. 'Yes,' she agreed. 'I think it is.'

'What was that all about?' Jess was still waiting by the front door with Dad.

'I'm just trying to work out the timings of Mr Pennington's library requests,' Laurie replied, as they walked out of the door and headed up the lane. 'And I think I have. He looked at all those books about pensions in the middle of May. Then there was a gap, and he didn't go back to the library until the end of June. Mrs Pennington just confirmed what I guessed. He was working out his notice.'

'That's a bit harsh of them isn't it? Making him work out his notice after they'd sacked him. I thought everyone in the City was sent on gardening leave the moment they were told to clear their desks.' Jess stopped herself and caught Laurie's eye. 'Sorry. You know "tactless" is my middle name, don't you?'

'It's OK. You see, the more I think about it, the more I don't think he was sacked. I think he resigned – he really did take early retirement.' Now she looked across at Dad, who was walking in step with the two of them. 'Just like Mr Sanderson said in his letter of condolence.'

'The one Margaret shredded? Well you might be right, I suppose, but I don't see why you're so sure. He might have known he was being forced into retirement and then gone to the library to check where that left him financially.'

218

'No,' Laurie felt even more certain as she spoke. 'Like Jess says, if you sack someone, you don't make them work out their notice. You want them off the premises as soon as possible. It's only if they resign that you hang on to them. In any case, those books weren't retirement guides. They were about pension schemes themselves. You said it yourself last night: you read books to find something out. Mr Pennington wanted to find out more about how his pension scheme operated. Whatever it was those books told him, it made him decide to resign.'

Dad looked as though he was marshalling his thoughts, preparing another challenge, or at least a question, but a loud 'Hello' from across the road prevented him: James and Alice Shilling, Dad's neighbours, also on their way to church.

It was Alice who had called them, and it was she who now spoke, bringing forth a stream of consciousness at a volume that made no allowance for the fact she had come up to within a yard of them. 'David, how lovely to see you – and Lauren as well. It's always a treat when you come down and grace us with your presence. And Jessica – lovely to see you again. You've got Lauren as your tenant now, is that right? Alice and James, dear, in case you've forgotten. Well, it's all I could do to tear myself away from the garden this morning. All this sun is lovely, of course. Don't think I'm complaining for an instant, but it does make a lot of work for us gardeners, doesn't it, David? You're lucky to have two young things to help you. Yes, I saw you out there yesterday. Well done. I mean, who would have thought things could get so out of hand so quickly? I said to James, "Isn't David lucky?" Of course we can't expect any help like that from our two. John's got the farm, of course, and the milking doesn't wait for anybody. He's busiest at the weekends when the cowman's off and I don't like to ask him to come into the village and look after our little garden. I mean, it would be like a bus-man's holiday for him, wouldn't it? Or do I mean coals to Newcastle? And of course Katherine has her two little ones now. I'm the one who has to pop over there to mind them while she snatches a bit of rest. I could hardly expect her to pull up my weeds now, could I? Anyway, I was in half a mind not to come this morning, but then James reminded me he was reading the lesson, so of course as a reader's wife I could hardly be absent, could I? I mean, it wouldn't be right.'

A sudden 'hmph' from Jess made Laurie turn around. She was clearly trying hard to suppress a giggle. Laurie looked at Dad. His cheeks were red and there was a tightness around his mouth. Either he was very annoyed about something and could barely keep his temper in check, or he too was strug-gling not to laugh. Both avoided Laurie's eye. Mrs Shilling, meanwhile, continued her monologue. She only paused for breath, and a short prayer, when she reached her pew, one row in front of them. Still puzzled by what was going on, Laurie took the opportunity to follow her example, bending her head as she sat and burying her face in her hands.

Long ago, Laurie had decided that the best way to cope with the boredom of Holy Communion was to join in the responses with as much enthusiasm as she could muster, but otherwise take the opportunity to let her mind wander at every available point. The sermon was therefore a blank to her, and if Mrs Shilling had asked after the service how she thought her James had read, then Laurie would have just had to lie, although there would never have been any risk of Mrs Shilling waiting for an answer. Other than that, there were the hymns. Laurie was quite happy to admit to herself that these were the best part of churchgoing; she had always enjoyed singing and this was as good an opportunity to let rip as any.

The processional was an old favourite, 'Holy, Holy, Holy'. Laurie began as she always did, giving it her all. By the third 'Holy', however, she was already moderating her volume. She had become aware of Jess's voice to the right of her, singing out, clear and true, entirely unselfconscious, not showing off in any way, but utterly angelic. Where had that come from? Laurie shot her a glance and saw Dad doing the same. Even Mrs Shilling looked like she was itching to turn round.

It was only a moment. Soon enough Laurie was back on autopilot, thinking about the conversation during the walk to church that Mrs Shilling had interrupted. She was pretty sure she knew what Dad had been about to ask, and by the end of the service she knew what her answer would be.

As ever, church ended with multiple introductions and invitations to coffee 'or something stronger' and it was some time before the three of them were alone again, walking down the lane back home. Dad was almost apologetic about his refusal of the several offers that had come their way: 'Very ungracious of me to curtail your social lives like that, I know, but I thought we should take advantage of the sun while we've still got it. Who fancies a picnic?'

'Sounds lovely,' said Jess, turning to Laurie.

'Ye-es, it does,' Laurie replied, the uncertainty there for both to hear.

'I detect a "but",' prompted Dad.

'It's just I've got an idea I'd like to follow up. You both go. I'll be bad company anyway until I sort it out.'

Dad looked at Jess: 'What do you think?'

'I think we can manage a picnic without your uncommunicative daughter – as long as we bring the Sunday papers, of course.'

That decided it. Laurie helped them make sandwiches and devilled eggs, keeping some behind for herself, watched Dad slip a Toblerone into the hamper – his sweet tooth remained as active as ever – then saw them off in the car. Jess had expressed a desire to climb Glastonbury Tor, and Dad had been perfectly willing, as he put it, 'to help you connect with your inner hippy'.

Laurie couldn't remember the last time she'd been home alone. The surrounding stillness made her more conscious of the sounds leaking in: high-pitched *pirrips* from the house martins that she could glimpse wheeling around outside the window, an occasional car moving down into low gear as it came round a corner in the lane; the almost continuous background rumble of a tractor somewhere up the hill. Perhaps she'd been wrong to let them go without her? Well, it was too late to worry about that now. She ate her lunch quickly, sitting at the kitchen table while she read Friday's *Times*, vaguely wondering if she should raid Dad's shelves for another Georgette Heyer. Then she went through to the sitting room, sat down at the desk, where Dad's laptop was already open, and started to surf.

Google sent her straight through to Companies House. She searched to see what was being held for Sanderson Recruitment. The simple answer was everything: or at least every filing for the last ten years, including the annual accounts for the year ending last December. That would do.

Three weeks ago, Laurie wouldn't have known where to start. Now she at least had an idea of what she was looking for. The details of the pensions scheme were in note 20. The text was dense and the language hardly designed for a lay reader. Nevertheless, it was not hard to draw an inference. At the end of the last financial year, the pension scheme had shown a deficit of over £3 million, up from £1 million the year before. Then there was another phrase: *It is estimated that the employer's contributions to the scheme during the next financial year will be £341,000.* That seemed a huge amount for a company whose profits – she flipped back to check – were a little under £80,000. It was hardly surprising that Sanderson's had not paid a dividend in either of the two previous years.

Moreover, Laurie knew from her reading on Friday that this was only part of the story. There would be the Pension Protection Fund levy to pay as well; that could be another £100,000 easily. And things could only have got worse since the date of these accounts. Sanderson's probably wasn't even solvent any longer.

Laurie got up from the desk and went for a walk around the garden. The air was close and humid. It seemed to amplify the scent coming off the one rose bush Dad had allowed to survive when he dug up the rest of the garden: the cloying intensity of over-liberal aftershave. She should look at the BBC website to see if thunderstorms were expected. It certainly felt like it. Just in case, she brought Dad's washing in from the line. All the time she thought about the implications of what she had just read.

There was William Pennington, financially comfortable but far from rich. He had worked for Sanderson's for years, looking forward to retirement on a pension from the same company. At some point he had put two and two together. He'd realised that the company he'd worked for all his life was going bust, taking his pension with it. So he'd retired. That was the counter-intuitive part. Two days ago it would not have made sense to Laurie, but it was one of the things she had picked up from her reading on Friday. She had thought at the time there was something faintly unfair about it: when a fund collapses, existing pensioners receive far more protection than members who are still in employment. William Pennington had read the same books. He'd worked out that

223

the only way to protect his pension was to retire immediately, so he'd gone back to the office and done precisely that.

This was an insight worth sharing. Laurie dialled Dad's mobile. It went straight through to voicemail; so did Jess's. They must be away from a signal. The second time, Laurie wondered about leaving a message, but hadn't worked out what to say before the beep came. She hung up, feeling faintly disappointed. Who would she share her triumph with now?

At least she could hear Paul's phone ringing before it clicked onto voicemail, and it was good to connect with him again, even as a disembodied prerecorded voice. She hoped her message back sounded suitably casual: 'Hi, it's Laurie. I can't remember if you're still seeing your children but I just fancied a chat. I've found out some more about that man on the Underground. It would be good to hear what you think about it at some point. Speak soon. Bye.'

Now what? Laurie had found a perfectly good reason for William Pennington to retire; it made the possibility that he had killed himself seem even more remote. Surely that made it more likely his death was an accident? She had been so sure. She'd seen him fall, hadn't she? What had happened to her old certainty? And yet somehow, now that she knew more about him, she was finding it harder to dismiss the possibility that he might have been murdered. Why was that? All she'd found out was that he was a harmless retired salesman living an unimpeachable suburban life, with an interest in nothing more racy than Alexandrine mythology.

Love and money: weren't those meant to be the only motives for murder? It sounded like the sort of thing Hercule Poirot might say, and Laurie realised it deserved an appropriate pinch of salt, but she had nowhere else to start. She got a sheet of paper from Dad's desk and wrote down the two headings. *Love*: was that a possibility? Might William Pennington have

224

been having an affair? Did that sort of thing happen to people in their sixties? Laurie thought back to the man she'd seen on the platform: well dressed, smiling at strangers. How might their conversation have progressed? If he'd asked her out for dinner she'd have said no, but that didn't mean that everyone would. Unwilling to impugn the honour of a dead man, Laurie tentatively wrote *?mistress??* in her left-hand column. Underneath, with equal uncertainty, she added *Margaret?*. Once again, Laurie cast her mind back to that crowded Underground platform. Might Mrs Pennington have been somewhere in that throng, reaching out a hand to push an errant husband just at the moment he turned to Laurie and the train came into the station. She had the air of a woman of action, Laurie had to admit. But murder? Anyway, how did you go about finding out if William Pennington had a mistress? Someone at work, perhaps? One of the employees at Sandersons might be good for a gossip. Laurie didn't relish the prospect.

With some relief, Laurie turned her attention to the right-hand side of her paper: *Money*. Who would be likely to profit from William Pennington's death? Well, if he'd left any life insurance, or if she hadn't fancied the cost of a divorce, then the answer was, once again, Margaret Pennington. Perhaps she was the one with a lover? Her name belonged in both columns; that much was clear. Weren't the vast majority of murders committed by someone close to the victim? Laurie was pretty sure that was a real statistic – nothing to do with Hercule Poirot or any other fictional detective. Anyone else? Well, no children, apparently. Brothers or sisters? Very probably. Might they have been mentioned in a will? It was a long shot, but worth checking.

Laurie sat and stared at her sheet of paper; it wasn't much to show for half an hour's hard thinking, but she had to be ready with her answers when Dad got back. Where were they, anyway? Laurie glanced at her phone to check the time. It rang as she did so, but it wasn't Dad calling to say when they'd be back. The screen showed the photo she'd taken of Paul beside the canal all those days ago – was it really only a week? He was returning her call.

'Hi you.' Laurie answered. 'Thanks for calling back. Is now a good time?'

'Yes thanks. Bethan's just picked up the kids, so I'm a free man once again. How have you been?'

'Fine, well apart from probably losing my job. So not really fine, I'm afraid, but there we are.' Laurie wished she had not giggled then; she could imagine how it made her sound. 'How about you?'

'Me, oh, fine, you know. Your job? Do you mind?'

'Well I can't live off thin air. But it's OK; I think I'd started to realise it wasn't what I wanted to do anyway.'

'Why? No, don't worry. You don't need to answer that. You were calling to tell me about that man.'

Was she? Laurie supposed she was. Anyway, it was good to be on solid ground: 'It was Dad more than me, really. He found out the man's name – William Pennington. And we went to visit his wife – widow, I suppose I should say – in Watford.'

There was a pause before Paul replied. 'Goodness, that's taking the sleuthing rather far, isn't it? Was she pleased to see you?'

'I wouldn't say pleased exactly, but she talked to us. Dad's quite good at that sort of thing.'

'But why on earth go to visit her in the first place?' Paul sounded vaguely incredulous down the phone.

'I know, I know.' Laurie laughed. 'It was Dad of course. He wouldn't let it rest. He hasn't said as much to me, but I think he's managed to convince himself that all the things that have been happening to me are related: you know, losing my phone and that break-in. He's not used to the realities of urban living, I guess. Anyway, he decided to investigate that accident, look for a link.'

'What?' If anything Paul's tone of disbelief had gone up a notch, to the extent that he almost sounded petulant.

Patiently, Laurie defended her father and the statistics that had convinced him that William Pennington was either a suicide or murdered. 'But I know it's all wrong.' She concluded. 'I saw him fall. I know it was an accident.'

'There's no accounting for parents,' Paul replied, sounding surprisingly flat. 'What did his wife say? What did you say he was called?'

'William Pennington. She was pretty sure it was suicide. He'd lost his job some weeks before but hadn't told her. I think she was angry with him for lying to her.'

'Well, that sounds convincing.'

'Yes, except I've just found out that he must have resigned. It's a long story, but basically he protected his pension by doing so. And he'd been spending the last few weeks going to the British Library, reading about his new obsession: Alexander the Great, would you believe?'

'Amazing. I'd never have guessed that. How did you find out?'

'Did I ever tell you that key came from British Library? I've been checking out the books he was reading there and trying to work out what it all means.'

'Oh, right. So is that where you are now?'

'The British Library? No. I'm at Dad's. It's amazing what you can do online. I'm just trying to figure out now if anybody could have had a motive for murdering him.'

'You sound like some latter-day Miss Marple, seeing

murder behind every village hedge. Your dad does live in a village, doesn't he? Where did you say it was?'

'Somerset, a little village on the Mendips. Nothing ever happens here. That much is for sure. People still talk about how Simon Parbrook was born six months after his parents' marriage. It's my antidote to London – better than Hampstead Heath. You should try it some time.'

Paul didn't take the bait that Laurie dangled out for him so temptingly. They talked for a bit longer, but he returned none of the warmth that Laurie tried to inject into the conversation. She brought the call to a close when she heard him tapping at a keyboard.

Putting down the phone, Laurie wondered what she had done wrong. She had been elated to make those discoveries about William Pennington, and her heart had genuinely leapt when she heard Paul's voice a few minutes earlier. How quickly her mood had changed. Should she call him back, have another go at a decent conversation? No – that way lay madness, or at least humiliation. Damn it. Why did their relationship leave her feeling so confused?

The front door opened to the sound of laughter. Dad and Jess were back from the Tor.

Monday 10 August – 12 a.m.

Laurie lay in bed feeling faintly woozy. The work they'd put in on the garden was partly responsible, of course, but there was no doubt that she'd had a bit too much to drink as well. She'd been surprised when Dad opened that second bottle of wine. He was normally so restrained, but he'd been on unusually expansive form this evening, telling the funny stories of his childhood that had always made Mum groan but were new to Jess, at least. At some point Jess had noticed the difficulty Laurie was having keeping her eyes open, and suggested she went straight to bed without worrying about the washing-up. It was strange how they'd never got around to talking about her discoveries that afternoon.

The creak on the stairs woke her. That must be Jess going to bed. Laurie and Dad knew the house well enough to avoid it. God, it felt like the middle of the night. How long had Jess been down there? Perhaps Laurie had only just fallen asleep. She reached for her phone to check the time.

She must have fallen asleep again, but something – a faint click, the hint of a draught, some imperceptible change in atmosphere – told Laurie the door of her room was opening. 'Dad?' she murmured, her eyes still shut. 'What time—' She never finished the sentence. With brutal swiftness, a pair of gloved hands clamped shut her jaw, while another slapped tape over first her mouth and then – before she had time even to open them – her eyes. Laurie felt for the mobile phone still in her hand. If she could just press the call button at least she'd get through to the last number she'd called? Who was that? Paul?

It was a vain hope. The sudden weight on Laurie's pelvis announced that she was being sat upon, mocking her efforts to buck the intruder off. Then, untroubled by her desperate attempts to resist, two pairs of hands grabbed her arms and swiftly taped them to each other, forearm to forearm, forcing the phone out of her grasp. Further tape around her bare legs, from knee to ankle, left her immobilised, lying on her back with her arms folded in front, like a corpse awaiting mummification.

Now Laurie had never felt more awake, but she was blinded and helpless. Frantically, she grunted as loudly as possible, desperate to warn Dad and Jess. Then she fell silent, straining to hear what was going on around her. Was that one set of footsteps or two? Perhaps there were more of them. Sounds came from the direction of Dad's room: a struggle, tape unsticking from a roll, then silence.

One set of footsteps returned; a click and a sense of brightness, discernible even through the tape and her eyelids, told her that the light had been turned on. Lightly, but audibly, the footsteps approached her bed.

With no warning at all, Laurie felt her t-shirt pulled down, exposing her right breast. A gloved hand caressed it, then took the nipple between thumb and forefinger, rolling it back and forth, and pulling it away from her body so she could feel the stretch, before releasing it with a disdainful flick. Used, violated, dreading what was to come, Laurie felt every muscle tense, as the hand was replaced by a mouth, once that sucked and nuzzled, pressing so hard that bristle felt like sandpaper against her areola.

'No time for that,' came a voice from the doorway. 'Check the rest of the house.' That wasn't a West Country accent, Laurie found herself reflecting as she heard footsteps retreat and then reapproach. Mum would have called it educated. Another hand – a different one? – cupped her naked breast, as if to feel its weight. Laurie felt leather against her nipple. Then the same voice that she'd previously heard in the doorway said, 'Pity,' as her t-shirt was pulled back into its proper position. The sound of exhaling breath filled Laurie's ears; it was a shock when she realised it was her own. How long had it been since she last breathed in? Now it seemed she couldn't get enough air. Rapid inhalations did little to fill her lungs, but seemed necessary to fuel the uncontrollable trembling that had taken over her body.

Two hands, fingers extended against her bare back, slid between Laurie and the mattress, until she felt herself cradled in the arms of the man leaning over her. Then, with one heave, she was off the bed and being carried, for all the world like a bride crossing the marital threshold. Laurie shook her head to rid herself of the allusion as she was taken downstairs and dropped onto – the floor? For one heart-stopping moment Laurie believed it. The relief when she felt herself hitting soft plastic at knee height brought on another bout of hyperventilation. And why the plastic? They must have put it on the sofa before bringing her down.

'All clear?' It was the posh voice again, speaking close to Laurie's ear. For a second she thought he was addressing her, but a 'yep' from across the room told its own story.

Presumably the house was now checked, and Dad and Jess were as securely trussed as she was.

'Right now, sweetheart. Don't bother shouting: it will only make things worse. Understand?'

Laurie nodded. In response, she felt gloved fingers search along her jaw, find the end of the tape covering her mouth and rip it off in a single swift motion that made no concession to the burning sensation it left behind. Laurie knew better than to scream but found herself trying to lift a hand in a reflex attempt to rub away the pain. The reminder that her arms were still taped together only reinforced her feeling of helplessness.

'Right, now then. Tell us your password.'

What was he going on about? The involuntary wrinkling of Laurie's brow must have conveyed her confusion.

There was a sigh, as if the man felt the inconvenience of having to deal with such patent stupidity. 'The password you use on this laptop, of course.'

'Why ...?' Laurie began, stopping as she felt a hand grab her chin.

The voice bent close to her ear. 'Because if you don't we will hurt you and your darling Papa, a lot.'

'Roxanne1,' Laurie said, dully. She spelled it out. 'All lower case.'

She heard the tapping of a keyboard and a grunt of satisfaction. What was going on? There was hardly anything on the computer. And why hadn't he mentioned Jess? Was it possible they hadn't checked her room? Might she still be sleeping soundly in her bed, unaware of what was going on downstairs? How could Laurie warn her without letting them know there was someone else in the house?

A bleep came from the computer, to a hiss of frustration from whoever had been using it.

'What is it?' The question was one that Laurie had wanted

to ask for herself, but it came from the other man. So – they were both in the room.

'Bitch has a different password for Gmail, but you're going to tell us what it is, aren't you, darling?'

Laurie knew what she had to do; she had to have an excuse to shout. She shook her head.

'I'm going to ask you nicely one more time.' The low voice was right in Laurie's ear and she had not even heard him approach. 'What is the password?' Laurie remained still, bracing herself for the blow that was bound to come. She breathed in, ready to deliver the scream that would warn Jess. But the chance did not come. Instead, she felt fresh tape being put over her mouth.

'You're not being very clever, are you, my love?' And then, directed away from her: 'Go into the kitchen and look for skewers. I'll get her father.'

Two sets of footsteps receded. One went into the kitchen, the other upstairs. Skewers? Laurie's skin began to prickle. For the first time, she wondered if she was going to die.

A crackle and muffled groan on the sofa beside her announced Dad's arrival. Laurie wanted to look at him, to check he was unhurt, to exchange glances of reassurance. The inability to connect was an unexpected corollary to her blindness. She felt so isolated, so alone, despite the certain knowledge that the person she loved most in the world was right beside her.

'Will these do?' It was the man back from the kitchen.

'Just perfect. Right, we need to keep their heads still. I don't want to risk any scratches. Let's use the table.'

There was a noise that Laurie struggled to place, strangely light, almost airy – and then the unmistakable sound of tape being unrolled, accompanied by a single odd command, 'Remember, we don't want to damage the varnish.'

Laurie was lifted, carried a short way, and laid down on a hard surface. Again, it was covered in plastic sheeting – that must have been the sound she had heard – and again she was surprised by the care with which the whole operation was carried out. What was it the devil said to Jesus in the wilderness? 'And in their hands they shall bear thee up, lest at any time thou dash thy foot against a stone.' What made her think of that?

More tape was being unrolled. Laurie attempted to wriggle. She shook her head from side to side, but as more and more tape was applied, encasing her head and sticking it to the table, she lost all freedom of movement. Now she truly was mummified. Only her ears and nostrils remained clear. It made her curiously aware of the sounds and smells around her: movement in the room, the pungency of her own sweat.

Something brushed against Laurie's leg. It was Dad, she realised, being strapped down next to her in much the same way. Since the comment about the varnish, neither of their captors had spoken.

After some time (how long was it? Five minutes? An hour?), the sounds of movement stopped. Laurie could hear Dad's breathing from the other end of the table – they must be lying head to tail – and nothing else. Were they being left alone? Was Laurie meant to stew in her fear, to become more likely to crack? If so, it was working.

They were not alone. Suddenly, a voice sounded right in her ear, little more than a murmur, but close enough that she felt her eardrum flinch. 'To tell the truth, my sweetness, I'd been hoping you might be a little bit uncooperative somewhere along the way. Of course, it makes things a little more difficult that we don't want to leave a mark on you, but that's just a challenge, more than anything else. Anyway, this is so you know what we're doing to him.'

Almost immediately, the voice was replaced by a strange tickling sensation, one that rapidly resolved itself into a sense of extreme discomfort. Something was being inserted into her ear. Laurie could guess what it was. NO . . . NO . . . NO. The tip of the skewer reached her eardrum and the fear that had been building within her resolved itself into a pain so acute that it occupied her entire being. Every muscle went rigid. Every nerve ending screamed for release. The membrane must have been perforated. Was the skewer still travelling on through her inner ear and into her brain/? Could eardrums repair themselves? Would she be deaf for ever?

Suddenly, the pain was no more severe than the worst imaginable earache. The skewer had gone. Laurie could take stock, could re-engage, first with her body, and then with the world around her. With relief, she realised she could still hear, but it took a moment for her to grasp that the insistent humming that filled her ears was no more than her own attempt at a scream, muffled by the tape that still covered her mouth. With the realisation came silence, or what passed for it; Laurie was more conscious than ever of the sound of her breathing, its rapidity matched by the throb in her ear, as her adrenaline-fuelled heart tried to keep up with the demands that terror was placing upon it. Then she heard the voice again.

'And of course there's the nose as well.'

Laurie stiffened as she felt the hairs inside her left nostril beginning to tickle. How far up would he push the skewer? Was there some sort of membrane there as well? Despite herself, Laurie found herself imagining the pain she had just felt in her ear, but this time focused on some area around the bridge of her nose, spreading out from there to her eyes and the rest of her head. She could feel the tears attempting to escape between her closed eyelids. Then she heard a low laugh in her ear.

'Except we want you conscious, don't we? Three grunts when you're ready to talk.'

The man paused, as if waiting for a response. It was all Laurie could do not to make the noises that he sought. Why was she holding out? For a goal that might be entirely pointless, and certainly didn't seem worth the pain? But she had come too far to crack now. She had to get things to the point where they removed the gag, where she could scream without arousing their suspicions. For the time being, silence was her only option.

'Hmm. So that's the way you want it? Well, let's see how brave you are when it's your Dad. Rip that off. I want her to hear this.'

Laurie heard the sound of tape unsticking, and then, in what briefly felt like a victory, Dad's voice. 'What are you doing? Laurie, don't tell them anything. No, stop. No ... no ... NO.' If he had been about to say anything more, it was lost in a marrow-piercing scream. Laurie was sure she would never forget it, and knew she would never forgive herself for it.

All thoughts of victory – of futile little goals – vanished. Let it end. Let it end now, please. Laurie grunted, and grunted again, and grunted a third time. Panic overtook her. What if the man hadn't heard? Would he carry on? She did it again, more loudly. He had to hear, surely? For all she knew, he was preparing now to stick a skewer up Dad's nose.

Suddenly, she heard the voice back in her ear. 'You get one chance: the password. Understand?'

Unable even to nod, Laurie could only grunt in reply. It was enough. The tape was ripped again from her mouth. The pain in her ear was so intense there was no way Laurie could have shouted, even without the warning. Instead, it was all she could do to whisper, 'Roxanne123,' taking a deep breath before she continued, 'same as before, but with a capital X and one-two-three on the end.'

There was tapping at the keyboard, then silence. Laurie waited, focused on her pain, panic building once again. What if she'd got it wrong? What would he do next? How was Dad? All she could hear from him was rapid breathing.

Then the man spoke. 'Right, clean these up and put them back exactly where you found them. I'm going to get on with this.' He paused before adding, unnecessarily in Laurie's case at least, 'One more squeak out of either of you and you'll both regret it.' The tapping started once again. She had got the password right. Surely this would all be over soon.

Sounds came from the kitchen. The man who'd sucked at her breast was, Laurie realised, busy washing up the instruments of torture. What would a running tap and scrubbing brush mean to her now? Would she ever be able to look at a skewer again? It was unlikely to matter, of course. Please God, let them kill her quickly. The kitchen drawer closed with a thud; returning footsteps indicated that the washer-up must have finished his task. Why hadn't he turned off the tap?

Whump! What was that? Laurie puzzled to make sense of what she just heard. Had her computer fallen on the floor? The tapping had stopped. Then, in quick succession, she heard two more thumps. The last of them including a cracking sound that instantly took her back to falling off Roxanne and the broken collarbone. Oh God! Had they started hitting Dad? No, the sound was further away than that.

Was that a groan? Where did it come from? The kitchen? Footsteps ran from the room, leading to three more rapid thwacks, then a clatter – something wooden had fallen on the floor – followed by a series of softer thumps, accompanied by Jess's voice, repeating with every thump, 'You bastards, you

237

bastards, you bastards.' Then there was silence, interrupted by occasional sharp sobs.

'Jess,' Laurie tried to speak, but got no further, as the pain in her ear crescendoed once again. Had she been heard? Yes: there was the sound of returning footsteps, accompanied by sharp, deep, rapid breaths. But they did not approach the table. Instead, Laurie heard a rustling sound. Was she taking the plastic sheeting off the sofa? Surely they should be leaving everything as undisturbed as possible for the police? 'Jess,' Laurie tried whispering, 'what are you doing?'

The reply came from Dad, and he sounded fine – no need to whisper for him. 'She knows we're here. darling. How are you?'

Dad! Laurie could almost weep with relief at the sound of his voice. She breathed in deeply before whispering again, 'Dad! Are you OK?'

'Don't worry about me, darling. They wanted you to hear me scream. Let's just say I gave them what they wanted without waiting for a reason.'

Despite the all-encompassing pain in her ear, despite the horror of what they had just been through, despite the uncertainty as they lay there, blind and immobile, Laurie had to allow herself a feeling of triumph. Trust Dad to be one step ahead.

Meanwhile, Jess had been moving around in the kitchen. What was she doing? That click and accompanying swoosh sounded like she was opening the outside door. The subsequent draught provided confirmation. Then there was silence; it lasted so long that Laurie tried another whisper – 'Dad?' – but before he could reply, she heard a car pulling up outside. Was that the police? Perhaps Jess had phoned them after all.

The car's door opened. Someone got out and came in through the open door, walking right up to the table.

Something dropped on the floor. Then, finally, Jess spoke, in a tone that sounded incongruously playful. 'Sorry about the delay my darlings. Laurie love, I hope you won't mind, but I think it would probably be better if I set your Dad free first.'

Laurie was in no mood to ask any questions and no hurry to move. She could only imagine how her ear would feel when she did.

Mummified, Laurie listened to the sound of Jess freeing Dad. If he was as tightly covered in tape as she was herself, then she could not be surprised at the time it was taking. Apart from a single 'thank you', Dad didn't speak. At least she knew he was OK. Nothing else mattered really. Jess, too, was quiet. Finally a creak from the table and muffled thud from the floor showed that Dad was free enough to shift from one to the other. The footsteps that followed must have been his, because Laurie now felt fingers picking at the tape that bound her as, in contrast to her earlier silence, Jess suddenly became voluble. 'Your Dad's just popped upstairs. I think it's probably best if I free your hands first. Then you can pull off the rest of the tape in your own time.'

It was Laurie's left hand – the one nearest the edge of the table – that Jess managed to unstick first. Laurie flexed it carefully, feeling pins and needles as the circulation returned, and brought it up to her face. Although she knew she was touching herself, and could feel the pressure on her cheeks through the tape that covered them, it was hard to connect it with the blank sensation coming from fingertips that were still numb. She felt strangely separated from her body. What could she look like, strapped down on a table like Gulliver in Lilliput? Was she even clothed? She moved her hand down her neck and felt the faint resistance of an elastic collar: yes, of course, she was still wearing the t-shirt in which she had gone to bed. What about Dad? Had he been naked on the table next to her? Had Jess seen him? It would explain why he'd gone upstairs.

Laurie's other hand was now free as well. She clapped them together, surprising herself with a noise that bore no relation to the dead weights she felt on the end of each arm, then shook and rubbed her wrists. Gradually, strength and feeling returned to her fingers. Now she could remove her blindfold. Jess guided her hand to the end of the tape. She grasped it, braced herself, and slowly peeled it off.

After all that preparation and worry, there was really very little pain – certainly nothing like what Laurie had felt when the gag was ripped off earlier; the area round her mouth still tingled with the memory. That must be because she was doing it for herself: good old Jess. Even so, it took some time for Laurie's eyes to adjust to the light, blinking as she saw the vague outline of her cousin carefully removing the other bits of tape attaching her to the table.

Gradually, Laurie took in other details. Jess was in a t-shirt, whose plain white design Laurie recognised as her favourite bedtime attire. The red splotches on it were unmistakable. She'll have to soak that in cold water, Laurie found herself thinking, before moving onto a more obvious concern: had Jess been attacked too? There was no sign of any injury, and she seemed to be moving freely enough.

'There, I think that's the lot.' Jess stepped back from the table.

Laurie was free. She thought about her ear, and realised the pain had reduced slightly. As if to test it, she lifted her head and gave it a little wiggle. There were no sharp stabs of agony, just a faint sense of incipient dizziness, enough to make her careful about sitting up, but no more than that. Using both elbows, she slowly raised her chest above the table and swung her legs round so that they dangled over towards the ground. For a brief moment she clenched her eyes shut, waiting for the rush of blood back to her temples that indicated the danger of a faint had passed. When she opened them again, she could, for the first time, look properly around.

Jess stood before her, head cocked to one side, pale, wide-eyed with concern. She had jeans on below her t-shirt. She must have just pulled them on before coming downstairs. Laurie frowned, trying to make sense of it all. Hadn't the men looked in her bedroom and found it empty?

'Tea, that's what you need.' Jess nodded to herself, confident in her diagnosis, and moved off into the kitchen, leaving Laurie's field of vision clear to see the rest of the room. The reason for the blood on Jess's t-shirt was obvious. Laurie's torturer was still sitting down, his face on the keyboard of Dad's laptop. She could see a gloved hand dangling by his side. That sight alone brought back memories that made her flinch. It was the back of his head, however, that drew her gaze: not just the bloodied hair but the unnaturally flattened shape of it, as if his neck carried on in a straight line from his shoulders to his crown. Mesmerised, drawn to the scene despite her better judgement, Laurie got off the table and moved over for a closer look, taking small steps like a ninety-year-old. That wasn't hair, she now realised – in fact, as far as she could see, his head was clean-shaven – it was . . . what? Gore? There was no other word for it. In any case, there was no doubt that he was dead.

Jess appeared in the kitchen doorway, carrying a mug. 'I've put two sugars in. Should be more, really, but you wouldn't drink it, so what's the use?'

'What about the other one?' Laurie asked.

'He's in here.'

'And . . .?' Almost diffidently, Laurie let the unspoken question hang between them.

'Dead too.' There was an edge of defiance to Jess's reply, as if she were daring Laurie to object. She walked over with the tea, which was trembling slightly in her hand, the whiteness of her knuckles testifying to the effort she was putting into the grip. Perhaps that wasn't defiance; what kind of strain must she be feeling?

Laurie knew she should sit down and drink it, should hug the cousin who had brought it, but she had to see for herself. With an apologetic smile at her saviour, she went over to the doorway. Another man lay sprawled on the kitchen floor, or rather on some clear plastic sheeting that lay underneath his body. Laurie looked back towards the sofa: yes, that was what she had heard Jess collecting a few minutes earlier; she must have rolled the body onto it already. Why on earth? Then Laurie saw the man's face. This was where the killing blows had landed: three separate indentations crossing his forehead. She remembered the crunching thwacks that had made them. And beside the man, she could see, covered in blood, the weapon that had killed him. She pictured Jess holding it as she ran back into the kitchen, fresh from doing for the man at the computer, ready to finish off the job in here too.

'Mum always swore that was the best rolling pin money could buy.' Had she said that out loud? Suddenly, it was all too much. Conscious of the tears rising up within her, and of the dizziness overcoming her, Laurie sat down at the kitchen table, rested her head in the crook of her elbow, and let the exhaustion take over.

242

Monday, 10 August – 5 a.m.

Laurie's ear ached, but no more than that. The stiffness in her neck and the numbness in her arms were some kind of indication of the length of time she'd been asleep; so was the grey light filtering in through the kitchen window. It was very quiet. Shouldn't the house be crawling with police? Surely a violent break-in merited some sort of attention – especially when there were dead bodies involved. Dead bodies? Laurie looked over to the floor in front of the sink, as horrified by her memory of the burglar's battered face as she had been by the sight itself only hours before. There was nothing there. Then she saw the note on the table beside her in Dad's handwriting: *DON'T WORRY. BACK SOON. CLEAN UP SOME MORE IF YOU CAN.* Beside it, very prominently, were his and Jess's mobile phones; the implication was clear: they did not want to be called.

Stretching cautiously, Laurie got up and went through to the sitting room. Dad's computer sat on the table, but there was no sign of the body that she could so vividly recall sprawled across its keyboard. Surely it hadn't all been a dream? The residual pain in her ear told her no. She looked at the computer. It had gone into hibernation. There were strange brown splotches on its keys, and a smear of something similar on the screen. It wasn't hard to guess what that was. Laurie recoiled from the thought. Would Dad ever be able to use it again? Then she sat down as she considered the wider implications.

For whatever reason, Dad and Jess had not called the police. That much was clear. Why not? Laurie was sure she would have done, so sure that she really didn't need to think about it very hard. For all her irritation with the Sergeant Atkinses of this world, it would have been her automatic response. And yet here was Dad behaving in a way totally at odds with everything she thought she knew about him. It made no sense.

So now what was she to do? She could make good the omission and call the police herself. Drop Dad and Jess right in it? No, of course not. She could wait for them to come back, have it out with them. The idea of hanging around aimlessly in a half-cleaned crime scene held little appeal. The way Laurie shuddered at the throught made her realise how close she was to breaking down, for all that a few hours' sleep had taken the edge off the horror. She needed to keep busy; that meant trusting Dad and doing what he said.

So how did you clean bloodstains off a computer? It sounded like the tag line to a Charles Addams cartoon. You'd have to use something that did not conduct electricity; the last thing Laurie wanted was to short-circuit the keyboard. After a moment's thought, she went up to the bathroom to fetch her nail-varnish remover and some cotton wool.

Back in the sitting room, Laurie spent the next few minutes meticulously cleaning the laptop. For good measure, she went on to wipe the desk around it. The activity was helping; it kept her from wondering what Dad and Jess were doing, kept her mind off the horror of the night before. Eventually, however, she had to look across to the table, feeling a reflexive twinge in her ear as she did so.

The plastic sheeting had gone. Only a few sticky patches provided any indication of what had taken place. Laurie cleaned them off with more cotton wool and nail-varnish remover. Now what? She could mop the kitchen floor, but that might get blood on the mop head. Laurie eyed her packet of cotton wool: just as well it was a nearly new jumbo pack; she would need it all.

An hour later, the packet was empty and the pungent smell of acetone filled both rooms, but every surface Laurie could think of had been wiped clean: floors, countertop, sink and taps. And it was obvious what she should do with the cotton wool. She opened the door of the wood-burning stove, realising as she did so that it was still warm. Inside she could see a few charred remains and several glowing embers. With a pang of sadness Laurie recognised a piece of turned wood from the rolling pin, and was that part of Jess's t-shirt? Good idea. Laurie stripped off her own top, added it to the acetone-soaked cotton wool and a few stray strips of tape that she'd found under the sitting-room table, and stuffed it all into the stove. She shut the door just in time. With an impressive *whoosh*, the whole concoction burst into flame.

The shower that followed was brisk and cleansing: not the long relaxing soak in the bath that Laurie would have preferred, but she wanted to be up and about when Dad and Jess got back. Besides, she had to tackle the computer sooner or later. Why had her passwords been so important?

Monday 10 August – 7 a.m.

The nail-varnish remover had more or less fully evaporated. Only a faint hint remained of the heady smell that had filled the room thirty minutes earlier. Laurie approached the laptop. It had been on for hours. Her first task was to recharge the battery. Carrying the computer over to the kitchen counter, she plugged in the lead and pressed the power button. As usual, it seemed like for ever, but eventually she got onto the usual password-request screen. Dad had never told her his password. She logged on as herself, just as the man had done however many hours before. Nevertheless, she hesitated before typing. What if he had taken the opportunity to lock her out? What had he been up to?

The relief Laurie felt when the computer responded to *roxanne1* vanished almost immediately when she saw the screen onto which it opened. She – or rather, her account on Dad's computer – was logged into a chat room: a suicide forum. Her username was lonelygirl73, and she seemed to be participating in a thread headed *My Dad feels the same way.* The last comment had been made a couple of hours before by *friend-in-need7* and read: *Hey Laurie. Getting worried here. Let us know your both ok.*

Heart pounding, Laurie scrolled back up to the top of the thread. As she suspected, lonelygirl73 had started it, at 1.30 that morning, with a post that read: *Hi all – me again. Id love a chat if anyone's there. Been talking to my dad and it turns out he feels the same way – has done since mum died. Feeling a bit blue. Laurie xxxx* The series of postings that followed from other users were hard to sift out from the emoticons and tag lines that seemed to be almost compulsory (lonelygirl73's was, Laurie noted, *Loving is easy, it's the living I find hard*), but the general gist was of supporting hands being stretched across the ether from one stranger to another.

The last few messages, however, had a worried tone similar to the one Laurie had first read. None of them spelt out exactly what their concern was, and every page on the forum carried a firm rule that explicit suicide notes would not be tolerated – for the sake of other users – but the posting she had just read from lonelygirl73 could certainly be construed as one. If at some point in the next few days, her body (and Dad's) had been discovered somewhere appropriate – hanging from the banisters on the top landing, for example – then anyone examining her computer would have been guided to an obvious conclusion.

Laurie was surprised to realise that her overwhelming emotion was relief – not because she was safe from whatever end those men had been lining up for her – after all, she wasn't necessarily safe, was she? – but because Jess's bloody actions had been so absolutely justified. Without them, she and Dad would surely now be dead.

Meanwhile, the message board shone back at Laurie's face. No more posts had arrived; the thread seemed to have died. Laurie was tempted to log off, to expunge her search history, to forget that lonelygirl73 had ever existed, but something made her hesitate. Should she put up a post that let everyone know she was OK? What if a vulnerable reader followed the apparent example of lonelygirl73? Would that in some way be her responsibility? How come all these people seemed to care about someone who was, in the end, entirely fictional? What was lonelygirl73's story? Sitting at the computer, Laurie started to investigate.

It was the first thing Laurie discovered that gave her the biggest shock. Lonelygirl73 had been a member of the forum for almost a year. Had someone been planning to kill her for that long? It was almost impossible to comprehend. Forcing herself to remain calm, Laurie clicked through to lonely-girl73's profile. It was little help. There was the tag line she had already read, and the choice of a cat as an avatar; all the posts she had seen had something similarly anonymous. The account was registered to the blatantly false 'Jane Smith' and an equally unhelpful email address (lonelygirl73@gmail. com). There was a physical address as well, one that appeared real, but a few minutes' search on a fresh internet page confirmed her suspicion that while Gauden Road, London SW4 really existed, its numbers did not extend up to 204. Laurie doubted that made lonelygirl73 all that different from many other posters on the forum. In a world where employers googled job applicants, who would use their real name or address on a site like this?

So in the end, lonelygirl73 only really existed as a series of posts. She had begun with a fairly standard opening gambit: *Hi, this is my first time, been feeling a bit low and came across this forum. Think it's just what I need.* This had elicited a series of encouraging welcomes and she had subsequently participated sporadically in various threads, with comments along the lines of *Hey hun, I know exactly what you mean.* Or *Hang on in there; you know you've got friends here.* In short, if she had not become one of the community's leading lights, she had at least become an accepted member of it. A few months in, she had posted asking for advice, which she had duly got, in spades: *Every day I go into work and nobody would know there was anything wrong with me. Does anybody else have trouble keeping up appearances? How do you get thru the day?* That, however, was the only point at which lonelygirl73 revealed anything about her personal life – until the previous afternoon.

For Laurie, the change was striking, although she recognised that a more casual reader might not have seen anything particularly different. It was the first time any of the posts contained a proper biographical detail: *Hi all. I really need some support right now. My life is collapsing around me. I lost my job last week. It feels like I can't do anything right. Help!* That had initiated a long conversation in which lonelygirl73 had been a full participant, gradually revealing details specific to Laurie: her mother's death; her panic after the accident on the Underground; the fact she was now staying with her father in the country. The thread came to an end with her accepting the suggestion that perhaps this was something she should talk to her father about. As friend–in–need7 put it, *Some things you need family for.*

Laurie got up. She needed to clear her head, to think things through. Was it really 11.30 already? Where had Dad and Jess got to? It no longer felt important to be around when they got back. Pausing only to leave an unambiguous note on the keyboard – *DO NOT TOUCH* – she went outside.

Monday 10 August – 10 a.m.

It was cold on top of the ridge, but not enough for Laurie to regret the impulse that had led her to saddle Roxanne and take her out for a ride. Here, with the wind against her face, she could free herself from the claustrophobia of chat rooms, shake off the lingering smell of nail-varnish remover, and acknowledge her stupidity. It made her so angry – with herself as much as anything. There was only one person who could have known all those details about her: one person, whom she had been preparing herself to love, but who had really wanted her dead. How could she have been so blind? She thought back through the events of the last few weeks, of Dad's attempts to question her, of her own wilful non-chalance. She'd been so keen to keep Paul to herself that she could have got them all killed. She very nearly had. She'd been an idiot.

It was only when she saw Roxanne's ears twitch in front of her that Laurie realised she'd said the last word out loud. 'Idiot!' She said it again, relishing the 'D' and stronger per-cussion on the 'T'. It was a good word – cathartic. 'IDIOT!' A flock of starlings took off from a nearby rowan. Roxanne shook her head, as if to laugh at this latest antic from the woman on her back.

What the hell? Why not? There was nobody around for miles. 'IDIOT!!!' This time Laurie really let rip. Did she imagine the echo coming back to her, or were her ears still ringing from the force of the shout combined with the residual pain from whatever it was that skewer had done? Now Laurie was the one who shook her head. She'd been going to take Roxanne for a gallop, but that was good enough. Why should she take any more risks? With the faintest tug on the reins and nudge of the knee she wheeled the horse back round; they headed for home.

Coming back along the lane proved to be a mistake. Mrs Shilling was out there, apparently weeding the front flower bed, although as far as Laurie could see it was already immaculate.

'Hello dear! So that was you. I thought it was someone calling a dog, but it sounded like you and I thought, well I said to James in fact, "Lauren hasn't got a dog, has she?" But he said you'd be back in London by now.' Mrs Shilling paused in full flow – a rare occurrence – she was clearly waiting for some kind of response.

Laurie really hadn't the strength for explanations but threw out a titbit that she hoped would prove enough. 'It's not very busy at this time of year. I thought I'd take advantage of the weather and make a proper holiday of it.'

'Lucky you. Well, it must be nice to be here for a bit longer. Your father and Jess are back, by the way. Drove past only a few minutes ago. Just went away for the night, did they? I must say it's nice to see him with someone at last.'

Another pause: Laurie did not know whether to laugh at Mrs Shilling for getting the wrong end of the stick quite so wonderfully, or object to the way she had so clearly engineered this meeting purely to recharge her gossip banks. Oh well, there was probably no harm in spreading a bit of misinformation, better that than have to explain exactly what Dad and Jess had been doing the previous night. 'Yes, she's lovely isn't she? Early days of course, but I'm keeping my fingers crossed.' Was that enough to satisfy Mrs Shilling's prurience? Who cared? Laurie squeezed her knees together, gave a cheery wave, and continued towards home.

Forewarned, Laurie was not surprised to see the Fiesta in the yard. She dismounted and tied Roxanne to the grooming ring just as Dad came out from the house. When he saw Laurie he did nothing but smile and spread his arms. God, it was good to be hugged by him.

But Laurie also needed explanations. 'What's going on, Dad? Why aren't the police here? Why did you tell me to clean up the house?'

'You did a good job, darling.' Laurie had never thought of Dad as shifty before, but he was clearly uncomfortable as he tried to come up with an answer to her question. 'It seemed the right thing to do. The state those bodies were in: well, that would have required some explaining. Jess . . .' Dad was struggling for words now. 'Well, Jess was quite definite. She told me about those men and what they'd done to her before.' He paused to compose himself. Laurie had last seen him this close to crying at Mum's funeral. 'That was bad enough for her. She really, really didn't want to tell it to the police. To tell the truth, after what she had just done for us, I thought that helping her – well, that was the least I could do.'

Laurie considered this, remembering the way Jess had already started disposing of the bodies before freeing herself and Dad from the table. She tried to imagine the whispered conversations that must have taken place while she slept – what 'helping' Jess had actually entailed. Surely it wasn't that easy just to dispose of two bodies? A look at Dad's face, however, convinced her that now was not the time for further questions. Instead, she tried lightening his mood. 'Where's Jess?' Then, smiling, 'You know Mrs Shilling's convinced you're an item?'

'An item?' Dad sounded puzzled. 'Oh, you mean ...' His voice trailed off before continuing, 'She's upstairs, having a shower. I'm going to do the same. Then we can talk.'

Monday 10 August – 12 p.m.

Dad was adamant. 'We spoke about this on our way back. We've agreed it's probably better if we don't tell you anything about what we did with the bodies. So please don't ask.'

Laurie was taken aback, not so much by what Dad was saying – she could see the sense of it, was relieved at being spared the details – but by the idea that from now on he and Jess would have a secret in which she could not share. Dad would never tell her; there was no point in trying to persuade him.

But why hadn't they called the police? The last thing Laurie wanted was an argument, but this was something she had to understand. She approached the subject as indirectly as she could: 'Jess? Those two men in the flat? Dad said—' She stopped, not sure what she wanted to ask. What had really happened while Jess was tied to that bed? They'd had all the time in the world.

'Well,' Jess replied, shortly but not unkindly, 'we'd be very unlucky if we'd attracted the attention of two different sets of shaven-headed thugs, wouldn't we?'

Shaven-headed? Yes of course, just like the two who had

chased her and Paul through Euston Station a lifetime ago. Except they hadn't been chasing Paul, had they? Laurie stopped to ponder this before starting again. 'Jess, you know you saved our lives last night? They'd logged onto a website in my name, were going to make it look like a double suicide.'

It was Dad who replied. 'I thought it must be something like that. Why else would they be so careful not to bruise us?'

Yes, Laurie considered, the men's actions all made sense, in some horrible psychopathic way. It was Dad and Jess whose behaviour she still couldn't understand. 'Anyway,' she continued, 'as far as I'm concerned, they deserved to die. The only thing is, I'm pretty sure the police would have seen it the same way.'

Dad wouldn't meet Laurie's eye. She could tell he agreed with her, but didn't want to say. It was Jess who eventually replied: 'This morning, in the cold light of day, I can see why you might be right, but last night I was absolutely certain you weren't. I was more than insistent, and David . . .well, he did as I asked.'

Dad was looking at Jess now, but he still didn't speak. Instead Jess continued, 'There's something else you need to see.' With that, she pulled over a chair, stood on it and reached on top of the dresser. When her hand came down, it was holding a Sainsbury's carrier bag. She dumped it on the table; a thin bundle of £50 notes fell out from the bag as she did so. Laurie picked it up and noted the NatWest logo on the tape that bound it: £2,500.

'There are thirty-nine more like that inside the bag.' Jess answered Laurie's unspoken question.

Laurie was starting to feel lost. 'I don't understand. Where did you find this? What's it for?'

'I found it in their car. They'd parked it along the lane. And I think it's fairly obvious what it's for. It's some sort of payment – for killing you; that would be my guess. Think about what we've all gone through. As far as I'm concerned, we deserve that money. By rights, it's ours.'

Laurie looked at the bag. The police wouldn't have thought it was theirs; she was pretty sure of that, but she could see Jess's point. By itself, of course, it wasn't a good enough reason for hiding the bodies. Combined with the fear of prosecution, however, and in the immediate aftermath of a night of horror, well she could just about understand it. One thing was certain; there was nothing to be gained by challenging that decision any more. Then a thought struck her. 'Where's their car?'

It was Dad who replied. Was it Laurie's imagination, or was he a bit too eager to change the subject? 'We dropped it off back at the hire office in London, put the keys through the letterbox. That's what took us so long.'

Then he reached down inside the bag and produced two mobile phones: 'We also found these by the way – by your computer – thought they might help us work out why they were here.'

Laurie immediately recognised one of the handsets. It was the new phone she'd had delivered only a few days before; the other was a cheap throwaway – the kind you buy over the counter when you need an emergency replacement. 'Have you looked at them?' She asked.

'One of them's yours, isn't it? The other has only been used to call one number. There are some texts as well – from the same number. One of them has my address here in it.' Dad stopped there, letting the implications of what he had said sink in.

'When was it sent?'
'Yesterday evening.'
'Is that the last one?'

'No – there's one more; just says "lonelygirl73 monday-blues". We're still trying to puzzle that one out.'

Laurie had to shake herself to drive away the tightness in her chest: 'I think I can help with that.'

Dad insisted they were systematic about it, writing down the date and time of every call and text the mobile had sent or received. Laurie recognised and appreciated the forensic nature of the undertaking, although she wasn't sure she or Jess would have had the heart to do it without him.

As a basic model, the handset only showed the last twenty calls in its register, but even those few entries covered several weeks. Working backwards, they included a call made early that morning; it was a shock to all three of them to realise that it could only have been made while Laurie and Dad were already tied up. One minute later, that 'lonelygirl73, mondayblues' text had arrived.

Gradually, the phone began to yield its secrets. The texts were most chilling. There were only three others, besides the ones Dad had already told her about. Each was preceded by a call and each contained a combination of username and password. The first was a few weeks old. One was from earlier in the week. The last of them had been sent only a few hours before the one with Dad's address. It was hard to avoid the implication that they had done this three times before. Done what? Dad and Jess wondered. So Laurie explained: 'It's what I was telling you they'd done with me. These will be usernames on some website for people considering suicide. Someone's opened the account and put up posts that sound like they're written by the person they want to kill. Then after the murder, they make sure the victim's PC is open on the site. I guess that's the modern version of a suicide note.'

Dad and Jess took in the implications. 'You mean,' Jess said 'they've already faked the suicides of three people? Who?'

'I think we know the name of one them, don't we?' Dad interposed.

'If you mean William Pennington, then I'm still not sure. None of the dates of these messages correspond with when he went under that train.'

'The first one's only a few days before,' Dad objected.

'But it doesn't fit the pattern. You only need the password when you're sitting at your victim's computer, just before you fake their suicide. With William Pennington that was the last thing they needed. Not only did he fall, hundreds of people – me included – saw it happen. No, if you want to know who, I think you've got to start off with *why*. In particular, why us.'

Dad and Jess remained silent, watching Laurie while she struggled to put what she had to say into words. Now that she was about to speak, she felt surprisingly calm.

'I think we'll find these people were all killed because of their pensions.'

'What, like those little old ladies who get mugged for the contents of their purses?' Jess was openly disbelieving.

'No – they'll be people who represent a big liability in the Sanderson pension scheme – ones with long service and high salaries.' Laurie appealed directly to Dad now. 'Don't you remember? Margaret said that the finance man – what was his name? – had left some sort of suicide note. I'll bet he's one of these.'

'And us?' Dad was looking at Laurie very directly now.

'I was just starting to work this out. While you two were out yesterday afternoon, I called somebody up and told him.'

'Somebody?' Jess had her head cocked to one side, frowning as her eyes flicked from Laurie to Dad and back again.

'Paul.' Laurie exhaled the name, forcing it to come out.

Jess had her arms around her in an instant. Laurie found herself racked with sobs, desperate to speak but hardly able to do so, snatching the chance to form words as her chest heaved with the effort of breathing. 'I'm sorry ... I'm sorry ... It's all my fault ... what those men did to you ... what they did to Dad ... I've been so stupid ... I thought he was someone special.'

Laurie felt better after she was sick: shaky but clear-headed – purged, in fact, ready to begin the task of working out who 'Paul' really was. She already had a pretty good idea. Dominic Sanderson was the owner of Sanderson Recruitment, the person who had the most to lose from the need to plug its pension deficit. Paul might, Laurie supposed, have been some sort of middleman, or a third member of the team employed by Sanderson – its brains, say – but why not go for the simplest suggestion first? She didn't even need Dad to go on about Occam's razor and how you should always select the solution that required the fewest assumptions.

Frustratingly, however, the internet was no more use in finding a picture of Dominic Sanderson than it had been when she was looking for Paul Collingwood. There was one image on Facebook that might have been him: the size of a postage stamp, it showed a man hugging a boy and a girl to his chest. Were these Aidan and Mia? Laurie found herself wondering, before remembering sharply that even if 'Paul' did have children, the names he had told her were no more likely to be real than his own. In any case, this man's face was in shadow and partially obscured by his daughter's hair. Had Laurie slept with him? She kept the disconcerting uncertainty entirely to herself. She couldn't even be sure – from the few details on the public profile – that this Dominic Sanderson was the one she was looking for.

'I suppose we could ask Margaret Pennington if she's got any pictures of him,' Dad mused.

'We could do better than that,' Laurie exclaimed in triumph. 'I took a picture of Paul, or whoever he is. We could show it to Margaret, ask if she recognises him.' She fumbled excitedly for her phone, looking for the photo she'd taken by the canal.

'Wouldn't that be the phone that was stolen?' Dad asked.

'Yes, but I reloaded it onto here the other day.' Laurie felt faintly embarrassed at the admission – this picture mattered so much to her that she hadn't just filed it and forgotten it like so many others.

'No, it's not that,' Dad started. 'It's just that it's given me an idea.'

Laurie cried out in disgust. 'They've wiped all the photos from the phone – everything I synced onto it the other day. It's gone. I'll look on the cloud.'

Ten minutes later, Laurie realised this was not going to be quite so straightforward. Only she would have noticed, but someone had been through her cloud account with meticulous care, deleting the email in which she'd sent herself that photo of Paul and removing the picture itself from the folder in which she'd stored it. That was why they'd wanted the password, she realised with a shudder of remembered pain.

Dad, meanwhile, was nodding. He didn't seem to share Laurie's frustration. 'What is it?' Laurie asked, unable to keep a note of irritation out of her voice.

'It's an explanation, isn't it? Why your phone was stolen, and the flat broken into. Your man – Paul, Dominic, whatever his name is – couldn't bear the idea of you keeping a picture of him, of you one day being able to track him down.'

'Not much of an explanation,' Jess complained, with an edge that reminded Laurie how she had been the one in the flat. 'What could Laurie do with a picture?'

'Look,' said Dad. 'This is a man who's gone to great trouble to plan the murders of however many people, making them look like suicide. He must be some kind of psychopath. He's using anonymous mobiles, false names; he'd be obsessive about making sure nothing led back to him.'

Try as she might, Laurie couldn't help thinking of him as Paul. She remembered his reaction over the phone when she told him that everything on her mobile had already been saved onto the cloud. 'I think Dad's probably right.'

'OK,' said Jess slowly, 'but in that case, why did he ever make contact with Laurie in the first place? I mean, you're a lovely girl and all, but that wasn't very careful, was it?'

Laurie had a flash of inspiration. 'He'd seen me talking to William Pennington, and the way I reacted after he died. He had to check I hadn't seen anything.' It all became clear. He must have followed her up, seen the problems she was having with her bike, looked for the opportunity to talk to her later in the evening. Christ, he must even have been waiting for her the following morning. It wouldn't have been hard to do if he knew that was her route into work.

'So,' Dad said. 'Now will you admit William Pennington was murdered?'

Laurie saved herself from answering this by musing along a different tack. 'I can't help thinking that we only went to see Margaret Pennington, and found out all this, because my phone had been stolen. If . . .' Laurie hesitated for a moment. 'If Paul had let sleeping dogs lie, not worried about that picture, never contacted me again, then none of this would have happened. Those men would never have come round last night. I suppose I'd be at work right now.' Laurie left unspoken the thought that encompassed the consequences of that visit, but it hung between them all, nonetheless. Could Jess really be as unfazed as she apparently was by the thought that

262

a few hours ago she'd bludgeoned two men to death? Laurie remained profoundly grateful that she had, but it certainly made her think differently about her flatmate.

Dad broke the silence. 'And those two thugs would still be on their little murder spree. And your man Mr Sanderson would have got away scot-free.'

'And,' Jess added, 'we wouldn't have one hundred thousand pounds in used notes sitting in a carrier bag in the kitchen.'

Monday, 10 August – 1 p.m.

The mobile phone yielded one more secret: there was apparently no routine for the men to re-establish contact with their controller after they had killed someone. Presumably, Dad suggested, the messages left on the website – and the associated open account – were evidence enough that they had done their work. Laurie remembered the concerned comments that had followed lonelygirl73's last post. Might one of them have been Paul, checking that his thugs had done their work?

So there was an outside chance that the controller – it felt better giving him an anonymous, functional name – did not yet know that his supposed victims were still alive. That surely meant they should return to London as soon as possible. If they could track down the man who had wanted them dead, and surprise him with their very aliveness, that could only put them at an advantage.

Laurie wanted to leave immediately, but Dad was more sensible. 'Having the benefit of surprise is one thing, crashing the car on the motorway because I've fallen asleep at the wheel is another. We'll have a quick lunch and then a nap.

A couple of hours either way will make no difference to anyone.'

Laurie might have argued the point, but she was too tired to put any energy into it. Lying down on her bed after lunch, she was asleep within seconds. When she came back downstairs an hour or so later, she found Dad and Jess sitting out in the garden, relieved from the necessity of watering by the morning's rain. There was a sense of relaxation about Jess's shoulders; her face looked different. There had been tension around her eyes, Laurie realised, something she had failed to notice until it was gone. She went to give her a hug, and got a satisfying squeeze in return.

Laurie's snooze had achieved something for her too. She'd remembered the email she'd sent Henry, the one that was meant to prove that she'd only sent herself a photo from work. It was still there, sitting in her sent items folder on Gmail. Laurie had to will herself to open it and print off the attachment. The picture of Paul by the canal came out inch by inch. Was this man a killer? Had he ordered her murder? The memory of what she had once felt for him – what she had done with him – had now changed so utterly into revulsion that she felt the bile in her throat even as she looked at him. She wanted to track him down; she wanted revenge.

Right now, there was no way Laurie was going to show the picture to Dad and Jess. She could just imagine the train of thought she would be setting off by doing so, but she had to admit to the photo's existence. Dad was suitably appreciative. 'Well done, darling. So that means we can make Margaret our first stop on our way back to London.'

Laurie tried to suggest to Jess that she didn't have to come too, that she and Dad had been the targets and that surely what made sense now was for her to keep as far away from things as possible, but Jess was having none of it. 'And miss the fun of a showdown? Not on your nelly. I think I'm in deep enough already, don't you? Of course, there's an argument that *you* shouldn't come. You're the only one of us he'll recognise. Why don't you stay here and guard the money?'

All three of them got into Dad's car for the journey back to London; the bundles of notes stayed behind, still in their carrier bag at the bottom of the tin dustbin that contained Roxanne's winter feed. She gave them a whinny from the paddock as they left, leaning over the gate as if to say, 'Off again?' It was noticeably cooler now, a foretaste of approaching autumn. In a few weeks Dad probably wouldn't even be able to leave her out overnight. For now, however, the Shillings had once again agreed to keep an eye on her.

By some silent agreement, Jess stretched out on the back seat while Laurie rode in the front with Dad. Was it a signal that she was back in favour, could once again be treated like a grown-up? Laurie knew it was absurd, but felt comforted nonetheless: they were a team; they had been through this together. Then her thoughts drifted to the last man with whom she'd partnered. Her head jerked: a nervous twitch, but also a physical effort to shake the memory away. Embarrassed, she looked across at Dad to see if he had noticed. His hands gripped the steering wheel, eyes fixed on the road; driving was a job that Dad always took seriously.

Twisting around in her seat, Laurie directed a question to Jess instead. 'I've been wondering how you managed to hide from those men when they arrived. I mean, didn't they check your bed?'

'Hid underneath it, didn't I?'

Wasn't it lucky they hadn't checked more closely, when they realised the bed had been slept in? Laurie considered asking Jess for her opinion, but then realised something else.

'So you didn't need to hear that scream? You already knew something was wrong.'

'Well, it certainly gave me a sense of urgency.' Jess smiled. Then her eyes shut, signalling an end to the conversation. Soon afterwards, a gentle snore indicated that she was using the opportunity to catch up on lost sleep. Clearly her afternoon nap had not been enough. Dad must be tired too, Laurie reflected. She really should be talking to him, to help him stay awake.

Monday, 10 August – 8 p.m.

Laurie opened her eyes just as the car came to a halt. How long had she been asleep? Long enough to feel as if someone had stuffed cotton wool into her brain. 'Where are we?' she asked through a yawn that turned into a stretch.

'Outside the Penningtons' house,' Dad replied. 'Look.'

Laurie looked. There they were, back on the same suburban road that she remembered from a few days before. The half-light of dusk made it seem even quieter. No car passed. The only signs of life were the faint sound of a lawnmower engine and the lights in various houses.

'Spooky, isn't it?' Jess's voice from the back seat put words to Laurie's thoughts.

They got out of the car and looked up at the house. Upstairs, one set of curtains had been drawn, but no light leaked out around them, or from any other window. Dad went up to the door and rang the bell, with the air of somebody who knew he had to try, but displaying no sense of expectation as he stood with his back to the door, looking around.

'She could be in the garden.' Laurie suggested, remembering their last visit. 'Perhaps that's her mowing the lawn.'

Dad frowned at that but said nothing as Laurie walked round to the side of the house in the direction of the engine noise. It sounded like quite a big machine. Did these gardens really have large enough lawns to make it worth using a ride-on mower? Laurie rounded the corner of the house and peered through the gate that blocked access to a side passage. No, the engine noise was not coming from the back of the house. In fact, it seemed to have got fainter. And it was no lawnmower. During all the time they'd been there, its note hadn't changed. Laurie could feel a small lump starting to form in her stomach as she turned around and walked back to the front of the house. Jess was standing there, in front of the garage. That was where the sound was coming from, and Jess was reaching out for the door handle.

'No!' Laurie shouted, with such force that Jess visibly jumped and Dad came running round from the front door. 'Don't touch anything.'

With dreadful, awful clarity, Laurie knew what was behind that door. When she'd thought about killing herself, in that period of self-obsessed torment after Mum died, that had been how she planned to do it: just sit in the car, fire up the engine and go to sleep. What could be easier? Had it only been the lack of a garage that had stopped her? Inside this one, Laurie knew, lay the slumped body of Margaret Pennington, her skin cherry-red with carbon monoxide poisoning.

When had they put her there? If the engine was still running, it could not have been that long ago. Laurie thought back to the message record they'd found on the mobile, the one sent the previous afternoon, around the time Dad and Jess were off on their picnic. That would make it a bit more than a day ago. Was that possible? They could have been with Margaret when they got the call from Paul that sent them down to Somerset that night. The noise behind that door was the evidence of what would have happened to her and Dad if it hadn't been for Jess. And somewhere in the house, Laurie suspected, the computer would be logged onto a website with messages confirming what the police already knew: that this was a suicide.

Laurie wasn't sure about the coherence of the explanation she offered Dad and Jess, standing there outside the garage door, but it was good enough for Dad at least. He nodded thoughtfully. 'All too plausible, I'm afraid. I don't suppose the car uses that much fuel while it's in neutral.' Then his emotions caught up with him. 'The bastards!'

'But why?' Jess asked. 'Why would they want to kill . . .wozzername?' She seemed to be frowning with the effort required to speak.

'Widow's pension,' Laurie replied shortly. She felt a bit light-headed, as if she still hadn't properly woken up from the nap she'd been having in the car. 'She told us so herself. She got half her husband's pension.' At least, that was what she wanted to say. She wasn't sure it had come out right. She shook her head, trying to get rid of the pain she could feel starting to spread out from behind her eyes. And what was Jess doing? Suddenly, it was hard to focus on her, but she seemed to be sitting down. Was she tired too?

Dad was shouting. What? Move? He was grabbing Jess – pulling her along. If he wasn't careful, he'd rip her dress. She wouldn't like that. Why wasn't she stopping him? 'Dad—' Laurie started to say, but that wasn't coming out right either. And what was the ground doing? She couldn't get a fix on it. It seemed awfully close.

'I'm sorry.' Dad was saying. 'I should have guessed, or at least made sure we were careful. I never would have thought there could be dangerous concentrations outside the garage.

271

I mean, carbon monoxide's lighter than air. It should have just dispersed.'

Laurie looked around. She had presumably been awake for a while. Dad was certainly behaving as though she had been, but she couldn't for a moment have said for how long. Anyway, here she was, on the ground next to Jess, sitting against Dad's car, looking back towards the Penningtons' house and still hearing the noise of an engine. Perhaps it was the headache that had woken her? It had the sort of throbbing intensity she remembered from those hangovers back in Cambridge. A low moan from beside her indicated that Jess felt much the same.

'You'll be all right,' Dad said, with less certainty than Laurie would have liked. She looked at the palms of her hands. Did they have a pinkish tinge to them?

'Deep breaths: that's the thing,' Laurie heard herself saying. 'That and plenty of water. Is there a bottle in the car?' She gulped down liquid and sucked in air, thrusting the bottle into Jess's face to make her do the same. As her head gradually cleared another pain came to the fore; the whole of her left side ached. She must have fallen on it. Jess had a cut above her eye, presumably from being dragged along the ground. Dad, on the other hand, looked unscathed. 'I don't understand.' Laurie began. 'Why weren't you affected?'

'You were there a bit longer than me. And I'm bigger. Perhaps you were just in the wrong place. Do you feel up to getting in the car?'

'But we can't just leave. Margaret Pennington's in there.'

'I thought I'd phone the fire brigade from that telephone box; at least they'll have breathing equipment, although I'm very much afraid they'll be too late for her. Apart from that, the best we can do is make sure we're not too late for anyone else.'

*

272

Whatever Dad said to the operator, it was enough for a fire engine to arrive ten minutes later. He had already moved the car a discreet distance away. The three of them sat inside and watched for long enough to see figures emerge with their features obscured by gas masks, before Dad put the car in gear and set off.

Laurie and Jess sat together in the back, making the most of the air that rushed in through the open windows. It was too loud to speak. So Laurie used the time to think. Too late for anyone else? What had Dad meant by that? Margaret Pennington's killers weren't going to be committing any more murders dressed up as suicide; Jess had seen to that. Paul was the only source of danger now; surely he was the sort of person who employed others to do his dirty work? And with any luck he didn't even know yet that he was now missing two assassins. As far as he was concerned, he had ordered several murders and had got away with it.

At some point, however, perhaps when they failed to make further contact, Paul would realise that his henchmen – Laurie grimaced as she thought of the word – that his henchmen had themselves been killed. From that it would be a short step to working out that Laurie was still alive. He would want to tie up that particular loose end. Laurie's smile ended in a little shudder as she followed the train of thought to its inevitable conclusion. Had Dad got there already? He was presumably in as much danger as she was. If anyone was 'anyone else', it was her and Dad. And, her musing continued, if Dad and Jess had phoned the police last night, as they should have done, then they would be in no danger at all. Would Dad be thinking that too?

Laurie looked out of the window. Dad was parking the car, but not in a street she recognised. That was sensible.

What if Paul was already watching the flat? But where were they?

Dad answered the unspoken question. 'We're in Finchley. This is where I left the car last week; it's about a twenty-minute walk to the Tube, I'm afraid. Anywhere nearer and we'd be in a residents' parking zone.'

Finchley? Laurie had never even considered before where Dad left the car on his rare visits to London. The realisation made her uncomfortable – guilty at this proof of the extent to which she had been so wrapped up in herself. He must have been to fetch it while she was at the library on Friday, so that they were ready to leave when she eventually came home. Well, the walk to the Tube would give them time to talk.

'I don't think we should go back to the flat,' she began. 'I'd feel safer if we just lost ourselves in London, at least until we work out if Paul really is Dominic Sanderson.'

'And how do you suggest we do that?' Jess asked. 'Go up to Sanderson's receptionist, show her the picture and ask if she recognises him?'

'It's an idea,' Laurie countered. 'How about if we watch the office and see if he comes out? That would give us a pretty good indication.'

'We'd get more specific data,' Dad said mildly, 'if we could watch Dominic Sanderson's own front door.'

'You mean find his home address?' Laurie stopped to think. 'Well, perhaps I can think of an idea for that. He is a company director, after all. She got out her phone.

Laurie's original thought came to nothing. The Companies House filing for Sanderson Recruitment listed all its directors, of course – that was a legal requirement – but it gave the same service address for all of them: 28 Great Portland Street, W1, the location, it seemed clear, of the company's head office. Briefly, Laurie wondered if they should revert to their original idea, stake out the building and see who came out. She looked at her watch: coming up to nine o'clock; not much likelihood that anyone would still be working that late.

Nevertheless, it was not a fruitless search. It also showed that Dominic Sanderson was director of another company: 74 FS Ltd. That company had a registered address of 74 Fitzwilliam Street, Surrey CR4. Of its four directors, three were shown as living at that address; only the elusive Mr Sanderson seemed to be based at Great Portland Street. She showed it to Dad and Jess.

'Looks to me like a freehold ownership company,' Jess volunteered.

'What?'

'It's the same for me. When I bought the flat I got a share in the company that owns the freehold of the house. Bet you didn't know I was a company director.' Jess preened herself. 'So you're saying these four people each have a flat in 74 Fitzwilliam Street, in CR4? That doesn't make sense. At least, I don't think Paul can be Dominic.' Laurie could feel the relief rushing through her as she spoke. She'd wronged him. He hadn't sent those thugs down to Dad's house. There was some other explanation.

'Why?' Dad was looking at her, reading the signs.

'Well, CR4 must be Croydon, isn't it? Paul lives in north London. It's how we met . . .' Laurie tailed off, trying to think if she had any definitive proof that Paul had been telling the truth. Of course, that second meeting, the one where they'd gone on to coffee, of course it must have been staged. Paul would have had to pretend he lived in north London for it to make sense.

'I'll tell you what I think is odd,' Dad interjected, relieving Laurie of the need to justify herself further. 'Why should a man who owns a reasonably big company be living in a flat in

Croydon? I mean, I realise Sanderson Recruitment isn't doing that well, but even so, surely he'd be able to afford something a bit bigger than that.'

'Not if he's divorced.' Laurie said dully, all her earlier elation vanished. 'Paul said he was – two kids living with their mum in Oxfordshire. I wonder if that's something he was telling the truth about.'

'OK. Here's the plan.' Dad was taking charge now. 'We'll all go and find some hotel now – get a good night's sleep. In the morning, Jess and I will go and watch Dominic Sanderson's front door.' He held up a hand to ward off the objection Laurie was dying to make. 'You can't go. If he sees you and recognises you then it's all for nothing. Thanks to that photograph you took, we at least know what the man calling himself Paul Collingwood looks like. If we see him coming out of 74 Fitzwilliam Street then that's good enough for me. We'll go to the police. There may be a bit of unpleasantness about why we didn't report things the moment we could, but we'll just have to weather that. I'll take responsibility.'

The rush of relief was so strong it was almost physical. The constricting nature of the anxiety Laurie had been feeling all day only became clear when it was released. At last Dad was going to do the right thing. What might the consequences be? Hours of police interviews at the very least, but they could manage that. They'd just have to tell the truth. Ah yes, the truth – could Dad really take responsibility? It was Jess who'd killed them, who had started the process of clean-up even before untying Dad and Laurie. And Laurie too, was hardly blameless, erasing evidence with nail-varnish remover. There must be some crime like unlawful disposal of a body. As she thought about it, Laurie's feeling of relief began to recede. Why should Dad take the blame for something that had, in the end, started with her own stupidity?

Jess interrupted the train of thought. 'It wasn't you on your own, David, not by a long chalk.'

'No,' Laurie agreed, 'we'll all have to take responsibility.' She took the photograph of Paul out of her back pocket and handed it over. 'There he is. I don't mind if I never look at him again.'

Dad took the printout and put it in his wallet without even unfolding it. Laurie loved him for that, as for so many things.

Tuesday, 11 August – 6.15 a.m.

Laurie woke to sunlight. For a moment, she didn't know where she was. She opened her eyes and looked around: of course, the Ibis Hotel by Euston station. The bed beside her was empty. Come to think of it, she vaguely remembered Dad dropping in at some unearthly hour to collect Jess, for her to join him on the long journey down to Morden at the end of the Northern line, where Fitzwilliam Street turned out to be. They must be long gone by now, sitting opposite that front door, waiting for it to reveal its secrets. Perhaps they'd already seen Paul and were on their way back? She'd better get up. It already felt like they were doing her dirty work for her; if they came back to find her still in bed, that really would be too much.

There was a mini kettle in the room. Laurie put it on to boil while she had a shower, and drank the instant coffee that resulted even before she had got dressed. The bitter taste it left behind was nothing that a quick brush of the teeth could not put right. That was when she noticed the clock, blinking away at the bottom of the television: 6.37.

Vaguely embarrassed at the way a few seconds' panic had

deprived her of an extra hour in bed, Laurie considered her options. She was awake now, that much was for certain; returning to bed held no attraction, nor did the idea of watching breakfast television until Dad and Jess returned. It would be good to get out and about, to have a bit of a wander on streets that should still be relatively empty. That sunlight was too good to waste.

Until she was standing outside, Laurie had not really thought about where she was. Then it struck her. Drummond Street; the Indian restaurant where she and Paul had gone for their first proper date was just around the corner. In the other direction were the bike racks where she'd first met him. If she decided to pop into Euston itself for another coffee, she'd probably end up in the coffee shop where she had found herself falling for him. Was that what different parts of north London would be to her now? Memory joggers of times when she'd thought herself happy? Two weeks ago she had gloried in the realisation that Hampstead Heath was practically on her doorstep. Would she ever be able to enjoy it again? She had to get away from here. More than that, she had to correct her memory of the man who was Paul from north London. If he was Dominic Sanderson from Morden, then so be it, but she had to see him again, to know him for what he was.

Twenty minutes' walk brought Laurie to Great Portland Street. Number 28 turned out to be a tall, narrow office block that had clearly seen better days. According to the column of doorbells beside the entry buzzer, Sanderson Recruitment occupied the third and fourth floors. A little bit of mischief within Laurie urged her to press a button and see what happened, but some residual common sense put paid to that. Besides, who would be there at seven in the morning? She needed to find some place in which she could wait and watch this entrance without being seen. The text she was expecting any moment from Dad would give plenty of warning when Dominic Sanderson was on his way.

Laurie looked across the road. The plate windows of a Starbucks caught her eye. It occupied a prime corner location, and had, Laurie could see even from here, an upstairs seating area. One of those sofas should provide her with the perfect vantage point. And the coffee would at least be better than the instant sludge with which she had started the day.

Laurie had bought her coffee and spent a good few minutes searching for the stairs before she realised her mistake. A quick conversation with the barista confirmed it: this Starbucks had no upper floor. Sitting in the window as she downed her cappuccino, Laurie tried keeping a watch on the building opposite, but soon had to give it up as a bad job. The traffic was already building up; the view of number 28 was intermittent, at best. She really needed a higher vantage point. What was that seating area she'd seen?

Outside the building, Laurie looked back up toward the first floor. Those weren't sofas, she could see now. They were rows of exercise equipment: treadmills, running machines and bikes. So there was a gym directly opposite Dominic Sanderson's office. She thought back to her conversations with 'Paul'. Hadn't he said that he worked in a fitness studio? Was that a total lie? Was this just a coincidence? There was only one way to find out. Laurie checked her phone to make sure there was still no message from Dad and headed for the doorway to the right of Starbucks, beside which a small silver plaque said *Portland Fitness*.

The layout at the top of the stairs had a familiar set-up: pass-reading turnstiles for members and a gate operated by the receptionist for the likes of Laurie. Encouraged by her smile, Laurie stepped up to the desk, still uncertain as to what she was going to say. Then she stopped, her eye drawn to the frame hanging behind the desk, from which four smiling faces stared back at her: the gym's staff.

There, among them, was Paul, except Laurie couldn't call him Paul any longer, nor Dominic. He was, apparently, Simon Egerton, Centre Manager. The photo looked as if it had been taken some time ago; this version had longer hair, and there was something about the tracksuit in which he was posing – was it the cut? – that made her think of her school PE teacher a dozen years ago. Nevertheless, there was no doubt about it. She had found him in the place where she had least expected him, doing the job he'd always told her he had.

What did it mean? Laurie gazed at the picture, willing it to reveal its secrets. As she did so, her eye was drawn lower, to the picture just below: shaven-headed, thirtyish, Brian Smith, Fitness Consultant. Laurie could feel her skin crawling as she returned his mocking gaze. Some atavistic response from deep within made her want to vomit, to run, to scream, to give some acknowledgment that this was the man, who, barely thirty-six hours earlier, had fondled her breast – made use of it – in a way that had left her feeling utterly helpless and vulnerable, even before his boss had put a skewer through her eardrum.

How could she be so sure? She had never really seen him properly: a hurried glimpse in the ticket hall of Euston Underground; his face battered almost beyond recognition as he lay dead on the kitchen floor. Nevertheless, it was him, she was certain.

Laurie brought her eyes back down to the receptionist's, to answer the question she must have been asked some time ago. The woman sat there, alert and welcoming, still prepared to treat Laurie as a potential customer. 'Er, hello,' Laurie began, before pausing to lick her lips. Her voice wasn't normally that squeaky, surely? 'I'm wondering if I could have a look around.'

The answering smile brightened a notch, as if Laurie had passed some little test. 'We're a little short-staffed at the moment. One of our consultants hasn't come in, but I'll see if I can get someone to help you. Would you like to sit down?' She indicated a couple of low chairs in the corner, in front of a table carrying an arrangement of magazines, and tapped into the computer in front of her.

Laurie acquiesced in the process she had started, to the extent of sitting at the table, but managed to resist the lure of the back issues of *Men's Health* without too much difficulty. So she was able to witness Paul's expression when he came through to the other side of the turnstile and saw her. What had she been expecting? Speechless shock? Anger? Some smooth and controlled attempt to pretend he didn't know her? Not, surely, this schoolboy embarrassment, indicated by a blush that put even Laurie's worst moments of excruciation to shame. He was stammering, too, 'L-L-L—' to the extent that the receptionist was starting to show curiosity.

Laurie decided to put him out of his misery. She stood up and walked over to him, holding out a hand to shake over the barrier. 'Hello. Are you the manager? I was wondering if I could have a look around.'

Paul found his voice. 'Of course, I'd be delighted, Miss er ...' He looked at the receptionist for the name, but Laurie wasn't going to let a chance like this go to waste. 'Collingwood, Pauline Collingwood.'

'Er, right, yes. Won't you come this way?'

Tuesday, 11 August – 8.15 a.m.

They began in the room that Laurie had seen from the street. One of the running machines and an exercise bike were already occupied, but their users, sweaty, red-faced, were both plugged into headphones that presumably played music to match the videos playing on the screens in front of them. They were oblivious to the pair standing in the doorway. It was as good a place as any to begin their conversation.

Laurie was determined to retain control. 'So, I guess I've got to learn to call you Simon.'

'Er, yes. Sorry about that. It just seemed . . . well, that is to say, I was told it would be . . . wiser.'

'Wiser?'

'Well, I was just meant to, you know, to get to know you. He said it would be better if you couldn't track me down afterwards. Paul Collingwood was just the first name that popped into my head.'

'He?'

'What?'

'The "he" who said it would be wiser.'

'Oh – Brian.'

285

'You mean the Brian from the wall there?'

'Yes.' Paul/Simon caught her eye and blushed once again. 'I'd no idea he was going to follow us down there. Honestly. It was horrible.'

Laurie studied the face of this man she'd almost loved. When she'd thought he was Dominic, at least it all made sense, in some perverted, horrible way. Now what was she meant to believe: that he was some sort of bit player, a pawn being given his directions by that shaven-headed creep?

'Is there somewhere we can talk properly? Your office perhaps?'

'I don't have one. This is it really, apart from the weights area and the changing rooms. It's really just for hardcore fanatics.'

'No swimming pool then?'

'Er, no. That was another lie. I'm sorry. To tell the truth, I'd never expected to see you again. When I did, I had to come up with a reason for being out of touch.'

Tuesday 11 August – 8.30 a. m.

Paul/Simon made no attempt to demur when Laurie suggested the Starbucks below the gym. His double espresso was being prepared even as they approached the counter. Laurie got a professional but brittle smile when she ordered a mint tea: she had no need for another caffeine shot. Simon looked at the brownies as if to think about ordering one. Surprised at the rawness of the memory they evoked, Laurie refused to catch his eye when he looked back at her, but accepted his offer to pay with a nod. Meanwhile, the girl behind the counter looked at Laurie with barely concealed hostility, as though Simon was her special friend, with Laurie a potential rival. There really was something about him.

The knowledge added to Laurie's determination as she followed Simon downstairs to the basement, and it gave her an opening line. 'So what are you, some sort of gigolo?'

'No!' Simon's reply was forceful enough for a couple at the next table to break their gazes from each other and look towards them – then, more quietly but equally insistently, 'No.' Laurie let the silence rest there as the colour rushed into Simon's cheeks. His third 'no' was quieter still, tailing

287

off as his eyes slid around, looking for escape. Finally, almost grudgingly, he produced the muttered answer that Laurie was looking for. 'It was a bet.'

'Go on.'

'We'd gone out for a drink after work. Brian said that you'd think that what with us being so fit and all, we'd have no problem pulling girls. I said I'd never had a problem, that his problem was the way he dressed. Who's going to fancy a guy in trackies? He said that was ridiculous, was I really saying I could pull anyone I fancied just because I wore a suit? Well, that wasn't what I was saying, but I'd had a bit to drink by then, so I just repeated that I'd never had a problem. He said tell you what, let's go to Euston station; I'll choose the girl; you show me what you can do. I said OK, but she'd have to be fanciable.'

Were men really that shallow? The story was unbelievable, wasn't it? 'So what was the bet?' Laurie found herself asking.

Having briefly found his voice, Simon seemed to be almost silenced by embarrassment. His response was small, and full of shame. 'Fifty quid. I had to spend the night with you within two weeks.'

Laurie could feel her jaw clenching in response, but this was not the time to give way to rage. She had to get the full story. 'So what happened at Euston station?'

'We wandered around outside for a while. Brian kept suggesting ones who were too old, or too fat, or too obviously married, if you know what I mean. You were the first likely prospect.'

Laurie could just about guess the rest, but it was worth getting confirmation. 'So what did you do?'

'Well, you were just walking up to your bike. I thought it might indicate a bit of solidarity if I put on my bicycle clips. Then I went up to see if you needed any help.'

'But then you let me cycle off without exchanging numbers or anything. You were taking a bit of a risk, weren't you?'

'Well, Brian said I shouldn't give you my real number. He said he'd get me one of those pay-as-you-go mobiles, in case you turned out to be a bunny boiler. Anyway, I'd got your number from the label on your pannier. Not that I needed it, as it turned out. I only had to wait for about ten minutes the next morning before you turned up.'

'Was Brian with you then, too?'

'No. He wasn't at work that day. The first he knew of it was when I told him about our date the next morning.'

Simon fell silent. Laurie guessed that he, too, was remembering that 'date': the kiss; the revelation about his first marriage; that business with the missing text message. She had to know. 'So how much of it was true?'

Simon lowered his eyes and then raised them again to meet Laurie's. 'By the end, all of it. I realised I didn't want to lie any more.'

Was that what Laurie had been hoping for? Was it far too late? Was it even believable? 'So what does that mean?' she asked.

Simon took her question entirely at face value. 'So, I am divorced; I do have two children; their names are Aidan and Mia; I did take them up to my parents the next day. I have even tried to make *dhosas*.' He looked up. 'But that whole business with the phone; well, that was earlier on. I was still following Brian's advice. The trouble was, things had happened so fast I hadn't even got around to getting myself a new handset like Brian said I should. I'd left that to him. Found it waiting for me when I got back to London on Sunday.'

'When you called me?'

'When I called you,' Simon confirmed.

Laurie thought this through. It still made no sense. He had

289

to be lying. 'But Brian and his sidekick were at Euston station that evening. How did they know?'

There was only one possible answer. Simon gave it. 'I told him. I mean, I didn't know he was going to turn up like that.'

What? Laurie could feel the pressure building inside her. Was it anger or just disbelief? But she didn't speak. Let Simon hang himself with his lies.

'He called me that evening. Asked how things were going. I didn't see any reason not to tell him. Well, not until I saw him coming down that escalator after you. That was when I realised things were going to get nasty. I mean, the two of them just ran past me, but the look Brian gave me as he passed – I knew that wasn't the end of it. I just ran, I'm sorry. I did what I'd told you, retraced my steps to Mornington Crescent, got back to the top, caught my breath, and there was Brian and the other guy waiting for me.'

Simon was almost crying now, with shame, or remembered fear, Laurie wasn't sure. 'They must have come up from Euston on their motorbikes, got a head start. They'd found the bolt-cutters. They put them around my finger. Said they'd go through them one knuckle at a time. I had to tell them what you'd found. All I knew was it was a key. They told me I had to find it.'

Laurie had a sudden memory of Simon's behaviour when they'd met again, of the way his hands wandered to her pants like he was some oversexed teenager. She'd been so caught up in the moment, in relief, that it hadn't seemed odd then. Was he really only looking for the key? What can he have thought when he realised she didn't have it? No – hang on. This still wasn't right. She still didn't have to believe him. 'But that whole night . . .' she countered, then faltered. 'The next morning . . .' she began again. It had felt so natural, so . . .

right. But she couldn't say that. She couldn't – wouldn't – admit that.

'Well, I really was that tired,' Simon began. 'And, well, in circumstances like that, you, er, well, you don't say no. I ended up having a lovely time. It felt so odd, being able to spend time with you like that, but also knowing that I had to get that key.'

'But you didn't get it.'

'No, but I didn't need to. I recognised it the moment I saw it, when you fished it out by the platform at Euston. Do you remember me telling you about getting too close to a client?'

Laurie nodded, hardly trusting herself to speak. Hadn't this whole conversation been as good as an admission that he'd got too close to many clients over the years?

'She was some sort of Chinese expert, spent years there. Companies used to pay her for advice. She based herself at the British Library. I always thought it was a bit odd. She wasn't the library type, if you know what I mean. She'd do things like the Great North Run. But she said that there were all sorts of people there, and if she needed to look up some bit of research, then that was easy too. Anyway, we used to meet at the Travelodge opposite. Often as not, she'd have one of those keys with her.'

Simon fell silent for a moment, surely allowing himself a moment of private reminiscence. Laurie resisted the urge to follow her imagination in the same direction. She had to decide what she was going to do next. In the meantime, she refused to catch his eye, so she was taken by surprise when he continued. 'Anyway, there was one afternoon when we ... well, when she didn't get back there until the next morning. It turned out her locker had been emptied by the security guards. She had to jump through all sorts of hoops to get her stuff back, describe exactly what was in the locker, show her ID. The moment I saw the key properly in your hand, I knew I had all the information Brian needed, or that's what I thought, anyway.'

'So you just left me there, in Euston station?' Laurie challenged. She looked up at Simon, wanting him to feel the force of her stare. Now, however, he was the one who avoided her eye. He lost the poise he'd recovered over the last few minutes and seemed to shrink back into himself. Laurie let the silence rest there. She wasn't going to relieve his discomfort by filling it.

It was probably only a minute before Simon finally spoke. 'I think I'd better show you something.' With that, he withdrew a mobile phone from his pocket and placed it on the table. Laurie recognised the model: it was the same as the one Dad and Jess had brought home the day before. She looked back at Simon, and this time he did meet her gaze. 'It's the one Brian gave me.' With that, he took off the back and removed the battery to reveal the SIM card underneath – or that was what it looked like, at first glance. Then Simon removed that too from the phone. Now she could see that it was some sort of adaptor; the real card was smaller, and slotted into it.

'I don't know if you've ever looked inside an iPhone,' Simon started to explain. 'Their SIM cards are smaller than the standard size. This is one. If you want to use it in another handset – like this Samsung here – you have to use an adaptor. It looks like this, except I don't think this is just an adaptor. I think it's more than that.'

Inwardly, Laurie shrugged. What did it matter? All she could do was ask, 'What are you trying to say?'

'You remember how I came round the next Saturday morning? The time I brought croissants?'

Laurie nodded. How could she forget?

'Well, the thing is, I'd decided I wasn't going to see you again – that it was too dangerous. I thought if I just didn't return your calls then, well, you know, we'd just drift out of touch.'

'I'd get the message, you mean?' Laurie returned sharply.

Simon flicked his eyes up to meet hers for a moment, nodded, and continued. 'So that morning, I went into work and Brian's there. It wasn't one of his days. He made no bones about it. He was there to see me.' There was a moment's silence while Simon swallowed. Laurie had no difficulty imagining how Brian had made his purpose plain, before Simon carried on. 'He said he knew you'd been calling me, that you'd found out more about the man who fell, that I had to find out what you knew, and that if not . . . if not . . .' Simon stopped, looked Laurie full in face, so she could see the anguish in his eyes. 'He showed me a photograph of Bethan's house, texted through to his phone that morning. He told me I had half a day.'

Laurie shut her eyes. She wanted to hit him, to say he still didn't have to follow Brian's instructions so well, to sleep with her, to make her want to see him again. 'Go on,' she eventually replied.

'Well, you know what happened next. After you left me – by the canal – I called Brian back, told him that I'd seen you but that you'd gone off to work without telling me what you'd found.'

'What did he say to that?'

'Nothing. Literally nothing. He just hung up. Anyway, that's when I started wondering how he knew you'd been calling me. Perhaps I should have worked it out earlier. That's when I looked inside the phone. And that's when I realised it really was time to bring it all to an end. I had to stop you calling me.'

That was a shock. Despite herself, Laurie couldn't help asking, 'What do you mean?'

Simon didn't reply directly. 'You didn't make it easy, I have to say: getting home so late that evening, taxi to the door. It made me a bit desperate. Luckily you got a taxi back the next morning; that gave me a bit of warning. Could run into you, make sure you didn't see my face under the hoodie, run off again with you none the wiser.'

Laurie was incredulous. Could she really not have recognised him? Was it even possible? She cast her mind back: maybe, just maybe, it had been him. All she really remembered was that hoodie. But he'd been taking an enormous risk. She said as much.

'Well, not really. Suppose you had seen me. What then? I was pretty sure you wouldn't go to the police. Even if you had, you couldn't have identified me. All it really would have done was give you a reason to hate me. I didn't want that, hoped it wouldn't come to it. I thought this was the best way of breaking off communications, but without making you suspicious.'

He was right, Laurie reflected. She hadn't been suspicious. That had been Dad, and even then it was only because there had been the burglary at the same time. The burglary! Those two men − Brian and the other guy − in her flat, searching for something, stealing her computer just in case it contained anything to link back to them. Had they been looking for the key too? What had she said in her phone message to Paul, the one that had got Brian to send him round? She'd found out something more about the man under the train? Would that be enough for Dominic Sanderson − if he really was behind all this − to send the boys round?

Should she ask Simon what he thought? There was no reason why he'd even know that they'd been round to the flat, was there? Somehow, she didn't feel like telling him about all of that.

In fact, Laurie realised, she didn't feel like telling this guy – Simon, Paul, whatever – anything. She'd had enough of this conversation. She could carry on questioning him, telling him more than she wanted to tell in the process, getting answers that might or might not be true, confirming that at best he was a weak-willed, self-centred bastard, or she could cut her losses, spend no more time with this ageing sex pest and move on to the rest of her life. It was time to leave.

Laurie made as if to ask another question, but as she did so let her eyes stray to the clock on the wall. 'Christ, it's past nine! I've got to go. Sorry. Look, I'm not sure if we'll meet again, but I'm glad we've cleared a few things up. I guess I know where to find you.'

That was it. Laurie had never before had reason to say anything like, 'Don't call me; I'll call you,' but now that she had, she found it empowering. Simon hadn't been expecting it, she was sure of that. She felt his eyes on her back as she left the table and went up the stairs. She did not turn around.

Tuesday, 11 August – 9 a.m.

Back in the street, Laurie looked across to Sanderson Recruitment's offices. She imagined Dominic Sanderson nipping across to the gym in his lunch break, unloading his problems to his personal trainer, gradually evolving a plan that combined misplaced ingenuity with a psychopath's disregard for life. Who brought what to it? Brian was a creep; he got off on the violence alone, but he hadn't been the leader; she felt sure of that. That had been the other guy – the torturer who enjoyed his work. Who was he? Were the suicide websites his idea? How had he got involved? Through Brian? That didn't seem right somehow.

No. Hang on. Wasn't she overcomplicating things? Yesterday they had all been convinced that Paul was Dominic Sanderson. Had that blinded them to the obvious, that Dominic Sanderson had, in fact, been much closer to the centre of things? Might he have been the other Mitchell brother, as Jess had so memorably described them? That would keep the conspiracy simple – bloody Dad and his bloody Occam's razor.

No time like the present. Was that also something Dad

might say? Probably not, but right now Laurie didn't care. She crossed the street, rang the bell, and pushed through the door as it buzzed in response.

The sign by the bell had said *Reception – 3rd floor,* but the lift opened out into a plain and grubby lobby, with locked doors to left and right. The narrow strip of glass that ran down each of them from top to bottom gave Laurie a view of a typical office environment: brown laminate desks, some occupied, a photocopier, a few people milling about in shirtsleeves and, through the left-hand door, a woman who caught Laurie's eye, reached for a button, and let her in.

'Can I help you?'

For the second time that morning, Laurie had the feeling she was being looked up and down. 'Er, yes, I'm looking for a job in IT.'

'What field exactly?'

Laurie was in too deep to back out now. She tried to sound confident. 'Systems support.'

'Well, that's not really where we recruit. We're looking for programmers.' The woman looked at Laurie, gauging the effect her words were having, and then seemed to come to some sort of conclusion. 'Still, no harm in taking your details I suppose. Sit down there and I'll get you a form.'

'There' turned out to be a chair whose orangey-brown ply and woven red upholstery had definitely seen better days. Laurie sat in it while the woman rooted around piles of papers on her desk before giving up with a sigh. 'Francis,' she called to one of the shirtsleeved men, who was standing beside what Laurie could now see was a water cooler, 'have we got any new client forms?'

'I'll print some off for you.'

*

298

Laurie's fiction was complete. She had filled out the form in the name of Tracey Craddock: education at Bristol High School (two Bs and a D at A level), a degree in PC applications from de Montfort University (that sounded reasonably likely, Laurie thought), holiday jobs helping with bookkeeping at the university students' union and two years' experience as a 'technical analyst' with one of Fitzalan Capital's competitors. It had all been so easy. Might this be the way to get another job? Or would it all come unstuck at the point an employer checked for references? She squiggled some sort of approximate signature and then obeyed the command to 'Turn over for terms and conditions'.

Dense columns of print greeted her, detailing the contract she was now, apparently, entering into with Sanderson Recruitment. If Laurie had really been Tracey Craddock, perhaps she would have read them, but she doubted that many people did. Instead, their eyes, like hers, would have been drawn to the final statement, in larger font, at the bottom of the page:

Our promise to you

Sanderson Recruitment believes that its clients are its lifeblood. We promise to treat you like human beings, to listen to your concerns, and to only recommend you for positions that we believe are well suited to you. If you feel at any stage in your relationship with us that we have not kept this promise, then please feel free to contact me and explain your concerns.

Dominic Sanderson

Beside the statement, putting a face to the name, was a photograph that Laurie had no difficulty in recognising.

She had first seen him at the top of the escalator at Euston, calling her 'an unexpected bonus'. He was the second of Jess's Mitchell brothers, the man who had taken such relish in torturing her, and whose blood she had cleaned from her laptop. She had been right. Dominic Sanderson did not, it seemed, delegate the job of murder.

The woman glanced up as Laurie handed her the completed form. 'Thanks. We'll be in touch if anything comes up.' Then, as though she felt that more explanation was required, 'I'm sorry you had to wait for the form. It's just that we don't get many walk-ins. Most people find us through Google.'

'Right, of course. I've just been to the gym across the road, and the trainer there suggested I drop in here.'

'Hmm. Never been into that sort of thing myself. Do you really find it worthwhile paying extra for the trainer?'

'It was a trial offer. It was good to have someone giving me new things to do. He seemed to imply that lots of you went there.'

'On our salaries? No. Just the boss.'

'Yes, Brian said he was the most dedicated.'

The woman looked puzzled. 'Brian? Who's that?'

'The trainer I saw. Seemed like he and Mr Sanderson were best buddies.'

'Really?' The woman smiled. 'Well, I don't know anyone called Brian, but I suppose he might have wanted to give that impression. No – my boss trains with the gym's boss. I know, because I'm the one who makes the bookings. He's called Simon, Simon Egerton.'

Tuesday, 11 August – 9.30 a.m.

Laurie took the stairs down. She thought about the picture she had started building up, of Brian and Dominic Sanderson plotting murder over the weight machine. Now she had to forget Brian – consign him back to the role of psychopathic sidekick – and reinstate Simon Egerton – Paul! – as something more than the innocent victim he had tried to pretend to be. It was obvious really, now she thought about it. Casting Dominic Sanderson as the second guy had never been the simplification that Dad would have appreciated. There had always been a third: someone who sent the messages to that mobile phone, the ones with the passwords and Dad's address. That would be the person who thought of using the suicide websites, who'd put the time into establishing all those fake personas, the one who must have come up with the plan. In fact, there had only ever been one way of keeping it simple: Simon was the third man.

Laurie paused in the downstairs lobby, trying to digest the implications. She knew it; Dad would know it; Jess would know it. But would anyone believe them? What evidence could they provide? Messages on a mobile phone? Her own story about being approached by Simon? Occam's razor? At least when they thought it was Dominic Sanderson there had been the gains he would make from killing off his pension liabilities. The link was complicated, but it was undeniable. With Simon Egerton they did not even have that. It was all a mess.

It was time to talk to Dad. No need to worry any more about radio silence; he and Jess were staking out a flat whose owner would never return.

Four rings ended in the familiar mobile message: the long pause, then 'Hello? . . . Er, David Bateman here. I don't use this thing very often, so probably best to try me at home. If you need to know the number, I probably don't want to hear from you.' It brought back the argument they'd had the first time Laurie had heard it. 'You can't say that' . . . 'Why not? It's the truth.' He'd been right, of course. No one who mattered had ever been offended.

When it came to someone likely to answer their mobile, Jess was clearly a much better prospect. No answer there either.

So what now? Go back to the Ibis and wait for them? Laurie started walking north while she considered her options.

The traffic on Euston Road had picked up in the couple of hours since Laurie had made the journey in the opposite direction. At the turnoff towards the Ibis, she paused. About fifty yards away, she could see the bus stop where the man had told her where the key came from. It seemed a lifetime ago. Had that all been a total red herring? Probably. Except that without it things would never have got to this. And what was 'this'? The knowledge that the last man she'd slept with was the guiding light behind a particularly nasty set of murders. The knowledge that she'd nearly got herself, Dad and Jess killed because of it; that the prospect of bringing this man to any sort of justice was remote. The knowledge that Dad had feet of clay, that the man she had always admired, the man who had sacrificed his career for her, was capable of mistakes – more than mistakes; was capable of doing the wrong thing.

Why had she let Simon Egerton know she was still alive? And in his gym too. At some point he'd put it all together, realise she must have been there to follow up her hunch about Sanderson Recruitment. He might even talk to the woman there, find out what Laurie had learnt. Dominic Sanderson and Brian were dead, but could she feel any safer as a result? Would she ever feel safe? What if she did die? Did she even care?

Laurie was fifteen again: suffering the overwhelming despair she had felt after Mum's death, skipping school, drinking cheap cider, experimenting with drugs and boys, letting the boys experiment with her, all the time wondering if she had the courage to kill herself. Dad had saved her then. So what if he had feet of clay? She had to talk to him. She knew the address. They shouldn't be hard to find.

The Euston ticket hall was a seething mass of humanity: so much for London emptying during August. Vacantly, Laurie joined the queue of people moving steadily through the ticket gates. Then she was riding down the escalator she'd climbed in the dark with Paul. The memory – of excitement, certainly, perhaps even exhilaration – only emphasised the blankness she could feel enveloping her now.

On autopilot, Laurie turned right at the bottom, heading for the Bank branch of the Northern line: that way she wouldn't have to change at Kennington. A curved mirror close to the ceiling gave her a view of the crowd: the way it carried on around into the passageway and the crush that pressed on behind her. And there it was, immediately recognisable even in this distorted reflection: the grey-splattered short black hair of Simon Egerton. He must have followed her from Great Portland Street. Of course! He'd never let her out of his sight now, not until she was dead. And now she was leading him to Dad. For an instant the weight of hopelessness was unbearable.

Hopelessness? Yes, but seeing Simon like this made Laurie angry too. She was angry at the way this man had treated her, angry at the way he had lied to her, angry at the way the thought of him had started to blight her life, angry that, even now, he was plotting her death – plotting something that, only minutes before, she had been considering for herself. Well, fuck him. If it all had to come to a head, let it be now, while she felt no fear.

Tuesday, 11 August – 9.50 a.m.

The platform was as crowded as Laurie had hoped it would be. A train was due in two minutes, but there was little prospect that Laurie or any of the people arriving now would get onto it. Ordinarily, she would have headed for the far end, but this time she let herself drift toward the middle, becoming one of the people who stood back to let passengers off the train that arrived, and then pushed forward to take the space they had vacated.

Laurie pushed with the best of them, but not with the aim of getting on the train. By the time it pulled out of the station she was in the position she wanted, just between the yellow line and the edge of the platform, but not too obviously endangering herself. The next train would be there in another minute. Ostensibly, she was well placed to get on it.

Laurie could feel, as much as hear, movement in the crowd behind her. It was all she could do not to turn around. Instead she pulled out her phone, as if to check for messages, actually using its screen as a sort of mirror, looking for some kind of warning of what was to come. Was that a familiar profile catching the light behind her? The space between Laurie's shoulder blades prickled at the possibility. Everything now lay in the timing, and in all those statistics being correct.

Her gaze still fixed on the screen of her phone, Laurie heard the change in roar as the train came out of the tunnel. She stole a glance to judge its progress as it slowed, flicked her eyes back to the screen of her phone to see the movement she'd anticipated, and felt the beginnings of a shove in the small of her back.

If Laurie had resisted, if she had attempted to keep her balance, if she had behaved in the way expected of her, then she would surely have been lost. The shove was too forceful for that. It had power behind it, the power of a man who spent all day in the gym, the power of a man who had done this before.

Laurie did not resist. Instead, she let herself be pushed out in front of the slowing train, stepping to the side off the platform so that she saw the driver, eyes on the signal. unaware of the woman apparently attempting suicide in front of him. Then, as she continued to turn, she saw the hand that had pushed her, reaching out from the crowd, continuing its now unnecessary progress. And she grabbed it. Dropping her phone beneath her, she grabbed that hand with both her hands. As Laurie fell down into the suicide pit, inches in front of the braking train, she had the satisfaction of seeing the look on Simon Egerton's face as he followed her, propelled by the force of his own push. Then the train came between them.

Tuesday, 11 August – 9.55 a.m.

Laurie lay sprawled beneath the tracks as the train screamed to a halt above her. What had she done? Was that the vibration of the rails, or was it her own body rebelling in a wave of uncontrollable trembling? Dozens of tiny creatures seemed to be crawling over her scalp; the itch was almost more than she could bear; her face had gone numb, as if with cold. Only the pain in Laurie's shoulder – whether from the wrench it had received as Simon's hand was pulled from her grasp or from the awkwardness of her fall into the suicide pit – gave her any connection with reality.

The train had stopped, but the screaming continued, reverberating through Laurie's head as though she were its source. Was she? No: she put her hand to her mouth to confirm it was closed, bringing herself back inside her body with the feel of her palm against her lips. This was the scream of a man – of a man in pain. In an instant she was back at home listening to Dad being tortured on the table beside her. The bastards! If that was Simon fucking Egerton she could hear, then it was no more than he deserved.

The screaming stopped. Laurie's ears ached for the relief

307

of silence, but instead she heard the hubbub of the reacting crowd, only a few feet away. One voice rose above the rest: 'Did you see that? . . . She was right beside me . . . He was trying to stop her . . . Poor bastard.'

Trying to stop her? 'No!' Laurie wanted to shout out in reply. 'He pushed me. He deserved it. Don't you understand?' Her mind raced ahead, to interviews with Sergeant Atkins and her colleagues. Would anyone believe her? Even if her police record really had been deleted, they'd be bound to dig up her behaviour after Mum died. All those counsellors' reports would be filed somewhere. And how would she convince them of the truth? Only by telling it, with all the consequences that would bring. She had to carry on with her plan.

Enough light leaked in under the carriage to mean Laurie could see perfectly well. The train had come to a halt about twenty yards in front of her, not far from its usual stopping point at the end of the station. Above her, shadows moved in synchronisation with the sound of a hundred shuffling feet. In the background, she heard muffled tannoy announcements, their words indistinct but their meaning clear, as network control swung into its well-rehearsed procedures for dealing with a body on the line.

Now there were two pairs of legs visible at the end of the train, standing on either side of the central rail, green-clad: paramedics dealing with whatever was there. At any moment they would surely start looking for a second body. The power must be off. It was time to move. Laurie ignored the protests from her shoulder, grabbed her phone from where it had lodged by the track, and started to crawl towards the back of the train.

Laurie's main concern was silence. Without it she would have made faster progress, but now she moved with exaggerated care, moving and settling a hand before following with a knee, minimising the risk that she might lose her balance, ensuring that she brushed nothing that might give away her presence. Every few yards she was presented with a small obstacle in the shape of a pillar, there to hold up the central rail. They weren't hard to squeeze past, but each time Laurie found herself holding her breath, gradually easing her clothing through the gap, lest any telltale rustle should give away her presence.

After a few minutes, the sound of footsteps above tapered to an end. More than ever, Laurie had a sense of being on her own. When she looked back, she could still see the legs of people gathered around the front of the train, but here, towards the other end of the platform, it was deserted. Good, that was how she wanted it.

Finally, Laurie reached the end of the suicide pit. She was still under the train. Obviously it went back into the tunnel for some distance, equivalent to however far it had stopped short at the other end. There was nothing to do but wait. Surely they wouldn't be keeping the network shut down for much longer?

Tuesday 11 August – 10.30 a.m.

The power rails began to hum. They were back on. That was a good sign, surely? Then, less encouragingly, Laurie heard footsteps approaching. Were they going to look under the train? Might she still be discovered? She buried her face against the wall of the suicide pit, willing herself into invisibility.

The footsteps came right up to Laurie's hiding place, and then, without a pause, changed tone. Whoever they belonged to was getting on the train and walking along to the end that was still in the tunnel. Laurie curled up into a ball and waited, listening to the sounds of a Tube train coming back to life: first the rhythmic pulsing as air was pumped into the brakes above her head, then the rising tone of the motor coming up to full power. Finally, there was a whoosh and accompanying thud, repeated along the train. The doors had closed. With that, the motor changed tone once again, and the train headed slowly back into the tunnel from which it had come.

Inch by careful inch, the train edged backwards. With her back propped up against the end of the suicide pit, Laurie watched the approach of the far end of the train. Torches shone underneath it. She supposed they were looking for her, for a second body. Somehow, she had not expected this. She had acted too quickly to think it all through. There was nowhere left for her to go. Laurie drew her knees up to her nose, wrapped her arms around her head, and waited.

Cocooned by her own body, Laurie imagined the figure she presented, and was comforted. Her discoverers would be sympathetic, not censorious. There would be psychological assessments, of course, and embarrassment, certainly. Dad would worry too, at least until she explained everything to him. But it wasn't as if she had a job to lose, or anything like that. Eventually the system would have finished with her, and she'd be free to get on with her life. They wouldn't see her as a murderer, surely? She'd lost her footing and instinctively grabbed onto her neighbour, only to find that he was falling too. Yes, that was it: a dreadful accident, the result of too many people on the platform. One she could hardly come to terms with. That was why she had crawled as far away as possible, why she was even now in the classic foetal position of a traumatised victim. It wouldn't be too bad to be discovered like that, would it?

With her eyes pressed into her legs and her ears covered by her arms, Laurie came late to the realisation that the train had stopped moving. She let herself peer over the top of her knees. She was still underneath a carriage, with at least two more between her and the end of the train. They must have moved it back by only thirty yards or so, enough to expose the spot where she had fallen, but not much further. And the torch beams had stopped as well. Presumably the searchers had satisfied themselves that there was, after all, nothing to find. Now what?

As if in answer, the train whirred back into life and started going forwards, beyond the place at which it had previously halted, to the point where it ran along the entire length of the platform. Above her head, Laurie could see the back end of the train, almost exactly in line with the end of the suicide pit. There was a space. Was it large enough for her to clamber out? Would she be seen from the platform? Laurie was debating her options when the train lurched backwards by a few inches, closing the gap.

Oh God, oh God, oh God. That would have killed her, no doubt about it: Laurie felt the pain in her midriff, almost as if she really had been crushed. This was crazy, wasn't it? She didn't want to die. What was she thinking of? Laurie slumped back into the suicide pit and listened to the sound of her blood pumping through her head.

Meanwhile, doors were opening above her. Laurie could hear feet – many feet – stepping onto the platform. A few came down to the back end of the train and got on. There were announcements – apologies for the delay, confirmation that this train was going to Morden, via Bank – and then the doors shut, the tone of the motor changed once again, and the carriages started to move off.

For a moment Laurie stayed where she was, savouring the light that fell upon her as the train moved away, the driver's cab empty at the back. Then the adrenaline took over. In a matter of seconds she would be discovered. If ever there was a time for decisiveness, it was now. She just had to be careful to avoid the electrified rail. Laurie manoeuvred herself around to face the back of the suicide pit and, in a single movement, hauled herself out, and into the tunnel's concealing darkness. From there, she risked a look back towards the platform. A new set of commuters was already arriving. If she made any attempt to return she would surely be spotted. It was time for her to trust her memory, trust her knowledge of Euston's Underground network. She crawled on into the tunnel.

Tuesday, 11 August – 10.40 a.m.

In a matter of seconds – at about the time she got to her feet – Laurie realised how stupid she was being. Yes, she'd been running in tunnels very similar to this one only a few weeks before, but now the rails were live. She had to stay close to the left-hand wall and make sure that whenever she shuffled forward there was no risk of losing her balance, of touching anything electrified. It made her progress slow, and she could not waste time, or she would still be in the tunnel when the next southbound train arrived.

Forty minutes earlier, Laurie had been so desperate to bring everything to a close that she'd been willing to play Russian roulette with a Tube train. Success had turned her around. Now she was desperate to live, to enjoy the rest of her life. What was she doing? And why was she still feeling solid wall to her left? All that stuff she'd read on the internet made it clear that the spur off to the old platform – the one they used before the Victoria line was built – should be coming up. Where was it?

Laurie continued edging along, feeling out against the wall with her left hand as she did so, the panic rising within her. Every step took her further from the safety of the platform.

315

Every second brought the arrival of another train nearer. Had the background noise changed? Had the general roar changed its pitch, become louder? Surely the rails were starting to ring? Laurie turned her head to the left, looking for her approaching doom.

She was right. There was a light; in less than a second it resolved into two separate pinpricks; they grew larger and moved apart. A familiar voice echoed down the tunnel from the platform: 'Please stand clear of the platform edge.' The air around her started to move, pushed by the piston of the oncoming train.

All this time Laurie was shuffling along the tunnel, away from the platform – it was too far away for her to reach by now – using her hand to search for the gap that would let her slip out of harm's way. She'd had it all planned: the day spent on the disused platform, the one she'd read about online, then, once the electricity was off, a return to familiar ground, back down the track, through the station, onto the right-hand fork that linked through to the Piccadilly line – the one she'd taken by mistake the other night – then on northbound through King's Cross to the disused station at York Way, and escape. She'd done it all before, much of it without a torch. It wouldn't matter that she didn't have one at all this time. The lights in the stations, York Way included, would have been all she needed. But first she needed to find that gap.

Then her hand met something: not a gap but a barrier. Laurie had been so focused on the approaching headlights that it took her a moment – a valuable moment – to understand what she was touching: some sort of metal box, about three or four inches deep, its top roughly level with her shoulder, its bottom with her pelvis. That was it; there was no way she could get around it with the train only seconds away. Nevertheless, the box itself gave hope.

316

There was no time to think, to calculate her chances. All Laurie could do was flatten herself against the tunnel wall, turn her head to the side, wrap her left arm around the top of the box, and hope that its existence meant there was enough clearance for the train to miss whatever parts of her body remained exposed.

So Laurie was looking straight at the train as it approached. The wind that came before it was deafening in its violence, forcing her to close her eyes just as she caught a glimpse of the driver, an indistinct human form, sitting in the front of the train. She had no idea if he (or she?) had seen her. Her hair streamed out behind her; it was all she could do to keep her grip on the box as she hugged it, one-handed, for protection. There was a thud as the train came level with her. For a moment she was convinced she'd been hit. How else to account for the sound, for the pummelling her body was receiving? But then the train was passing her, slowing down as it came into the station.

Laurie opened her eyes. She did not dare move her head, but she could see the shadows cast by the lights inside the last carriage, moving along the wall towards her. Any passenger looking out would have seen her torso. Laurie had time to register the thought and then the train was gone. She looked back over her shoulder to see its tail lights come to a halt at the end of the tunnel. Black spots danced around them. Flies? No, these were entirely in Laurie's head.

The possibility of fainting made Laurie's heart lurch, as if she really had touched the live rail a few feet away. It shocked her into clarity. She might have been spotted; she might not. What was important was that she was still alive, and she wanted to stay that way. All other concerns were secondary. She had to get back on the platform, away from trains, and live rails, and terror. With the tail lights as a beacon, and the light from the platform silhouetting the train, Laurie started back towards humanity.

It seemed to take no time at all. There she was, standing at the back of the train, listening to the doors close. The pitch increased; there was a moment of fear: what if this train reversed as well? And then it pulled off to the south, opening a gap through to the platform on Laurie's right. No point wasting time on thought. With just a brief glance down to check she wasn't about to step into the suicide pit, Laurie brought up her knee and levered herself onto the platform. The manoeuvre completed, she indulged in a small internal acknowledgment that she had just contravened the one cardinal rule she still remembered from that rock-climbing course when she was eleven ('Don't use your knees; it throws off your centre of gravity'). Then she got to her feet and looked around.

Further up the platform were the backs of the people who had just got off the train, now queuing for the escalator that would take them up to the connecting concourse above. Between them and her, however, a man had just stepped out of the archway connecting through to the Victoria line. For a moment Laurie thought it was Dad, before a part of her subconscious dismissed the notion: 'Of course not; he's with Jess.'

And that was enough. Dad was with Jess. Of course. Laurie stared at the man as understanding dawned, ignoring the odd look that he was giving her in return.

Then another thought kicked in. This man had just witnessed Laurie's reappearance at the end of the platform. He probably hadn't seen her climb out of the tunnel, and he might not raise any alarm even if he had; all he wanted was to get on the next train with as little delay as possible. Nevertheless, it probably wasn't wise to stick around.

Through the tunnel behind the man, Laurie could hear the whirr of an approaching train. With a grunt of apology, she slipped past him, arriving on the Victoria line platform in time to join the people waiting to board.

One minute more and Laurie was through the doors, hearing them shut behind her. She looked like God knows what; both her arms were immobilised by the crush of other passengers; her face was pressed into an armpit; a briefcase jabbed into her thighs; but she had never felt more exultantly alive.

They were leaving Oxford Circus before Laurie was struck by another thought. She had just been on the platform where, only a few weeks before, she had watched William Pennington die. He had been pushed, she could be pretty sure of that now, as sure as she had once been that he fell. Laurie looked back on her earlier self, on her certainties and insecurities. She'd been so wrong about so many things, so wrapped up in herself that she had thought about no one else – been blind to the blatantly obvious. But she was still alive. She was in a position to put things right. The question was, how?

Tuesday, 11 August – 11.05 a.m.

Seats were plentiful beyond Victoria. It was only when Laurie sat down that she realised how tired she was. For the first time in her life 'take the weight off your feet' seemed more than just an expression. As the ache in her legs eased, she examined the map on the opposite side of the carriage. Yes, as she thought, the Victoria and Northern lines crossed again at Stockwell. She could get off there, continue on to Morden, go and find Fitzwilliam Road; it shouldn't be that hard to track down Dad – assuming he was still there – to tell him everything that had happened this morning, let him decide what to do next.

Two weeks ago that was what Laurie would have done. Even now, she found the thought ridiculously tempting. Dad would listen, be sympathetic, continue putting his own life on hold while he sorted out hers. When the train came into Stockwell, however, something more than weariness kept her in her seat.

Laurie was thinking. She carried on thinking when the train arrived in Brixton, ignored the flashing carriage lights that indicated it had reached the end of the line, remained in her seat as those around her started to fill again. By the time the train was heading back north, she knew what she needed to do. She would sort things out herself, do the right thing, or something that approximated to it. Dad – Dad and Jess, to be more accurate – could be left undisturbed.

Laurie had thought she'd remember the route from Watford station, but last time she'd been following Dad and hadn't really been paying attention. She got out her phone to check the route. Somehow she'd missed two calls, one from Jess, another from a private number. The voicemail icon was flashing. Laurie held the phone to her ear as she walked.

Both messages were short and to the point. She recognised Jess's voice immediately. 'Hello you, we're back. No joy, I'm afraid. Where are you?' That was to be expected, but comforting nonetheless.

The second was a shock, a reminder of a life that seemed to have vanished in the space of only a few days. 'Hi Laurie. This is Linda. Can you call into the office please? Henry is trying to get hold of you.' Oh God, Henry. What could he want? Did she even care? What would she do if he asked her to come back? Laurie was surprised to realise that she wasn't sure. Her only certainty was that she didn't need to call back right now. She could give herself some thinking time first.

Jess, on the other hand, deserved an immediate reply. Laurie stopped walking as she keyed in the text: *All fine. Will call soon. Don't do anything until we've spoken.* That should hold things for a while. A conversation was the last thing Laurie wanted at the moment.

Laurie carried on walking into Chestnut Avenue. There was the house. A police car stood outside. Good, that would make things easier. She stepped across the road to ring the bell.

Tuesday, 11 August – 5 p.m.

The wind and overcast sky made Parliament Hill a far less inviting spot than it had been on Laurie's last visit. Or perhaps it was simply the effect of being a weekday. Either way, she faced no competition for the bench at the top. She was glad she had suggested to Dad that they meet there. It would mean she could associate Hampstead Heath with a memory that had no connection with the man who had called himself Paul Collingwood. She hadn't wasted time on the phone asking Dad about the morning. He didn't have to justify himself to her. In fact, that, as much as anything, was what she wanted to tell him, to let him know it was OK, to give him whatever blessing he might feel he needed. So she had suggested that Jess came too.

Laurie gazed out at the view. Once you knew where to look, the top of the London Eye was fairly easy to see, poking out above the top of that nearby tower block. Was that when she should have realised Paul wasn't all he claimed to be, at least not a north Londoner? Now that she thought about it, so many things should have made her suspicious. She got up from the bench and walked around. If she wasn't waiting for

Dad and Jess, she would have ignored her tiredness and gone for a run.

What would she tell the two of them about the morning? She'd have to explain why they didn't need to worry about Dominic Sanderson any more, what had happened to 'Paul', who he really was. And yes, she'd have to persuade them there was no point in going to the police, that she had said all that needed to be said – no need for Jess to admit to what she had done, or for Dad to take responsibility for anything. They had this one chance of an uncomplicated future together. Laurie would never forgive herself if it were spoilt.

Inspector Carmichael had been interested to hear that Laurie had an appointment to meet Mrs Pennington: not just interested, pleased in fact, that she had thereby explained the phone call from a house in Somerset on Sunday morning; it saved him a line of inquiry. Laurie allowed herself a few a tears at the news that Mrs Pennington was dead; they were genuine enough, even if the surprise wasn't. And then she had let the story emerge: her proximity to Mr Pennington when he fell; how she was sure it was an accident and had gone to Mrs Pennington to say so; how she had ended up offering to look at the books he'd asked for at the British Library, to see if they gave any insight to his state of mind.

'And did they?' The inspector had asked, without Laurie needing to prompt any further.

'Well, what they told me was that he was worrying about pensions. Mrs Pennington had told me he was due a good one. So at first I just thought that if he was going to be comfortably off then that at least meant he was less likely to kill himself. That might have been what he was checking at the BL, but looking at those books made me aware of something else.' Here Laurie had paused, as if to gather her thoughts, before continuing, 'I wasn't sure whether I was going to say this to Mrs Pennington, but I guess it can't do any harm if I tell you. Promise you won't think I'm crazy.' She had looked directly at the inspector then, waiting for the consent that came with his, 'Go on.'

'What I realised was how expensive he was going to be to the company as a pensioner. Only now he was dead, of course, he wouldn't be. That's when I remembered Mrs Pennington telling me that another of his colleagues had killed himself. That was someone who had just retired too. It just strikes me as a bit of a coincidence, I suppose.'

That was it, but surely it was pointer enough to anyone with any curiosity? At least the inspector had asked for the names of the books at the BL, even if the statement Laurie eventually signed made no reference to them or the little bit of speculation she had dangled before him. All she could attest to, after all, was that she had spoken to Mrs Pennington on Sunday morning, and that they had made an arrangement to meet on Tuesday afternoon.

Even if there was no proper investigation now, Dominic Sanderson's disappearance would soon become obvious. Would anyone link it with the fatal fall of a gym manager across the road? Or with the disappearance of a trainer at the same gym? It was hard to see why. The deaths of several Sanderson pensioners, on the other hand, was another matter. In the absence of a body, the assumption could only be that Dominic Sanderson was on the run. He'd almost certainly withdrawn the cash that was now sitting at the bottom of Roxanne's feed barrel. The police would find out about the withdrawal; it would only add to the impression of a fugitive from justice.

One thing was for certain. There was no reason for anyone to think Dominic Sanderson would have paid a visit to Dad's house in Somerset. That part of his story – of the circumstances of his death – would never emerge. Dad and Jess were in the clear.

Laurie looked back towards the bench. Somehow, while she had been lost in her thoughts, Dad and Jess had arrived. They stood there, side by side, looking at her, wondering what she had to say.

Words could wait. The two of them were close enough to each other for Laurie to catch them both in her hug, pressing them together, willing their happiness to last.

Acknowledgements

I'm very grateful to all the kind friends who read early drafts and were either encouraging, or suggested improvements (in many cases significant), or both. Charlotte Robertson was particularly supportive at a crucial time, and through her I came to have Peter Straus as my agent. His faith in the book was inspiring and his editorial comments insightful. I am so pleased to have been taken up by Sarah and Kate Beal at Muswell Press and am looking forward to the adventure of publication with them. This has already included significant enhancements first (and crucially) in the structural edit by Laura McFarlane and then in the copyedit by Kate Quarry. As ever, my greatest thanks are to my wife, Amanda, both as a reader, and for everything else.

About the Author

Toby Faber was Managing Director of Faber and Faber and remains chairman of its sister company Faber Music. He has written two celebrated works of non-fiction, *Stradivarius* and *Fabergé's Eggs*. His history of Faber and Faber comes out later this year. This is his first novel. Toby lives in London with his family.